Voyage
of the
Redeemed

Deborah
McDermott

Published by

MELROSE BOOKS

An Imprint of Melrose Press Limited
St Thomas Place, Ely
Cambridgeshire
CB7 4GG, UK
www.melrosebooks.com

FIRST EDITION

Cover designed by Jeremy Kay

ISBN 978 1 907040 60 3

"Unless otherwise indicated, all Scripture quotations are taken from the
Holy Bible, New Living Translation, copyright 1996.
Used by permission of Tyndale House Publishers, Inc,
Wheaton, Illinois 60189. All rights reserved."

Printed and bound in Great Britain by:
CPI Antony Rowe. Chippenham, Wiltshire

FSC
www.fsc.org
MIX
Paper from
responsible sources
FSC® C013604

CONTENTS

III

Historical Background and Author's Acknowledgements

Voyage of the Redeemed is based on Noah and the Great Flood, recorded in Genesis chapters 6–7 of the Bible. Although the story takes place in approximately 2276–2160 BC, the people of the day were by no means primitive or ignorant. Evidence of their intelligence is documented in Genesis chapter 2, verses 19–20, where Adam was tasked with naming all the animals. Building a boat the size of the Ark would have required advanced technological know-how and equipment. Bronze, tempered steel and other metals must have been in common use, together with beasts of burden.

There is much speculation as to exactly where the Ark was built. The record in Genesis chapter 8, verse 4 indicates a familiarity with the mountains of Ararat. I have therefore set the story in eastern Turkey, near Armenia. It is to be noted that weather conditions prior to the Flood would have been more temperate, resulting in a wider range of flora and fauna than what is in the region today. The terrain would have also been less rugged.

With regard to the history of the principal characters, Noah's age and the birth of his children can be found in Genesis chapter 5, verse 32. From the time of his call to the completion of the Ark was approximately 100 years. The only people to board the great ship were Noah and his wife, their three sons and their wives. We therefore know that Noah's grandchildren were born subsequent to the Flood. I have based the chronological order of their birth on Genesis chapter 10, which records Japheth's genealogy first, Ham's second and Shem's third.

As the Book of Genesis was written by the Jewish Patriarch, Moses, I have used Hebrew culture and language as the backdrop for the story. A glossary and list of Bible references is included at the end of the book for your convenience.

All quoted Scripture has been taken from the New Living Translation of the Bible (NLT). Any characters, places, events or names not recorded in the principal Biblical text are fictional.

The superscripted reference numbers throughout the text refer to the Glossary and Bible Cross-References to be found at the end of this book.

TIMELINE (APPROX. YEAR BC)

3760	Creation and the Fall
2276	Prophecy concerning the Ark is given.
	Noah and Seraphina wed.
2275	Noah's eldest son, Shem, is born.
2273	Noah's second son, Japheth, is born.
	Work on the Ark begins in earnest.
2262	Shem comes of age.
2261	Noah's youngest son, Ham, is born.
	Noah celebrates his 500th birthday.
2245	Ham and Dinah wed.
2240	Shem and Hadassah wed.
2166	Lamech dies at 777 years of age.
2161	Japheth and Tabitha wed.
	Methuselah dies at 969 years of age.
	Noah and his family enter the Ark on the eve of the Flood.
2160	Noah and his family disembark the Ark.
	Gomer is born to Japheth and Tabitha.
	God makes a Covenant with mankind.

In loving memory of my husband, Sean, without whose encouragement and input this story may never have been written.

PREFACE

V *oyage of the Redeemed* is about a small group of people determined to obey God in a depraved world. It is also about this Most High God and His fervent desire to save those enslaved by sin. He is the true Hero of this narrative, repeatedly undertaking for those who trust Him.

The record of Noah and the Flood in the Book of Genesis is more than an historical event. It foreshadows the imminent return of Jesus Christ. The Lord Himself declares in Matthew 24:37–8:

When the Son of Man returns, it will be like it was in Noah's day. In those days before the Flood, the people were enjoying banquets and parties and weddings right up to the time Noah entered his boat.

Despite the lapse of time and the vast differences in longevity, *Voyage of the Redeemed* is very much a story for today. Wickedness is as rampant now as it was then, and God yearns for Man to repent before the final Judgment Day.

While I have attempted to remain true to the historical facts, this story is primarily about relationships. It is here that real life happens and I have created ordinary, everyday situations to underline this fact. Share with me in the joy of broken hearts mended and desires fulfilled. Weep for those who are crushed by bitterness and stubborn pride. Feel the hope and fear, the joy and sadness that so often walk side by side.

Above all, rejoice in the Sovereign Lord, to whom nothing is impossible. The miracles recorded in *Voyage of the Redeemed* are not uncommon to those documented throughout the Bible. God would have done whatever was necessary – supernatural or otherwise – to accomplish His will in the pre-Flood world. May this story touch you as much as it challenged me while writing it.

Deborah McDermott

PART 1

THE GREAT COMMISSION
3760–2275 BC

Then I said, "My destruction is sealed, for I am a sinful man and a member of a sinful race. Yet I have seen the King, the LORD Almighty!" ...Then I heard the Lord asking, "Whom should I send as a messenger to my people? Who will go for us?" And I said, "Lord, I'll go! Send me."
Isaiah 6:5 & 8

PROLOGUE

In the beginning...
Genesis 1–3

In the beginning, God, whose name is Elohim[7], created the Heavens and the Earth. But the Earth was without form and void, and the Spirit of God hovered over the face of the deep. Then God spoke and said, *Let there be light*, and there was light. God separated the light from the darkness, and the one He called day, the other night.

Still the world was empty. So God spoke again and called forth Life. And thus was Earth made verdant and teeming with creatures, both small and great. God looked upon His creation and saw that it was good, but incomplete. So He made Man in His own image, male and female, to have fellowship with Him and to reign supreme over the Earth. And God called the man Adam and put him and his wife, Eve, in a garden called Eden. God brought all the creatures He had made to Adam, to see what he would name them. He also allowed the man and his wife to eat of all the trees in the garden except one – the Tree of Knowledge of Good and Evil. To partake of its fruit would result in death.

And thus it was that Lucifer – that ancient serpent of old – deceived the woman as she worked alongside her husband.

"Surely God did not *really* mean it when He said you would die," he whispered. "How could He when the Fruit of Knowledge can only serve to make you as wise as He is?" Eve looked at the forbidden fruit and felt her mouth begin to water. Of all the trees in the garden, this one was the most beautiful. *Could the serpent be right?* she asked herself as she tentatively touched the heavy, blood-red fruit.

"That's it! Go on! Go on!" Lucifer hissed from somewhere behind her. The woman hesitantly turned to confer with her husband. But he had his back towards her and was unaware of the temptation she faced.

"Well, what're you waiting for?" the serpent urged. "Nobody's looking. No one will see." No longer able to resist, Eve snatched a fruit from the tree and sank her teeth into it. The flesh tasted out of this world and she eagerly turned to share her delight.

"What have you done?" Adam demanded as he stared in horror at his wife's stained mouth.

"But it's good, Adam," she answered, inviting him to also partake.

"What about the Curse?"

"Do I look like I'm dead or dying?" she teased. "There's no curse, Adam, merely a chance to increase our fellowship with Elohim[7] through the knowledge this fruit imparts. So eat!"

Although uneasy in himself, Adam admitted Eve's argument had merit. The thought of communing with the Most High at a higher level of understanding was appealing. Taking the fruit from her, he bit into it, then gagged. But it was too late! The darkness had already descended upon his soul.

He turned to accuse the woman, but what he saw chilled him. Looking down at his own body, he wept. The Glory that had covered them had been stripped away, leaving them naked and ashamed. In that moment, Adam realized death was not the end of life. Death was separation from God through disobedience!

Covering himself with his hands, he cried out for mercy. But sin had already entered the world, and with it the iniquity that would corrupt the generations to come.

Chapter 1
Divine Appointment

I knew you before I formed you in your mother's womb.
Before you were born I set you apart and appointed you
as my spokesman to the world.
Jeremiah 1: 5

The sun was high in the sky when Methuselah[16] awoke from a deep sleep. Easing his stiff joints out of bed, he shuffled across the cold stone floor and nudged the wolfhound with his toe.

"What's this letting me oversleep, Abner?" he muttered as he stooped and gently fondled the hound's ears. But the old dog merely yawned and turned over to warm himself in the patch of sunshine beneath the window. Chuckling, Methuselah poured some water into a basin and washed his face before dressing for the day. He regretted not having roused sooner. Slipping away before daybreak was the only way he could avoid being accompanied. He was aware that his great age was cause for concern, but found the restrictions imposed on his dignity offensive – especially when they intruded into his time of prayer. And he had awoken that morning with a greater desire than ever to have a time of solitude.

The large house was full of noisy activity, but the Patriarch[23] knew his son and daughter-in-law ate an early breakfast. The empty dining hall would be an ideal escape route. Throwing a stylus and clay tablet into the pocket of his robe, the old man shuffled from the room, the dog trotting happily at his heels.

Methuselah's yearning to pray increased as he entered the forest. Such a sense of urgency meant God had something important to say and he walked as fast as he could towards his destination. Months had elapsed since his last visit to the grotto. Its deep stillness enveloped him as he sat on the mossy ledge, gasping for breath. Noah was the only other person who knew about the secluded spot and had accompanied him here often. But today Methuselah was grateful to be alone. In this case, the exuberance of his grandson would not be appropriate.

1

Sunlight filtered through the forest canopy and danced with dazzling brilliance on the river. The Patriarch[23] felt hot and dusty after his exhausting walk and wished he had had the foresight to bring a towel. A quick bathe would have been refreshing. He sighed deeply and lifted his hands in praise, but the words that filled him would not come. Falling to his knees, he silently waited for the Lord.

Methuselah lost track of time and was suddenly aware the day had darkened. Thinking dusk had begun to fall, he rose unsteadily, then gasped. The black shadow spreading like ink across the blue *shamayim*[27] made him feel dizzy and he collapsed, striking his head against the grotto wall as he fell. The startled dog sat up and licked his face.

"Alright, boy, alright," Methuselah said, pushing his pet away and dabbing at the cut with the corner of his robe. "A small accident is all it is."

But the old man became increasingly alarmed as the shadow continued to darken the sky. A few minutes more, and it would be black as night! Much as he loved Abner, the dog was no tracker and he worried they would have difficulty finding their way back home. A shiver ran up his spine as the phenomenon moved across the face of the sun. Would he ever see daylight again?

The far end of the grotto suddenly burst into flame. Methuselah flung up an arm to shield his eyes from the brilliant blaze and fell to his knees in terror.

"Oh God, no!" he cried as the tongues of fire reached for him. He knew how painful seared flesh could be. But his fear rapidly turned into amazement. The flames touching his arms were almost unbearably hot, like heated oil, yet they did not consume him.

Methuselah's heart palpitated with excitement as he dared to look into the midst of the fire. There he saw One so dazzling that he knew he was in God's most holy Presence. The Shekinah[29] Glory of the Lord was here, in this place, all around him! Awestruck, he tried to look away, but the eyes of the Most High held him fast, stripping him of all pretence and pride. The old man nervously knotted his fingers in Abner's wiry fur and together they stood, trembling.

"Elohim[7]?" he whispered.

The Voice that answered Methuselah was like the thunder of many waterfalls and shook the cavern to its core.

Come! the Almighty commanded.

Captivated by the resounding word, the Patriarch[23] released his hold on the whining dog and walked into the light. He then sat on the floor of the cave and removed his writing materials from his pocket.

Methuselah was never sure afterwards just how long he sat in the glorious circle of light. It was as if time stood still and he was oblivious to everything except the Voice that filled him until he thought he would burst. Ablaze with wreaths of spectral light, he fell on his face, quaking in fear of what was to come.

A chill as cold as the light was hot swept over him. He stared in awe as the Holy One began writing on the grotto wall. His amazement turned to horror when the four indecipherable words bled from the rock onto his clay tablet.

"What does this mean?" he asked, his heart drumming with terror.

The Lord extended His hands palm upwards. They, too, were bleeding! The torn, ragged wounds filled Methuselah with sorrow, and he sobbed as he placed his hands into those of Almighty Elohim[7]. A shock of exquisite energy shot through his veins, making him shudder.

"What would You have me do, Lord?" he whispered hoarsely.

It was impossible to look upon the glorious One's face without being blinded, but the divine nod of approval was unmistakable.

You are to guard these words for the man I have appointed to interpret them, came the simple answer.

"Do I know this man?"

You know him well. He is one of your descendants with a heart to love and obey me, and will one day become the father of the age to come. Until then, I command you to diligently watch over these words. They are the key to my calling upon his life.

And this is the sign that what I have said will come to pass: You will go from this place blind for a season. The unrighteous will scorn your testimony but do not be afraid of them. I have given you strength to withstand their unbelief. I will protect and watch over you. Never will I leave nor forsake you. I, the Sovereign Lord, have spoken.

With these parting words, the light in the grotto began to dim, leaving behind a palpable darkness. Exhausted, Methuselah slumped against the rock and drew his knees up against his chest. Unsure of what to do next, he closed his eyes and fell into the deepest sleep he had ever known.

Several hours passed before Methuselah awoke feeling cold and out of sorts. His eyes were gummed up and the gash on his head tender to the touch. *Must be blood*, he thought, rubbing away the sticky muck. But the blindness remained and he grimaced when he recalled the sign God had promised. He pressed his hand against the precious tablet in his pocket and sensed the urgency of the moment. It was time to do something about getting back home. He chuckled with relief when he felt Abner's warm tongue on his face. Clutching the animal's wiry fur, he rose unsteadily to his feet. The evening chill had set in and he could feel every muscle in his aging body.

Despite Abner's willingness to help, the going was tough. Struggling to his feet after a bad fall, Methuselah leant against the dog in an effort to catch his breath. He was shivering with cold and did not think he could last much longer.

His fears were soon allayed by the sound of barking in the distance and he grinned when Abner howled in reply. Within minutes, the glade was ringing with shouts of relief and Noah warmly embraced his grandfather.

"What on earth have you done to yourself?" he scolded as he threw his mantle around the old man's quaking shoulders.

"This isn't the time for niceties, Noah," Lamech[13] interjected harshly. "Your grandfather's not supposed to go out alone."

"That's a fine way to talk about your elders," Methuselah retorted as he groped for his son's hand.

Lamech lifted his flaming torch and instantly knew something significant had happened. Not only had his father been struck blind, his shock of grey hair had also turned white and he wore that look Lamech had resisted all his life. Feeling uncomfortable, he pulled away and beckoned his physician.

"Attend to the master," he ordered.

Enos stepped forward and quickly examined Methuselah. He thought the blindness had been caused by the Patriarch's[23] fall, but the old man's grey pallor and clammy skin were of even greater concern. It was imperative he be warmly wrapped before something worse befell him.

"Bring that litter and blankets," he instructed the servants. "We need to get the master to bed as soon as we can."

Lamech anxiously watched the men carry Methuselah away. Despite his resentment, it was distressing to see his father looking so frail.

Methuselah's blindness remained a mystery. Lamech did not understand how his crusty old father could accept his infirmity with such grace. Not only did the Patriarch[23] allow the servants to assist him, he actually welcomed their help.

Sensing his son's presence in the room, Methuselah swallowed a spoonful of broth before waving the dish away.

"I know what you're thinking," he said as Beulah removed the napkin from under his chin. "But who am I to argue with the Almighty?"

Lamech scowled. He disliked it when his father talked about God in such an intimate way. He himself had tried to believe once, but that had been before the death of his first wife. Orpah would still be alive had the Most High not been deaf to his prayers for her healing. He had distanced himself from religion ever since. The cost of faith was too high, the disappointment too great.

Lamech was so deeply lost in thought that he started when Methuselah prodded him with the clay tablet. For weeks the old man had been pestering him to look at it, but he had refused. There was something ominous about the thing. He could not resist Methuselah's request for much longer, however, and wondered what had happened to his father on that awful day.

It had been a morning much like any other. Lamech had been working in the vineyards when the air had begun to get cold, and had stared in terror at the shadow fingering its way across the vault of Heaven. Throwing down his tools, he had fled to the safety of his big house and barred his door against the unknown thing. But his relief had turned to fury when he discovered that Methuselah was missing. Cursing loudly, he had called for a search party and spent hours scouring the woods. They would never have found the old man in the eerie darkness had they not heard his dog howling.

Sighing, he reached for the clay tablet and winced when Methuselah laughed heartily.

"Curiosity finally got you, did it?" the old man chuckled.

"No!" Lamech snapped. "I've given in to your persistence, that's all. What's so important about this thing that you want *me* to read it? Wouldn't Enos do? Or even Beulah here? What's in it for me, for goodness' sake?"

"A lot more than you realize," Methuselah answered with tears in his eyes. Feeling embarrassed, Lamech shifted uncomfortably in his chair.

"What happened that day?" he asked. Methuselah became very still but his face was alive with the memory.

"I know you'll have trouble believing me," he answered quietly, "but I saw the Lord. Not as a man would look upon another man, mind you, for no one can look upon Elohim[7] and live. But I saw His Shekinah[29] Glory, Lamech. Beauty like I've never seen. There are no words to describe Him and His Voice is like nothing I've ever heard. Magnificent, marvellous, call Him what you will, the Lord Himself wrote the words on this tablet. And He wrote them not for me, but for a descendant of mine able to interpret them. I think you're that man, Lamech. You must look at this – please!"

Lamech stared at his father, perplexed.

"Very well," he agreed reluctantly, "but not here. I want to be alone." Leaving Methuselah's room, he wondered what he had let himself in for.

Several days passed before Lamech sat down with the clay tablet. It felt strangely hot beneath his fingers, and he once again wondered what he had let himself in for. Methuselah's insistence that he read it was disturbing. While he had never doubted the existence of the Creator, the pain of Orpah's illness, and his doubts about God's mercy, had filled him with a determination to exclude the Most High from his life. Yet now here he was, a faithless man, about to read a divine message! The prospect was terrifying and it was with a heavy heart that he plucked up the courage to do so.

His throat tightened as the words began to pulsate like a living thing. Throwing the tablet down, he took a deep breath to steady his nerves. Surely what he had seen was a trick of his imagination. Why, then, was he so afraid? Bending down, he retrieved the tablet and peered at the unusual writing. The ink was crimson red and clotted in places, like blood. Shuddering, he tried to interpret what was written, but in vain. The characters were indecipherable.

Sitting back, he rubbed his eyes. He could not remember when he had last felt so tired. Strange, he thought. It was not yet mid-morning and he had been wide awake earlier. Resting his head against his high-backed chair, Lamech was soon asleep – only to awaken to the worst nightmare of his life.

Although not fond of his stepmother, Noah made a point of visiting his parents once a week. Hearing his father's cries for help, he burst into the house to find Lamech on all fours, gasping for air, eyes wide with horror.

"What's wrong?" Noah cried, shaking him.

"Let me go!" Lamech screamed, striking out wildly. "You're pulling me under! I can't breathe! I can't…"

"It's alright. I'm here. I've got you," Noah said as he wrapped his arms around him. Lamech went limp and emerged out of the nightmare with a low groan. Leaning on Noah for support, he slumped down into his chair and nervously reached for the tablet. Although frightened by the thing, he had to try reading it one more time. But it was useless. The words meant nothing to him.

Noah was intrigued when he saw his father had the clay tablet. For weeks he had begged Methuselah to tell him what was written on it, but the old man had been unable to enlighten him. Moved by curiosity, he peered over his father's shoulder at the Ne'um[20], the Oracle of God. The first word stirred him and he leant forward to decipher the rest of the message when Lamech suddenly snatched up the tablet and left the room. The reaction took Noah by surprise and it was several seconds before he followed.

For days, Noah pleaded to see the tablet, but Lamech stubbornly refused. He feared the Ne'um[20] of God and would not let anyone near it. Had he been aware of Noah's ability to interpret it, he might not have been so foolish.

It was a fortnight after Lamech's first attempt to read the tablet when Noah arrived unannounced.

"Father, you have to let me see the Ne'um[20]," he insisted. Lamech stared at his son blearily. He had been plagued with dreams from the moment he had first looked at the

6

tablet, and had come to a decision he knew would upset both Methuselah and Noah. Laying down his stylus, he sat back in his chair.

"Why's it so important for you to see Methuselah's tablet?" he asked dully. "It contains nothing but a jumble of words no one can read. I know. I tried."

"That may be true for you, Father, but when I saw those two words over your shoulder, I *could* understand them!"

"Then tell me what they say," Lamech demanded. Noah hesitated. He was convinced the message was a forewarning of divine judgment, but would not know for certain until he had read it in its entirety.

"I'll be able to tell you once I've seen the tablet," he answered quietly. Lamech stared up at his son's earnest face, then groaned.

"If only you'd told me you could interpret it!" he said ruefully. "I threw the tablet into the river this morning." Noah glared at his father in disbelief, then ran from the house down the hill to the Tigris and wept.

Noah's desire to read the *Ne'um*[20] would have consumed him had it not been for his preoccupation with Seraphina. The couple were due to wed within the fortnight and looked forward to the consummation of years of devoted companionship. Unlike most marriages within their society, their relationship would be based on love and equality.

Having grown up together, it had taken years for the pair to realize their feelings ran deeper than friendship. Their new-found awareness had initially been embarrassing, but it had not been long before they had begun to openly express their love for one another. In an era where women were considered little more than the chattels of men, Noah's display of affection was mocked. But the many protests and snide comments had little impact. The Son of Lamech cherished Seraphina and did not care who knew it.

The couple's decision to marry late in life was a standing joke in the community. Although it was common for people to live for as long as 800–900 years, most folk married before attaining their first century and produced families of 20–30 strong in their lifetime. Noah, however, would be 486 next month and she a year younger. Hopefully, they had not left it too late. Few women fell pregnant beyond middle age, and both longed for a family of their own.

Seraphina was proud to be having a white wedding but doubted anyone but Noah believed she was still a virgin. Little was held sacred now, least of all sexual morality, and her insistence on chastity before marriage was scorned by many. Abstinence was becoming more difficult by the day, however. She had begun to ache for her betrothed in ways she had not thought possible and longed for when her desires could at last be satisfied. Smiling dreamily, she looked up into Noah's brown eyes.

"I'd give anything to know what you're thinking," he prompted.

"Not this time," she laughed. He laughed with her, and together they strode off to the river in search of the watercress they enjoyed eating.

Seraphina found the clay tablet in a secluded backwater and extricated it from the cleft where it was wedged. It was only when she had rubbed the mud off its chipped surface that she realized what she held and gave a whoop of joy. Hearing her shout, Noah scrambled over the rocks towards her, then came to a skidding halt.

"Dear God!" he whispered in awe. Although the fired clay was damaged, the writing remained untouched and Noah noticed for the first time the crimson-red ink. Kneeling beside him, Seraphina peered at the four strange words.

"Are you really able to understand them?" she asked.

"Strangely enough, yes," Noah nodded.

"Well, what do they say?"

He turned from her and stared at the clay tablet. His throat tightened.

"I can't tell you. Not yet. This is just the beginning. There's more Elohim[7] wants to say." Sensing Noah needed to be alone; Seraphina rose reluctantly to her feet.

"You know where I am if you need me," she murmured. Noah silently watched her go, then fell on his face and cried out to the God of his fathers.

For hours Noah lay staring at the *Ne'um*[20] of God, the words throbbing like a hammer in his brain.

"Why won't you speak to me, God?" he eventually cried. "Or have I also been weighed on Your scales and found wanting?" A gust of wind stirred the leaves in the willow above him. Closing his eyes, Noah pressed his fingers to his aching temples. He had no right to be frustrated. He was just as prone to sin as everyone else.

"Forgive me, Lord," he whispered. "I will wait for however long it takes for You to reveal Your will." The air erupted with the sound of tinkling laughter. Noah spun round, thinking Seraphina had returned. But the forest was empty. Again he folded his hands in prayer.

"Not my will, Lord, but Yours be done," he stated firmly.

In that instant, the Earth stood still and Noah knew he was no longer alone. Almighty Elohim[7] was with him, inside him – a still small Voice speaking to his soul.

All have been weighed on my scales and found wanting, Noah. But you have gained favour in my sight because of your faith and repentance.

Tears welled up in Noah's eyes. He did not know what to do or say. He sensed the Spirit stir within him and sat up as the Voice grew louder.

The Earth has become defiled and full of violence before me. Man has become desperately wicked and the thoughts of his heart are continuously evil. He has filled the Earth with iniquity and I grieve that I created him. I will therefore send a Flood of waters to destroy all humanity, and every creature that moves along the face of the earth, and the birds of the air.

But you, Noah, are to make an Ark of cypress[6] wood – a boat 300 cubits[5] long, 50 cubits[5] wide and 30 cubits[5] high. You must make a roof for it and finish it to within a cubit[5] of the top. Put a door in its side and make lower, middle and upper decks for it. This Ark will be a place of refuge for you, your wife and sons, and your sons' wives. You are to also take along with you seven of every kind of clean animal and two of every kind of unclean animal, as well as seven of every kind of bird – male and female – to keep them alive during the Flood. Ensure you stow enough food for your family and the creatures onboard. I, the Sovereign Lord, have spoken.[33]

The Voice faded and Noah ran a trembling hand across his eyes. He was drenched in his own sweat and heart-torn by what he had heard. Never had he seen an expanse of water larger than the Tigris. Neither had he witnessed a drowning. To try and imagine a flood swamping the entire Earth was more than he could manage.

Although a large part of him resisted the idea of a flood, he knew the penalty for ongoing sin was death. Methuselah had often preached on this very topic and been scorned for it. But no longer would God allow His word to be mocked or wickedness tolerated. From now on, His mercy could only be invoked through repentance.

Placing the tablet in the pocket of his robe, Noah got to his feet. It was vital he record the Prophecy while it was fresh in his mind, but he wanted to confide in Methuselah first. He just could not believe Elohim[7] would entrust him with such a task.

Noah had never liked to be kept waiting and paced the room while Methuselah completed his evening ablutions. He felt the clay tablet pressing against his thigh and removed it from his pocket before flopping down onto a stool. The anxiety he had felt after Elohim[7] had spoken washed over him again. He might be a carpenter of some note, but he had never seen a shipwright at work. It would take much research if he was to come anywhere close to what God required.

The sound of shuffling feet preceded Methuselah into the room and Noah eagerly rose to help settle his grandfather next to the glowing brazier. The old man had aged considerably since the incident at the grotto and insisted a fire be kept burning in his quarters. With the windows shuttered against the cool evening breeze, the room was stifling hot.

"It's good to see you, Grandfather," Noah said, as he edged his seat away from the hot embers and wiped his forehead.

"Just wish I could say the same," Methuselah chuckled wryly. "I can't even remember what you look like, for goodness' sake! I tell you, Noah, never again will I take my eyesight for granted once I get it back."

"How much longer do you think the blindness will last?" Noah asked. Methuselah shrugged.

"It all depends on when the Ne'um[20] of God is read and understood. I gave it to your father weeks ago, but he's sitting on it like a chicken waiting for her eggs to hatch. He probably doesn't realize how important it is."

"Oh yes, he does," Noah responded. "He tried reading it weeks ago but couldn't understand it."

"Not even one word?"

"Not even one word. The letters and symbols are different from ours and can only be divinely interpreted."

"I couldn't understand them either," Methuselah said with frustration, "but I'd hoped your father would."

"What would you say if I tell you I'm the one able to read what Elohim[7] wrote?"

"You? You mean you've actually read the Ne'um[20] of God?" Methuselah cried, clutching Noah's hand. "When?"

"This afternoon."

"But your father has had it for weeks. Why have you only read it now?"

"Because Father was convinced the tablet was under a curse and refused to give it to me. He eventually threw it into the Tigris, but Seraphina found it this morning, washed up on some rocks."

"How could Lamech be so presumptuous?" Methuselah cried. "The Ne'um[20] was not his to dispose of! What if it had been lost forever?"

"Come now. The Almighty is above our foolishness," Noah admonished. "You yourself said the Ne'um[20] was merely a key to unlock God's future call. Elohim[7] would have found another way of making His will known if the tablet had been destroyed."

"I still can't understand why Lamech would do such a thing. Surely he realizes how much I long for him to be the one through whom God's word will be fulfilled? Your father lives such an unhappy life, Noah. Just think of what it would mean for him to be entrusted with something like this." Methuselah's uncharacteristic sentiment revealed the full extent of his love for his son, and it was a while before Noah could respond.

"There are more ways than one to bring the lost back into the sheepfold," he said softly.

"So there are," Methuselah agreed. "But come. Won't you tell me what the Most High wrote?" Once again, Noah read the words etched into the clay tablet. He then proceeded to tell his grandfather all Elohim[7] had said He would do.

Methuselah sat transfixed as he listened to the solemn words. The room was suddenly flooded with light and he gasped when he saw the glistening Dove. One look into the Bird's compelling eyes and he knew he was again in God's awesome presence. The

Prophecy forgotten, he fell to his knees and cried when the Voice he had heard only once before spoke.

The time has come, old friend. From now on, your sight will be restored and you will be a mentor to this one I have called to build my Ark. Although he is small in his own eyes, he will learn to obey me with an undivided heart.

Methuselah waited with bated breath. There was much he wanted to know, much he wanted to say. But the vision had faded. He sighed and stared for several seconds at the hot coals before realizing he could see the brazier. Leaping to his feet, he seized hold of his grandson's hands.

"What's wrong?" Noah asked in alarm. Methuselah chuckled, then gave a hearty bellow of laughter.

"Nothing's wrong, lad. Can't you see? I'm no longer blind!"

"You're jesting!"

"What's this then?" Throwing aside his shawl, Methuselah whirled Noah around the room. He then flopped down on his chair, tears running down his face.

"The Lord touched me, Noah. He was here, talking to me. I feel younger than I've felt in years, much younger!" Methuselah paused at Noah's blank expression and realized his grandson had not been privy to the divine visitation.

"Didn't you hear Him at all?" he asked quietly. Noah shook his head ruefully.

"Was it anything like the first time?" he probed.

"Different, yet very much the same. You'll experience it yourself one day, Noah. Elohim[7] has destined you for great things."

"So He says, but I've done little to deserve it. You, now, have always been diligent in your work for the Lord, so why didn't He choose you instead?"

The remark made Methuselah laugh.

"Why, indeed! But aren't you relieved to know you and Seraphina will survive the Flood?"

"I suppose so, but that doesn't solve my immediate problem. How am I to build such a massive boat when I've no idea where to start?"

"Simply continue to be the good carpenter you are and God will help you with the rest. And so will I," Methuselah replied. Noah shrugged uncomfortably.

"But why should *I* be so privileged, Grandfather? Being able to interpret God's word does not put me above anyone."

"Don't waste time on issues you may never understand, Noah. God has given you a destiny to fulfil."

Left with nothing more to say, Noah rose to his feet and bid his grandfather good night.

CHAPTER 2
EMBRACING THE CALL

*If I say I'll never mention the LORD or speak in His
name, His word burns in my heart like a fire... a fire in my
bones! I am weary of holding it in!*
Jeremiah 20:9

Noah could hear it rapidly gaining ground as he ran, his lungs burning like fire. Hampered by the tunic entangling his legs, he fell down a heaving slope and gasped when he felt the sting of pelting droplets. Rolling over, he stared at the approaching flood and knew he could run no further. The wall of water was upon him.

"No! No!" he shouted as his head broke the surface of the raging torrent. A chill ran through him when he heard the frantic screams of the others.

"No!" he cried, swimming towards them. But it was too late. He began to sob, then froze as he heard his name being called above the howl of the wind.

"Wake up, Noah!" Seraphina said, shaking him. Noah slowly opened his eyes. His body ached with exhaustion and it was several seconds before the tightness in his chest began to subside. Reaching up, he pulled his wife into his arms.

"Is it the same dream, Noah? The one that frightens you so?" she asked sombrely. He shut his eyes and nodded. The icy water had seemed so real, the terror so crippling! The nightmare was clearly a foretaste of the Prophecy and he knew he could no longer delay building the Ark. Deciding to begin first thing in the morning, he sighed and drifted back to sleep. Seraphina watched the gentle rise and fall of his chest and knew he had finally accepted Elohim's[7] commission. Building the Ark would be costly, but their obedience would reap eternal rewards. Snuggling up to her husband, she slept peacefully for the first time in days.

It had been several minutes since Noah had given his drawing any degree of concentration. His urge to begin work on the Ark was strong, but he was reticent to proceed without Methuselah. Frustrated, he threw aside his apron and stormed out the door. He

12

had sent a message to his grandfather hours ago, asking him to come to the workshop to discuss the project at length. But the old man had not responded. Knowing how inquisitive the Patriarch[23] was, Noah suspected his invitation had been arbitrarily refused by Lamech.

Unlike Noah's modest dwelling on the banks of the Tigris, Lamech's large, rambling house occupied the highest hill in Je'el. Pausing to catch his breath, Noah turned to look at the terraced city below. The river was dotted with boat traffic and he sighed when he saw the barge carrying his latest consignment of sandalwood. Sadly, he would no longer have a use for the fragrant timber. The enormous task of building the Ark would leave him with no time for anything else. Smiling ruefully, he unlatched the gate and strode up the path towards his childhood home.

To his dismay, Lamech was waiting for him in the dining hall. The expression on his father's face confirmed Noah's suspicions.

"You had no right to intercept my message," he stated angrily. Lamech sourly curled his lip.

"I had every right," he snapped. "Methuselah is almost 900 years old, for goodness' sake! Why should he answer your every beck and call?"

"My intention was not to inconvenience Grandfather, but to avoid your interference. There're important things I must discuss with him, decisions I need to make if I'm to fulfil my calling."

"What calling, Noah?"

Seeing his father was genuinely perplexed, Noah strove to calm his anger.

"It's Methuselah's clay tablet, Father. I've read it," he answered in a low voice.

"You've read it? But how? I destroyed it!"

"So you thought, but Seraphina found it down by the river weeks ago."

Lamech's jaw tensed at the news.

"Then you'd better tell me what it says," he said through clenched teeth. But Noah was reticent. He doubted his father would believe the tablet was simply a key to something greater.

"Lamech has a right to know about the Prophecy, son."

Noah turned to see Methuselah in the doorway, the *Ne'um*[20] of God in his hand. A feeling of shame washed over him. This was not the time for anger or judgement, but for compassion. Nodding, he led the way to the stone bench in the courtyard and listened for a few moments to the chattering birdsong. He then removed the tightly rolled linen scroll from his pocket.

Lamech listened to the Prophecy in stony silence, his face lined with worry.

"I know it's true because I've seen it," he said when Noah had finished speaking. Surprised by the statement, Noah looked intently at his father.

"Seen what?" he asked.

"Everything the Prophecy talks about. The Flood! The screaming! The drowning!" Lamech's voice had risen to an uncharacteristic pitch and his hands trembled violently.

"I've never felt so afraid! So without hope!" he exclaimed hoarsely. Noah suddenly understood.

"You've had the nightmare too, haven't you?" he asked.

"Often," Lamech nodded. "It recurred each time I tried deciphering the tablet. That's why I threw it in the river. I would never have been so foolish had I known the dream was a vision of judgment to come. But how could God do such a thing, Noah? And why are you and your family the only people with any hope of salvation? What about us?" Noah squirmed. He had repeatedly asked himself the same question.

"I don't have the answers," he replied slowly. "All I know is that I've been instructed to build a boat in preparation for when God cleanses the Earth of sin. I also have a deep desire to call people to repentance."

"Repentance? Repentance!" Enraged, Lamech stuck his finger in Noah's face. "Don't talk to me about repentance or mercy! The Prophecy says that everyone except you and your family will be swept away by this Flood."

"You're taking the Prophecy out of context, Father. Yes, the Most High *will* sweep away the wicked. But He is always merciful to those who repent. I believe He will somehow keep them safe from the terror of the Flood. Who knows? They may simply vanish, like Great-grandfather Enoch[34]. No sickness, no leaving his body behind, just – gone."

The disappearance of Methuselah's father was a mystery Lamech still refuted.

"I don't believe Enoch left this world supernaturally, and I'm not alone in my thinking," he declared. "He died, just like we all will!"

"How Enoch departed counts for little, Father. What matters is that he remained true to God all his life and went in peace. The Ancients say that to be absent from the body is to be present with the Lord. But that state of grace only applies to those who are united with God through repentance."

"Granted, but who wants to be united with a God who allows suffering? Your mother loved the Lord, Noah. Why, then, didn't He heal her? And why does He allow so many of those who are alienated from Him to remain healthy? Repentance should give us the assurance of a happy, pain-free life, but it doesn't. So what's the point?"

Noah longed to say that true inner health and happiness could only be obtained through being in the right relationship with God. But he kept silent. Lamech did not have the faith to understand. Sighing, he rose to his feet, then sat down again as a thought occurred to him. "Repentance may seem pointless now," he said. "But what if the majority of people did it? Perhaps the Lord would change His mind and not send the Flood after all." Lamech merely gave a derisive snort and marched back into the house.

"At least hear me out!" Noah pleaded. But his cry was met with silence.

"There are none so deaf as those who refuse to hear," Methuselah murmured, giving Noah's arm a comforting squeeze. "But come now. We have a boat to build and no time to waste."

Drawing up plans for the Ark proved easier than anticipated. The only foreseeable problem lay in obtaining the timber. The nearest cypress forests were over 100 mil[17] away, at the foot of the Aldarg Mountains. Although the journey and felling of hundreds of trees would be arduous, floating the logs downriver to Noah's workshop would be relatively easy.

Noah wasted no time in proclaiming the Prophecy. Sadly, his pleas for repentance were met with the same derision Lamech had displayed earlier that month. Outraged, the citizenry of Je'el reacted to God's warning by indulging in sin more than ever.

As if this disappointment was not enough, Noah's efforts to recruit a labour force were frustrated at every turn. Desperate, he asked the City Elders for a public audience. As he stood to address the crowd, he knew he should not have brought Seraphina. Her beauty fuelled the audience into such loud vulgarity that he had to shout to be heard. But the effort was wasted. His request was denied long before he had finished speaking.

"The Son of Lamech jests," Eli Thomas mocked at the conclusion of Noah's speech. "He pleads for our support when the only interests served by this project are his. What's so special about him or his wife that they should be chosen to sail in the Ark? Are we not *all* sons and daughters of Adam?"

The barbed comment elicited a roar from the crowd and it was several minutes before Eli could resume his accusations.

"Defend yourself or be damned," he goaded. "Why should you escape the Flood, Noah? Why not Methuselah, or Lamech, or the many children in our midst? There are surely *some* here worthy of rescue. Or maybe you think your chastity puts you a notch above us. If so, you've been deceived! God commanded us to multiply and fill the earth. How else can we obey except by planting our seed in every available receptacle?"

Pausing, Eli winked lewdly at the amused crowd, then turned to Noah with a scowl.

"This Prophecy is a manipulative ploy, Noah. God forbid that we should become a religious hypocrite like you!" The blasphemy made Noah angry.

"How could Elohim[7], who is righteous and true, forbid you from becoming more like He is?" he retorted. "Are you too dull to understand? God is more concerned about the salvation of your souls than He is about death. That's why He commands you to turn from your wicked ways. He wants to be merciful. He wants to transform your lives into something beautiful. Something like Him. God is not lewd or adulterous, Eli. So how could He possibly condone your behaviour? If anyone's deceived, it's you!"

15

The crowd gasped. Disrespect for the Senior Elder incurred a severe penalty. Seraphina paled when she saw two Guardians elbowing their way towards them. Noah would receive at least a severe beating and she feared she would be similarly punished. The thought of a flogging made her tremble. *Oh, Elohim[7]*, she cried silently, *please, please help us!*

Feeling a breath of hot air against her face, she opened her eyes and was amazed to see an enormous tongue of fire rising up against the burly men. The crowd drew back in terror, then frantically began clawing their way out of the city square. Noah begged them to stop and repent. But they were too fear-crazed, too steeped in sin, to listen. Overcome, he knelt in the dust and wept for their souls.

Jasper arrived at work the following morning to discover Noah had already opened shop. The foreman knew something was afoot. His master seldom beat him to the bench.

Noah called for a meeting as soon as all his men had reported for duty. He wanted to ensure they understood what the future held in store. As he spoke, he could sense they had been talking among themselves. Not only did they take his news calmly, they listened to his call to repentance with respect. He concluded by apologizing for having to close shop to all business except that concerning the Ark, and hoped they would agree to help with the enormous task. His request was met with silence.

Jasper finally took it upon himself to speak for the team. Respectfully touching his forehead, the wizened foreman smiled widely, his teeth cracked and broken with age.

"Would we get paid for working on this boat, Sir?"

It was a fair question, demanding a truthful answer.

"Building the Ark will cost me everything," Noah admitted. "There will come a day when I won't be able to pay your wages. Hopefully the ship will be complete by then, but you are under no obligation to stay on if she isn't."

Nodding, Jasper turned to the men.

"Should I put our idea to the master?" he asked. There were several murmurs of agreement and the foreman once again addressed Noah on their behalf.

"Well, Sir, it's like this, see. We guessed you'd not be able to afford us much longer, what with the cost of timber and all. But what if some of us run the shop while the others work on the Ark? The profits could be used to pay our wages, while you use your own tender to buy the materials for the boat."

"A good scheme, Jasper, but it still won't be enough."

"What if we buy the business from you?" Obed, the record keeper, suggested.

"You have sufficient gold?" Noah asked in surprise.

"We've enough between us to give you a fair price for it," Obed confirmed confidently. Noah was impressed. Although his men were well paid, they would have made costly sacrifices to save such a large sum.

"You do realize how difficult it can be to run a business?" he hedged.

"Ah, Sir, anything worth its salt is risky," Jasper laughed. "I reckon we've worked side by side long enough to make a success of it. Besides, it's the chance of a lifetime, isn't it, lads?"

The group agreed unanimously.

"What about my reasons for building the Ark?" Noah asked sombrely. "Folk despise me for what I stand for. I suspect they'll hate you just as much if you assist. Are you able to stomach being ostracized for a cause you may not uphold?"

"What you believe is your own affair, Sir," Obed replied. "Some of us agree with you and some of us don't, but we all respect your honesty. You've done right by us and we want to do right by you."

Noah was deeply touched by the loyalty of his workforce.

"Very well," he said with feeling. "You can have the shop when I'm ready to sell – but only on one condition: I am to be granted ongoing access to the yard and tools, for the purpose of completing and storing the Ark until she's needed."

The proviso was immediately agreed to, and it was with a sense of relief that Noah concluded the meeting. As the men filed out of the room, he drew Jasper and Obed aside.

"I want you to consider who should be given the job of managing the shop and who should be part of the crew tasked to build the Ark," he instructed. "Ensure the men in each group are compatible and have an aptitude for the work."

Agreeing to present Noah with their recommendations in the morning, the two men left. Noah shut the door and leant heavily against it. He had not expected the meeting to end on such a positive note. Even so, a split workforce would result in a smaller team than anticipated and he decided to ask his father for help. Although Lamech had kept his distance since their argument three weeks ago, he might be willing to consider Noah's request.

Lamech's attitude was as chilly as it had been on the day he had heard the Prophecy, and Noah doubted his plea would be heard, let alone met. The presence of his stepmother made matters even worse. Miriamne was reputedly immoral, yet Lamech was like clay in her hands, and just as blind! Even after six years of marriage, he refused to believe the reports attesting to his wife's adultery. Noah frowned. Miriamne invariably put him into a dark mood. Casting off the unwelcome distraction, he cleared his throat to speak.

"I hear you've had a plentiful harvest and that your cellars are full of good, new wine," he said.

"Cut the niceties, Noah, and get to the point!"

"The completed harvest *is* my point, Father. Your labourers have little to do at this time of year. I'd like to borrow them for a few months, on full pay."

"What do you want them for?" Lamech growled.

"I need more men to help build the Ark if I'm to avoid taking years to complete it."

"Why should I help you?" Lamech retorted. "There's no mention of a workforce in the Prophecy, is there? No! You've been called to build the Ark, Noah, not us!"

"You're being unfair!"

"The only one who's unfair in all of this is God! As far as I'm concerned, you can jump in the proverbial lake before you get any help from me!"

Noah glared at Lamech. He was tempted to remind his father that it was he and all mankind who were destined for the proverbial lake, but refrained. The accusation would widen the breach that already existed between them. Speechless, he turned to leave, but stopped when Lamech called out to him.

"You say it'll take years if you don't have sufficient labour?"

"Yes, Father. Years!"

"Then there's little likelihood of the Prophecy being fulfilled in my lifetime," Lamech said with a broad grin. "The Flood will remain what it is now – a horrible nightmare, nothing more."

Noah was shocked to hear his father jest over such a grave issue, but knew nothing he said would change Lamech's outlook. Once again he turned to leave, but was rudely intercepted by Miriamne.

"Get out, Noah, and don't come back!" she hissed.

"How dare you!" Methuselah thundered from the open doorway. Miriamne nervously stepped back as the old man approached. She feared her father-in-law and would not have maligned Noah had she realized he was within earshot.

"You've no right to treat my grandson with such disdain," Methuselah continued, his brown eyes glinting angrily. "He has more right to be here than you do."

"How so?" she countered. "This is *my* house."

"Since when?" Methuselah answered hotly. "The title deeds remain in my name until I die." Realizing she had gone too far, Miriamne inclined her head and smiled winsomely.

"Agreed, Father, but the care and running of the home are customarily entrusted to the firstborn son and his wife."

"That only holds true for as long as I permit it, Miriamne. Indeed, I would demand you leave if I wasn't sure Lamech would follow. Your husband belongs in his ancestral home. Yet even *he* lives here at my pleasure. I can bequeath the family estate to any relative I choose, and leave you and Lamech out of my will altogether."

The threat rendered Miriamne speechless.

"You obviously haven't thought the matter through, daughter," Methuselah jibed. "In future, I suggest you only speak when you're sure of the facts."

Miriamne's eyes snapped with rage but she wisely remained silent. A response would show her up in an even worse light. Tossing her head, she flounced from the room.

"There's no fury like that of an arrogant woman proved wrong," Methuselah muttered as he watched her go. He then turned to Lamech and shook his head. "You've got yourself a handful in that woman, son."

"Don't talk about her like that!" Lamech protested sullenly. "She's my wife!"

"Yes, and sorry I am for you, Lamech. I don't know why you allow the wench to wrap you around her finger. God forbid she should try it with me! But enough said on that score. Beulah and Enos have come to me expressing a desire. Since Noah's here, I've asked them to put it to us as a family."

Turning, Methuselah invited the hesitant pair into the room. They had heard the bitter altercation and feared their request would not be welcome. Lamech, however, had already guessed the two servants wanted to team up with his son. They had been Noah's boyhood mentors and were as devoted to him as ever.

"I suppose you want to join Noah," he said bluntly. Beulah's plump face broke into a hearty grin.

"Yes, and isn't that a fact, Sir," she confirmed. "Old Master says he's in good health and doesn't need me anymore. So, I think, if he doesn't need me, then who does? 'Course, when you and Miss Miriamne get around to having your babies, I'll come right on back, won't I?"

Lamech scowled. There had been a time when he had hoped to sire many children. But Orpah had become too ill after giving birth to Noah to endure another pregnancy, and Miriamne was barren. He considered his second wife's infertility fortunate. She disliked infants with an intensity that was cause for concern.

"We both know I'll never sire another child, Beulah," he said bitterly. "Besides, it's time for you to retire. I'll not object if you want to spend your twilight years working for my son."

"Oh, thank you, Sir. I was hoping you'd say that," Beulah enthused, bobbing her head up and down and smiling toothlessly at Noah.

"Welcome to the crew, Beulah," Noah smiled back. It was unlikely the old lady would be capable of heavy labour, but she was a fair cook and would be good company for Seraphina.

Lamech turned to address Enos. He had shared many long nights with the doctor at Orpah's bedside. Releasing him would be like losing a part of himself.

"I suppose you also want to be involved in this hare-brained scheme?" he asked.

"Yes, Sir, I do," Enos admitted. "I'm not sure what it's about, but I have great faith in Noah."

"What will my household do without a doctor?"

"Not get sick, I suppose."

Lamech grimaced at the physician's gentle humour.

"I'm sorry," Enos apologized. "That remark was uncalled for. But you really don't need to concern yourself, Sir. I've found a good doctor to take my place, and many more are looking for work should you find him unsuitable."

"I trust your judgment, Enos, but not your wisdom. You're no carpenter. Can my son afford your lack of skill and strength?"

There was no denying the truth of this observation. The physician was slim as a boy and had never wielded anything bigger than a surgeon's saw.

While Enos knew he would never match Noah for size or strength, he remained undeterred.

"I know I'm not muscular," he said, "but I am willing. Besides, you might need my doctoring skills from time to time." This last point was inarguable. The risk of injury would be high and Enos's input could prove invaluable.

"You're welcome if my father will let you come," Noah responded warmly.

"With respect, Sir, I am a free man. The decision is mine." Lamech flushed angrily at the tacit remark. Family policy dictated that bonded servants be given their freedom and liberty to resign at any time. His arbitrary refusal to allow Noah the use of his labourers had been an unlawful breach of their free will.

"Very well," he said irritably. "Go with Noah if you must! You, too, Beulah. I hope you realize my son's project will one day bankrupt him. When that happens, don't come begging at my door. I will never re-employ either of you."

"But, Sir ..." Beulah began.

"Enough! Go get your wages and be off with you!" Lamech watched the servants leave the room, then turned bitterly to Noah.

"As Enos pointed out, I can do nothing to prevent my staff from following you. Just make sure they know they are not welcome here once they leave. It will be your responsibility to look after them – whether or not you can afford to do so. And as for you, Father," he said to Methuselah, "you can threaten to disinherit me all you like, but I'll not support Noah in this."

"You're making a grave mistake, Lamech. The Prophecy must be fulfilled. I dread to think what your fate will be if you continue resisting Elohim[7] so!"

Lamech shook his head vehemently.

"What does it matter? We're all doomed, even you."

Methuselah smiled sadly at the acid remark.

"You're so wrong, Lamech! Weren't you listening when Noah spoke to you the other day? It's not death we escape through repentance, but terror and separation from God. Fear dogs the heels of those who refuse to turn to Him, and they will be cast into an eternal hell when they die. Please, Lamech – don't let that happen to you. Repent!"

20

Methuselah's cry was more than Lamech could bear.

"Do what you have to and go. I don't want to talk about this again. Leave me alone to get on with my life as I think fit." He then strode from the room, a desperately unhappy man.

Noah used his remaining oak to build two wagons, increasing his existing fleet to five. He expected to be away for months and needed at least three of the vehicles to transport the team's equipment and supplies. He had considered taking a fourth to provide extra living space for the women, but had decided against it. Obed and the workshop crew would be unable to manage with only one.

Jasper was disgusted when Noah purchased three teams of oxen to haul the wagons. The foreman was accustomed to sweet-tempered carthorses and regarded bovines as second rate.

"Cattle can be mean," he objected strongly. "Why can't we take the horses instead?" Noah raised his eyes from inspecting the harnesses and cocked a quizzical eyebrow at his foreman.

"Who's been spinning you tales, Jasper? Oxen are generally more placid than horses. Hardier, too. Our gentle giants would baulk at having to pull such heavy loads for any length of time."

In reality, the aging animals had been in Noah's family for generations and he was unwilling to put them to the test. They were, however, experienced in hauling logs out of the river.

"You've given me pause for thought," Noah said after a few minutes. "We'll take Shalom and Boaz, but not for hauling wagons. They'll be used to tow logs once we start felling trees. The women will also prefer riding them to sitting for hours on hard wagon seats."

Jasper grinned. He loved the draughthorses and knew taking them would not be a mistake.

CHAPTER 3
ONWARD

Forgetting the past and looking forward to what lies
ahead, I strain to reach the end of the race and receive
the prize...
Philippians 3:13b–14a

Noah inspected the wagons once more, then stepped down and wiped his hands on a rag. It was getting late, but he wanted to ensure there was nothing to stop them from leaving by sunrise. Exiting the city gates was a lengthy business and the first day of a journey was often fraught with problems. Yawning, he secured the house, then snuggled up to Seraphina. Although bone-weary, he had much on his mind and doubted sleep would come easily. Closing his eyes, he quietly prayed for God's hand to rest upon him and his family. The barely audible petition had a calming effect and he was asleep within minutes.

He awoke with a start to Seraphina's gentle shaking and groggily rose from his bed. The men were already busy with final preparations for the journey, leaving him with nothing to do but supervise. Once the oxen were in harness and the horses saddled, the women served a breakfast of porridge and milk. The hot fare was welcome in the early morning chill.

Returning his empty bowl to Seraphina, Noah anxiously surveyed the small group. How could he possibly manage with only ten men and two women? Methuselah noticed his grandson's concern and quietly drew him aside.

"I know what's bothering you, Noah, but Elohim[7] can do whatever He pleases – even with so few. Numbers mean nothing to Him, but faith and determination do. You have here a dozen people who really want to do this thing. Therefore it will get done. Don't worry about when or how the Ark will be completed. Simply remain steadfast to God's will."

Noah smiled with gratitude. He had initially resisted Methuselah's request to accompany him to the Aldargs, but was now glad he had conceded. The old Patriarch[23] might be incapable of heavy labour, but his insight had already proved invaluable. Linking arms, the two men rejoined the group and Noah raised his hand for silence.

"Almighty God," he said. "We commit this journey and our lives into Your hands. Be with us, we pray!" His team responded with loud amens, and Noah watched them pull out of the yard, the two draughthorses and milk cows loosely tethered to the rear of the third wagon. Locking the door of the small limewashed house, he slowly followed.

Having expected their departure to stir up some reaction, Noah found the deserted streets oppressive. Stopping, he gazed up at the house on the hill. He had hoped his father would be waiting for them at the gates, but the streets were empty of all but the nightwatchmen. A lamp suddenly flared to life in the window of Lamech's room and Noah grinned when he saw his father's silhouette against the backdrop of light.

"Come with us, Father!" he shouted in the pre-dawn hush. "It's not too late to change your mind!" But the lamp was abruptly extinguished and the shutters slammed shut. Noah stared in defeat at the darkened window.

"You've done all you can," Methuselah consoled him. "Your father is lost to us, Noah. Only Elohim[7] can restore him again."

"But what if we remain forever estranged?" Noah responded quietly.

"You know there can be no reconciliation until there is a softening of Lamech's heart towards God. Perhaps it is good for us to be apart from him for a while. He needs time to think. But, come. We have delayed our departure long enough."

Nodding, Noah turned his back on his childhood home and walked towards the city gates.

Dawn made way for a glorious blue sky and the warmth of the sun soon dried the dew-drenched grass. Discarding sandals and coat, Seraphina revelled in the early morning freshness. The day would soon be too hot to enjoy. She bent to pick a wild flower, then gasped. Pressing her hand to her abdomen, she laughed in delight when the child moved again. For weeks she had known she was pregnant, but had not told Noah for fear he would insist she remain in Je'el. The thought of being separated from him made her cringe. He could not send her back. Not now.

Slipping her sandals on, she gathered her skirts in her hands and ran up the river-bank. Noah was riding alongside the small wagon train, and she eagerly beckoned him to join her.

"You called, dear heart," he teased, as he swung down from the tall draughthorse. Seraphina grinned and flung her arms around his neck.

"It's happened!" she exclaimed. "We're going to have a baby!" Noah was incredulous.

"You're not serious?"

"Never more serious than I am right now! I'm pregnant with our first son!"

"So soon?" His obtuseness made her laugh.

"I'm about four months pregnant. I felt the first movement today."

"Why didn't you tell me before?" he scolded.

"And take the risk of you leaving me behind? I know you think I'll be too frail for the trip, but I couldn't face being apart from you for so long."

"But what if the journey *is* too hard for you? What if you miscarry?"

"I believe there's little likelihood of that happening, Noah. The Prophecy talks about us and our sons. We therefore know Elohim's[7] hand is already on the fruit of my womb. He will watch over and keep us safe. Why else would He provide us with a doctor?"

Seraphina's argument had merit. God had indeed taken care of every contingency.

"Just promise you'll be careful," Noah admonished as he gathered her into his arms.

"I'll agree to anything as long as you don't fuss me to death," she answered, tugging playfully at his beard. Grinning, Noah caught her hand and held it against his chest.

"What impudence!" he exclaimed. "I don't suppose you've decided what we're going to call our son?"

"Yes, I have. Shem[30] is a name meaning 'one of renown'. A good reputation is worth more than rubies, and I pray the Lord will bless us with many sons who will make us proud."

Noah looked down into her eager green eyes.

"You may think differently once you're in the throes of childbirth," he said.

"There is no pain that can compete with the privilege of bringing forth a child, Noah. I praise God for enabling me to give you a family. It seemed so unlikely at my age."

Noah gently squeezed her hand. His wife had endured much in the short time they had been married, but would undoubtedly remain steadfast. Knowing that filled him with gratitude.

Even on good days their progress was slow. It was three weeks before the group reached the foot of the Aldarg Mountains, where grew the finest cypress in the world. The vast forests were owned by Ben Salassi, a hard man who capitalized on the needs of others. Noah's bitter encounters en route had revealed just how unpopular his message of repentance was. He hoped the merchant's greed would outweigh his prejudices. Drawing up a trade agreement would have to wait until morning, however. The day was too far gone. Turning in his saddle, Noah waved the wagons towards a clearing.

"This'll be a good place to settle for the night," he said.

While the men set up camp, the women organized their kitchen and soon had a lentil stew bubbling over a crackling fire. Noah enjoyed a hot meal after a long day's trek and smiled appreciatively across the rim of his steaming bowl. The first stretch of their journey was now over. God willing, the second would commence on the morrow.

Ben Salassi's refusal to sell his cypress had little to do with prejudice. He simply enjoyed bringing the elite to their knees. Noah shook his head in frustration. He had expected the timber merchant to drive a hard bargain, but had never thought he would refuse to trade altogether.

"Is there nothing that will persuade you to sell me your trees?" he asked. A sly look came over Salassi's face and he stroked his goatee in anticipation.

"There *is* one thing," he answered smoothly. "I've been told your wife is a handsome woman." The suggestive remark was like a blow to Noah's stomach and he drew back in disgust. Salassi merely shrugged.

"Why so shocked? Sharing women isn't out of the ordinary. It's not as if I'd be taking her away from you."

"Even so, I'd never agree!" Noah exclaimed indignantly. "Adultery is an abomination to God!"

"Ah, yes. God! I've heard it all before, Noah, and it's nothing but drivel! Have it your way, but from now on you're trespassing. I want you off my property by tomorrow."

Methuselah, who had been sitting quietly to one side, stood and glared at the timber merchant.

"Not so fast!" he thundered, his face suffused with anger. Noah had never seen his grandfather so upset and quickly rose to intercept the Patriarch's[23] wrath.

"Sit down, Noah!" Methuselah growled. "You've had your say. Now it's my turn." Swinging round, he thrust Salassi back into his chair and towered over him with clenched fists. With his flashing eyes and long white hair, he cut an imposing figure, and Salassi knew he had cause to fear. There was something familiar about the enraged old man.

"You obviously don't remember me, Ben," Methuselah remarked as his anger subsided. "That's a pity. I clearly recall the day I had mercy on you." Troubled, Salassi looked at Methuselah with a bravado he did not feel.

"Who *are* you?" he asked. "And what are you talking about?"

"I refer to when you stood before me on charges of murder and begged for your life. You claimed to have accidentally killed someone while stealing whatever you could to feed your starving family. I believed your testimony and had the charges reduced. Ten years is all you served in the end, but it could've been a lot more had I not intervened."

The timber merchant nervously licked his lips. He would never have recognized the feisty judge had Methuselah not spoken. Shamed by his prison sentence, and rejected

25

by family on the day of his release, he had decided to settle in a small village where he was unknown. Creating a new identity had been easy and he was quickly accepted into the community. To have his past exhumed now would not only result in a loss of credibility, it would also raise suspicions regarding his current state of affairs – something he wanted to avoid at all costs.

"I paid for my crime," he said sullenly. "Why are you digging it up now?"

"You force me to, Ben. To be recognized after all these years must come as a shock, but you've nothing to fear if you agree to sell Noah your trees."

"And if I refuse?"

"That would be foolish. Folk around here will not be happy when I reveal how you've deceived them all these years. Deal with us or risk losing everything."

"You're bluffing!"

"Just try me, you old charlatan! Noah needs your trees more than I want to keep your business and reputation intact." Salassi heard the ultimatum and knew he would be stupid to ignore it. Reaching for a pen, he drew up a trade agreement and pushed it across the table. Satisfied with the terms of sale, Noah affixed his seal to the contract.

"I appreciate this, Ben," he said.

"It's not I you should thank," Salassi answered tightly. He then leant forward on his elbows. "There's an old logging camp on the southern boundary of the estate. It's yours if you want it, at no extra cost. The cypress trees in that area rank among my finest. You'll need to be careful when felling them."

Noah nodded and silently applauded Methuselah's timely intervention. The meeting would have been disastrous without it.

Salassi had not exaggerated when he had described the southern-boundary cypresses. The enormous trees would provide Noah with at least a third more timber than the average pine. Built on a low promontory overlooking the Tigris, the logging camp was within shouting distance of the heavily wooded area. Such close proximity to the river would cater to their daily water requirements and facilitate the transport of timber downstream.

The camp had been out of operation for decades, but the buildings needed little more than a clean-up and some minor repairs. Although somewhat meaner than home, both men agreed their new quarters would be preferable to living in the wagons.

"It'll be a relief to have more breathing space," Noah said.

"I've known worse," Methuselah chuckled. "Just think of it. The women will now have a kitchen to themselves." Noah threw back his head and laughed.

"Have you seen it?" he spluttered. "I don't think it's ever known a woman's touch!"

"All the more reason for them to enjoy fixing it up. Strange creatures, women, but we men don't enjoy life half as much without them." Methuselah's veiled reference to his years of joyful marriage did not go unnoticed by Noah. His grandmother had died when he was a boy and he recalled his gawky attempts to console his grandfather. Methuselah's grief had softened with time, but not his memories. The old man's reminiscing brought to life what little Noah remembered of that happy time.

"You still miss Grandmother, don't you?" he said.

"Not a day goes by when I don't think of my Naomi," Methuselah answered without hesitation. "You never get used to being alone, Noah – especially when what you had was so good. But enough said. We need to strike camp if we're to move everything here by nightfall. I don't want to delay another day. Do you?"

"No, I don't," Noah replied, swinging into the saddle.

Beulah gave a cry of alarm when Noah cantered into camp with Methuselah in hot pursuit.

"What's this, Master Noah?" she demanded with hands on hips. "You've ridden these horses into a lather, and your grandfather, too, by the looks of it. What if he'd fallen off and broken a leg? Have you forgotten he's an old, old man?"

"Goodness, Beulah!" Methuselah laughed. "I'm not *that* old! Besides, a little exercise is good for me."

"It's not just you," Seraphina complained. "She's been making much ado about everything this morning!"

"And why would that be, I wonder?" Noah asked.

"Well, I had to tell her sometime," she retorted. "Now I wish I'd kept silent." Noah grinned and gently patted his wife's stomach.

"I'm surprised she hadn't already guessed."

"What on earth are you two talking about?" Methuselah asked, baffled. Seraphina laughed.

"Can't you see?" she said, laying her hand over Noah's.

"See what?"

"My word, he's gone blind again, I'm thinking!" Beulah exclaimed in mock horror, then clapped her hands in delight. "Really, Sir, I think you've forgotten what it's like!"

"Forgotten *what*?"

Seraphina was, by this time, pink with mirth.

"Dear, dear Grandfather! I'm pregnant with your first great-grandchild!"

"You're what?"

Everybody was now laughing uproariously. Feeling somewhat foolish, Methuselah grinned back at them.

"I hope I'm not blushing," he quipped, "because I really *am* too old for that." He then pulled Seraphina into his arms and hugged her warmly. "What wonderful news. When can I expect to hold my first great-grandchild?"

"In another four months or so."

"Can I ask why you didn't tell us sooner?"

"And have Beulah fuss over me for the whole trip? She's known for less than half a day and look how she is already! What would she have been like had I told her three weeks ago?"

"My Lady! You're not being fair!"

"Am I not? Come now, Beulah. You simply can't help yourself when it comes to expectant mothers! But to be honest, I'm grateful for your concern."

"As we all are," Noah said, fondly embracing the old nurse and grinning when she flushed with pleasure. He then turned to address the rest of the group.

"There's a logging camp a couple of mil[17] from here that Ben Salassi says we can use. We need to leave now if we're to be settled in before dark." The men immediately set about striking camp, while the women packed up their kitchen. Beulah saw Seraphina hoisting a sack of potatoes into the back of a wagon and scolded her soundly.

"You want to come on this trip while you're pregnant, My Lady, then you'll live by my rules. I'll not have you losing your baby because you've been foolish." Frustrated, Seraphina let her hands fall to her sides.

"Alright, Beulah, but I can't stand here idle. There must be *something* I can do that is safe." Beulah nodded in satisfaction.

"Why don't you fix lunch while I load the supplies? There isn't much to cooking and the fire's already lit."

"I'll get on to it right away," Seraphina answered, stirring up the hot coals with a stick.

Seraphina woke late the following morning to the sounds of the busy camp. She touched the cold space on Noah's side of the bed and was annoyed to realize he had left her to lie in. She disliked being unnecessarily pampered. Pulling back the wagon's canvas flap, she looked out on a day that made her glad to be alive. Jasper was busy offloading supplies and warmly greeted her as she joined him.

"It's some porridge you'll be wanting, My Lady. Beulah left you a bowlful warming by the fire. She's busy fixing up the logging camp's kitchen, which is worse than a chicken coop for muck and suchlike."

"I'm sure it is, Jasper," Seraphina said as she savoured the creamy oatmeal. The air was heady with the smell of cypress and she looked up at the tall trees stretching heavenward. They were captivatingly lovely. It would be a pity to fell them. Sighing, she turned to see Noah in the distance and strolled towards him. He was busy scribbling on a piece of bark with some charcoal and gave her a brief smile as she approached.

"What's that?" she asked when he had finished.

"A rough sketch of the area."

"For what purpose?" she pressed. Smiling, Noah leaned back against the tree under which he stood and held the piece of bark out to her. Seraphina was an apt student. He enjoyed it when she showed an interest in his work.

"Look at the drawing closely and you'll see I've marked the trees I want chopped down. I've also indicated the angle at which they should be cut. A tree falling in the wrong direction can cause untold damage. We must minimize confusion right from the start if we're to prevent that happening."

"But surely the trees will come down on top of each other, regardless of which way they fall?"

"Agreed, which is why most of them will be chopped down in sections, from the top downwards. The section being worked will be secured with ropes and hoisted to the ground once cut. As will the axemen, to prevent them falling to their deaths." Craning her neck, Seraphina looked up at the forest canopy. The thought of working at such a height made her dizzy.

"It's more than just cutting down a few cypresses, isn't it?" she murmured.

"That it is," Noah answered. "I've never undertaken such a task and doubt anyone else on the team has, either. You need to pray for us, dear heart. This is an expensive exercise we can't afford to botch."

"You won't," Seraphina asserted strongly. "Not with Elohim[7] strengthening you for the battle ahead."

"You speak as though I was a Guardian."

"Well, aren't you? We're not here for fun, Noah. We're in a war to win the world!"

"Granted, but is this a war that can ever truly be won?"

"Not by us, perhaps, but the Lord God will ultimately triumph over evil and set the world free from sin. Why else would He command us to build the Ark, or talk about an age to come? We're His Guardians, Noah, and must not give up – ever!" Noah looked at his wife with new appreciation.

"You're quite the preacher when you get going, Seraphina. How about taking over that side of my calling?"

"I would if men didn't treat women with such contempt. No, it's your job to preach, Noah. Mine is to support you in any way I can. I know we've a long road ahead, but we *will* finish victoriously," she said, stamping her foot for emphasis. Noah snapped to attention.

"I'm at your command," he said with a solemnity that belied the twinkle in his eye. Laughing, Seraphina threw a playful punch and returned to camp. After a quick bathe, she went to help Beulah. The sooner they got the kitchen organized, the better. Men always worked more efficiently when the heart of the household was fully operational.

CHAPTER 4
FOUL PLAY

Be careful! Watch out for attacks from the devil, your
great enemy. He prowls around like a roaring lion,
looking for some victim to devour.
1 Peter 5:8

Despite Seraphina's optimism, the project was fraught with setbacks from the moment they moved into the logging camp. The latest incident confirmed her suspicions. They had a traitor in their midst! She had tried voicing her fears to Noah once before, but with little success. The situation was now too serious to ignore. They had just lost two barrels of flour to the mysterious fire. Another delay and they would run out of supplies before they were ready to return to Je'el. Folding her arms, she turned and looked her husband straight in the eye.

"None of this is coincidental, Noah," she said. "Somebody is doing all they can to undermine our work on the Ark. To force us to give up. But we can't do that. Neither can we allow whoever it is to continue. Each incident is worse than the one before. Someone may get hurt if we don't put a stop to it."

"But who would be so malicious?"

"I suspect it's one of the men on our team."

"How can you be sure?" Noah asked sharply. "It could be anybody, hiding and watching what we do."

"But you agree there *is* a perpetrator?"

"I've come to that conclusion, yes, but I find it hard to believe it would be one of the men. And even if you're right, we can't accuse anybody until we're sure of our facts."

"But we *must* find out who's betraying us, even if it means laying blame prematurely. Missing tools and a shattered wagon wheel may seem harmless, but crippling one of our horses in the process is not. As for the ladder to the loft, I could've fallen when that loosened rung broke. What if I'd lost our baby, Noah? Now we have this fire.

I was with Beulah when she doused the embers in the woodstove and am convinced it was not an accident."

Noah sighed and rubbed his hand across his eyes.

"Point taken," he admitted. "But whoever is undermining us is stealthy as a cat. So how are we to catch him?"

"By setting a watch, I suppose," Seraphina answered. "We'll have to be crafty, though, if we're to avoid raising the scoundrel's suspicions."

"Which means only those we trust can be part of this watch."

"We already know who we can trust, Noah, and should meet with them soon."

"Very well, but we should first talk to Methuselah. He's crafty as a fox and will be sure to come up with something ingenious." Taking Seraphina's hand, Noah led her from the charred remains of the lovingly restored kitchen. It would be at least a fortnight before the room would again be fit for use.

Nobody had seen Methuselah since the alarm had been raised in the early hours of the morning. The old man seldom went off by himself and Noah had begun to fear the worst when they found him lying on the floor of a nearby glade.

"Grandfather!" Seraphina cried as she knelt beside him.

"Hush," Noah cautioned. "He sometimes prays like this."

"Prayer? I'm not praying! Repenting of my stupidity is what I'm doing!" Methuselah growled into the dirt. The Patriarch[23] pushed himself up with his hands and rose stiffly to his feet. His colour was alarmingly high, and the couple wondered what could have agitated him.

"I don't understand," Seraphina spoke gently. "What stupidity are you talking about? What have you done?" Methuselah stopped his angry pacing and spun round to face her.

"I could've got us killed, that's what!"

"Surely not! Whatever you're guilty of must've been a mistake."

"Yes, and a fatal mistake it could've been, too!"

"This is getting us nowhere!" Noah scolded. The old man took a deep breath, then proceeded to confirm what they already suspected.

"When did you realize?" Seraphina asked, wide-eyed.

"Right from the beginning," Methuselah answered. "I worked with Jasper for years before Noah took him on. Nothing breaks or gets mislaid when he's in charge."

Bemused, Noah scratched his head.

"Are you suggesting the tools haven't been lost, but stolen?" he asked. Methuselah nodded.

"Stolen, or hidden in a place where no one would think to look for them."

31

"I only wish you'd said something when you first suspected," Seraphina said.

"So do I, but I don't like speaking until I've sufficient evidence. In this case, I was wrong. Last night's fire could've killed us all."

"How can you prove it was arson?" Noah asked.

"Simple. What's left of the kitchen is smeared with lamp oil to facilitate a blaze. There's also some on the walls of our sleeping quarters. Had Beulah not spilt that jar of water over the kindling during dinner, the place would have gone up like a torch and burned us all to death. Whether you admit to it or not, Noah, we have an arsonist in our midst. And I'm convinced that person is Hophni."

"Obed's son? Surely not!" Noah exclaimed. Methuselah smiled grimly.

"The evidence points to him, but I doubt he's working alone. I think Ben Salassi is his accomplice."

Noah was unconvinced.

"How can you be certain Hophni is the culprit?" he asked.

"This fire and the flux[8] we went down with the week before last clearly indicate his involvement."

"But how could anybody be responsible for a disease caused by bad food or water?" Seraphina asked with an innocence that made Methuselah smile.

"He used poisonous mushrooms, granddaughter. None of us noticed them in Beulah's stew that night and we would've died had Hophni not dropped one by the kitchen door. I immediately recognized that mushroom for what it was and knew how to counteract its poison. Even so, we were ill for days, and it's only by God's grace that you didn't miscarry."

"You don't think Beulah picked them by mistake?" Seraphina suggested sombrely.

"Considering how sick the old lady was with the flux[8], I doubt it," Methuselah answered. "Besides, she knows her herbs too well to make such a blunder."

"I still don't understand how you can accuse Hophni," Noah argued. "He was away from camp on both occasions, delivering my weekly payments to Salassi."

"You're right," the Patriarch[23] agreed. "He *was* away from camp. Or so we thought! How else could the rascal provide himself with an alibi?"

"I hadn't considered that possibility," Noah muttered. "For goodness' sake, Grandfather! Why didn't you say something?"

Methuselah shrugged uncomfortably.

"I've rubbed enough salt into this old dog's wounds to last a lifetime," he grumbled. "There's no need to dump burning coals on my head as well! Now, it's time to stop Hophni. And this is how we're going to do it."

CHAPTER 5
A TRAP SPRUNG

He [God] catches those who think they are wise in
their own cleverness, so that their cunning schemes are
thwarted.
Job 5:13

Enos was astonished.

"You can't be serious!" he exclaimed.

"Never more so," Methuselah answered. "You're the only one with a plausible excuse for leaving camp."

"Why don't you just let Hophni know you're on to him and be done with it?"

"I would if I didn't suspect Salassi of being Hophni's mastermind," Methuselah explained. "If he is, we run the risk of him ganging up on us if we come out into the open too soon. His men outnumber us three to one and we have few weapons with which to defend ourselves."

"But I don't see how we *can* avoid a confrontation. Hophni's no fool. He'll soon realize we're wise to him and tell Salassi."

"You're wrong, Enos," Seraphina said confidently. "Hophni will never guess if we pretend to play into his hands. Once he thinks he's got us where he wants us, he'll become careless. And that's when we act."

"I'm still unhappy about it," Enos objected, "but I suppose the longer we wait, the closer we move to disaster. Very well. I'll do it."

Seraphina gave the physician a resounding kiss on the cheek, then stood back to allow Methuselah to go over the plan again.

Hophni was in a quandary. Standing in for the doctor would make his life even more complicated than it already was.

"Surely there's someone more capable than I?" he said tentatively.

"Apart from Noah and Methuselah, you're the only man able to read my instructions, let alone anything else," Enos answered. Hophni flushed with pride.

33

"True," he said. "But how will I manage my other duties?"

"If carrying Noah's weekly payment of gold to Salassi is what you're worried about, Noah has given John that task."

"John? But he's as illiterate as I am lettered!" Hophni exclaimed indignantly.

"Come now, Hophni! You know the lad's honest and well capable of making the delivery. Besides, your abilities may entice me to take you on permanently. I'm getting old and need someone to replace me when I'm gone."

The physician appeared sincere, but it was several seconds before Hophni nodded in agreement.

"You still don't seem certain," Enos observed.

"I'm concerned about the added responsibility," Hophni admitted shrewdly.

"I promise you'll be well paid for it."

"Then how can I refuse?" Hophni extended his hand and Enos shook it warmly.

"Thank you," he said. "All I ask is that you commit to being in camp at all times. Sickness strikes when least expected."

"I'll do as you say, Enos." Hophni's solemn expression masked his inner feelings. He had always envied the prestige of the elite and was ecstatic to be in a position of authority. Had he known what this day held, he would never have got involved with Salassi. Now it was too late. He had to honour his side of the deal if he did not want to end up with his throat cut.

Enos was already at work when Hophni walked in and donned his apron. Oblivious to his student's presence, the doctor added another sentence to what he had written.

"What are you doing?" Hophni asked curiously. Enos looked up sharply, then laid down his pen.

"You startled me, Hophni!"

"Sorry. I couldn't sleep and thought an early morning start might clear my head. Are those more notes for me?" Enos looked down at the linen scroll beneath his hand.

"Merely a letter I've written home," he answered with a crooked smile. "I thought I might send it with Sheba." He affectionately rubbed his finger across the pearly green feathers of the pigeon perched on his desk. She had been an injured chick when he had found her, and the two had bonded quickly. The bird seldom left his side except to convey messages. Her usefulness as a carrier had often proved invaluable. Slipping the scroll into his pocket, Enos turned to Hophni.

"I've taught you all I can for now, but we need to recap before I leave. It's easy to do more harm than good if you're uncertain about anything."

Hophni's eyes gleamed. He knew all he needed to know, but it wouldn't hurt to go over old ground.

Enos uncorked the jar of green liquid.

"This extract of marsh nettle is used to bring relief from bowel disease and food poisoning," he said. "It's doubtful we would have survived the flux[8] without it. I could prevent the disease recurring if I knew what caused it in the first place, but I've not a clue. I don't suppose you do?"

Caught off guard, Hophni flushed guiltily. "W-why ask me?" he spluttered. "I wasn't here when it happened!"

"Sorry! I was hoping you might suggest something I haven't considered. Seraphina still hasn't fully recovered. Another bout could put her and the baby at risk."

"I never realized the mistress was in danger," Hophni said with apparent concern.

"Why else would I need to stock up on my supply of extract so urgently?" the doctor retorted. Hophni nodded.

"Then the sooner you go looking for the nettles, the better," he said, taking the jar from Enos and recorking it.

Enos smiled to himself. How easy it was to spin a lie!

"You're sure he suspected nothing?" Noah asked. Enos shook his head.

"If anything, his self-confidence got the better of his good sense," he said.

"Well, we all know how pride goes before a fall," Methuselah chuckled. "You've done well, Enos."

"You're taking quite a risk," the doctor warned. "Seraphina could miscarry if she has a recurrence of the flux[8]."

"Do you really think Hophni will use poisonous mushrooms again?" Noah asked.

"That, or something worse. You must strike tonight, before he does."

"But what if he makes his move earlier?" Seraphina argued. "What if he tampers with today's lunch, for instance?"

"That's highly unlikely!" Enos guffawed. "Hophni wants to enjoy his moment of glory. He will only put his plan into action when it suits him."

Noah nodded grimly.

"Very well. Tonight it is," he agreed.

"I'd better make a start, then," Methuselah said.

"Whatever you do, Sir, Seraphina must *not* get sick at this late stage of her pregnancy," the doctor warned.

"I promise she'll have nothing harmful to eat," the Patriarch[23] assured him. "Now go before Hophni wonders why you delay." Enos turned to see the man lounging against one of the wagons and raised his hand in farewell.

"You're right," he answered. "It is time to leave. Now, remember to take four drops of my stimulant every six hours."

"We've already had our first dose," Methuselah answered, holding up a small wooden bottle. "I've also got plenty of my own remedy on hand, in case Hophni strikes before we do. *Shalom*[26], Enos. May the God of peace watch over you."

"And peace be with you," Enos answered as he mounted Boaz and rode away at a slow canter. The small group watched the departing figure in silence.

"May Elohim[7] keep his heart, mind and body safe," Methuselah prayed. Noah and Seraphina responded with a solemn amen. They had each other if their scheme went wrong. Enos was alone.

Methuselah turned to Seraphina and smiled.

"Now it's your turn, granddaughter."

"Do I have to?" she protested lamely.

"Come, come," the old man urged. "You know it's the only way to get Beulah away from the cook pot."

"I suppose so," she admitted reluctantly. Then, without warning, she grasped her swollen belly and fell to the ground. Alarmed by Noah's shout for help, Hophni crossed the yard at a run and stared at the unconscious woman.

"What's wrong?" he asked fearfully.

"She grabbed her stomach and fainted," Noah answered. "I think it's the baby coming."

"Oh God!" Hophni protested. "I don't know what to do."

"Then we can thank Elohim[7] that Beulah is both a midwife and a nurse," Noah growled. "Now, get out of my way. I want to lay my wife down." Scowling, Hophni stepped aside from the open doorway of his mistress's quarters.

"I suppose I'd better find Beulah," he muttered as Noah pushed past him. Methuselah watched him go, then followed his grandchildren into the room.

"That was quite an act," he teased. Seraphina's eyes sparkled with mirth, but she quickly closed them when she heard Beulah approaching. Hopefully, she would be able to fool the old lady as easily as she had fooled Hophni.

Beulah once again examined Seraphina, then stood back and shook her head.

"It isn't the baby, My Lady," she said, rinsing her hands in the basin of water Noah had brought. "He's only likely to enter this world in another month or so."

"But that's weeks away!" Seraphina exclaimed. "What are these terrible stomach cramps I'm having, then? I'm in agony!"

"They're a mystery, they are," Beulah answered dryly "A sore stomach will grumble and growl in complaint, but yours is doing neither. What am I to say, My Lady? My fingers and ears tell me nothing's amiss." Shamed by the nurse's stony stare,

Seraphina lowered her eyes. It was several seconds before Beulah spoke again, the hurt evident in her voice.

"You may have a good reason for pretending to be sick, My Lady, but I refuse to stand for it." Seraphina realized she had to tell Beulah everything, or risk the old lady exposing their plan. Sighing, she propped herself up against her pillows.

"I *have* tried to mislead you, Beulah, but only because I wanted to protect us both. If you're not going to allow me to keep my secret from you, then you'd better close the door and shutters. I don't want to be overheard."

Beulah silently obeyed, then sat with folded arms at the foot of her mistress's bed. Her eyes widened in disbelief as Seraphina told her all that had happened over the past weeks. Not once had she suspected Hophni of such wickedness.

"You now understand why I'm pretending to be in labour," Seraphina concluded. "It's a good smokescreen for our plan, and it's unlikely Hophni will guess my pains are feigned."

"But surely he'll give you some nettle extract if you pretend to be sick like the rest of us?"

"Yes, he will, Beulah."

"Won't it affect the baby, My Lady?" the nurse asked in alarm.

"Enos has given me medicine to prevent that happening. What we've got to avoid is the possibility of Hophni rounding up a gang to do us harm. Fortunately, Shalom is lame and the doctor has Boaz. It's doubtful the scoundrel will walk to Salassi's unless he's desperate. But he won't be if all goes according to plan."

Beulah shuddered.

"You're scaring me, My Lady!" she cried.

"I'm sorry you're being subjected to this, Beulah, but you're going to have to cooperate if we're to avoid bloodshed."

Seraphina's final argument persuaded the old nurse. She had seen much blood over the years, but it had been the blood of life, not violence. While she did not entirely agree with the trap they were laying, she would do anything to keep her mistress safe.

"Are you sure it's the baby coming and not just a stomach upset?" Hophni asked irritably. "Enos said she hadn't fully recovered from the flux[8]."

"Which you escaped," Beulah reminded him caustically.

"True, but 'twas no fault of my own," he retorted. "Now, what of Lady Seraphina?"

"It's the baby alright," the old lady answered with a conclusive smack of her lips. "Little fellow's too lively to be staying inside much longer. He's bound to be born soon."

"How soon?"

"That's hard to say, Hophni. It's her first and could come quickly. On the other hand, the babe could take days to crown. The pains aren't regular, so the mistress will probably be a while – especially if she's in false labour."

"False labour?"

"Why now, aren't you the one?" Beulah mocked. "Not that it's your fault. You've a long way to go before you know as much as Enos. Good at delivering babies, he is."

"Of course I've a lot to learn," Hophni admitted impatiently. "So get on with it and tell me what you mean by false labour." Beulah smiled at the young man's ill temper.

"False labour is when all the signs are right, but the baby's just pretending to be coming. It can be scary for a woman."

"Do *you* think it's false labour?"

"Well, like I already said, it could be. But then again, it might not. Whichever, I don't want to risk treating the mistress's pains lightly. Do you?"

"No, I don't. Very well, it's over to you, then. I'm clueless when it comes to women."

"You can't expect Beulah to look after Seraphina as well as the kitchen," Noah pointed out. Hophni nodded.

"I realize that," he said. "What if I make up for my ignorance by standing in for her? My cooking's not half as tasty but it'll sustain us for the time being." Beulah threw her hands up in horror at the suggestion.

"There's only one man I trust in my kitchen, and that's my Lord Methuselah," she declared. "He's already volunteered to prepare our meals until Lady Seraphina's well again. Now, I must return to the mistress. She'll be wondering where I am."

Hophni smiled. Methuselah's offer was an unexpected bonus. Sneaking the mushrooms into Beulah's stew had been easy enough the first time, but it would nonetheless be expedient for him to be distanced from the preparation of food.

Methuselah dipped his ladle into the pot and sipped the rich gravy. He then spat it out and rinsed his mouth. Yet a little more honey was needed to mask its acridness. Pouring a generous measure of the syrup into the pot, he again gave the stew a stir and sampled it. To his satisfaction, the flavour was now as good as anything Beulah ever concocted. Chuckling to himself, he struck the dinner gong and waited impatiently for the crew.

Jasper did not have a strong stomach and was first to double over in pain.

"What's wrong?" John asked, anxiously twisting his hands.

"My belly feels like it's being pulled inside out, it's that agonizing!" Jasper groaned. "Oh Lord, I can't take much more!" Pushing his stool away from the table, the pallid foreman collapsed to the floor and retched.

"I don't feel too good either!" Obadiah cried, running from the room, his hand over his mouth.

It was soon apparent they had all been stricken. Clutching his stomach, Methuselah stared helplessly at Noah. Even with the drops Enos had prescribed, the pain was excruciating.

"I hate to think what the others are experiencing," Noah muttered through clenched teeth.

"Hush!" Methuselah whispered. "I'm about to be questioned." The two men watched Hophni stagger across the room to slump down next to them.

"What on earth did you put in the food?" he demanded hoarsely.

"I've never had anyone complain about my cooking before," Methuselah objected.

"Then explain why we're all down with stomach cramps and vomiting, you old fool!"

"Watch your mouth!" Noah warned with clenched fists. Hophni's eyes flickered. He knew he could never match the strength of the larger man. But his time would come. Tonight he would do it – tonight, when no one would suspect a thing! Meanwhile, he had to act as Enos would in the circumstances. Turning to Methuselah, he inclined his head.

"I'm sorry I was impudent, Sir, but I, too, am sick. We've all been infected by the same thing. I can only conclude you put something poisonous in the stew."

"No, Hophni. There's nothing harmful in this meal."

"Perhaps not, but I must check every possibility if I'm to treat the symptoms. Isn't that what Enos would do?"

The Patriarch[23] ran his hand across his eyes.

"You're right. Enos would ask what I put in the food, wouldn't he?" he conceded. "Let's see. I used plenty of potatoes, carrots, lentils, corn and flour. I also tossed in some wild turnips. We're out of cabbage and I needed a substitute."

"You didn't tell me you'd found turnips," Noah said.

"Well, I did and pulled enough for two meals. The rest are over there." Reaching to the shelf behind him, Noah picked up one of the bulbous roots and smelled it.

"These look like turnips, but they don't smell the same. Are you sure they're alright?"

"You've got me thinking now, Noah. What if I have poisoned us all?"

"Why, those aren't turnips," Obadiah interrupted from the doorway. "They're morning glory[18] roots. My mother used to grind them up and give us no more than a pinch or two whenever our stomachs needed purging. What you've given us is opening medicine, Sir, and plenty of it, too! Little wonder our innards are being turned inside out! Oh mercy! There it goes again!" Holding his hand to his belly, the carpenter ran from the room.

"Well, that explains it," Hophni grunted. "Fortunately, Enos showed me what to prescribe if you went down with the flux[8] again. But I can't treat any of you until I've treated myself. I'm not well enough." Overcome by nausea, he staggered from the room. He really was ill and hoped the nettle extract would work as effectively as Enos claimed.

Shaking with pain, Hophni uncorked the jar and mixed a measure of the green liquid with water. It was bitter as gall and he held his hand over his mouth to stop himself retching. Knowing it would taste even worse undiluted was sobering. His scheme would come to nothing if what little he had of the extract was vomited up before it had time to take effect.

To his surprise, the heaving in his stomach rapidly subsided. He had not expected the extract to work quite so quickly. Picking up the jar, he left Enos's room at a trot.

The condition of the men had worsened considerably during his short absence and he wondered if Obadiah was wrong. What if the turnips were in fact poisonous? He considered withholding the extract and letting nature take its course, but decided against it. He did not want his motives questioned. Putting the jar down, he clapped his hands for silence.

"As you can see from my renewed state of health, Enos's extract really does work," he said. "Unfortunately, it tastes vile. But I suppose you already know that."

"We managed to stomach it before," Jasper groaned.

"True, but I'll be giving you a double dose, and not watered down."

"Why so much?" Matthias asked.

"Enos suggested it," Hophni answered smoothly. "Not only will a double, undiluted measure work faster, it will also make you drowsy – which is a good thing. Sleep is often the best medicine of all. My only worry is that you'll not be able to keep the extract down, it's that bitter."

"We'll keep it down," Methuselah stated firmly.

"Are you sure?" Hophni asked dubiously. "You know I'll soon run out of the stuff if you don't."

"Vile or not, Hophni, I can't take any more of this," Obadiah cried. "For mercy's sake, do something!" Hophni poured a double measure of the potion into a wooden beaker and watched Obadiah gulp it down, his face twisting in disgust. The tense moment quickly passed and Hophni nodded with relief. If Obadiah had managed to keep the undiluted extract down, so would the others.

"Who's next?" he asked confidently. Jasper immediately stepped forward, a look of apology on his haggard face.

"If I don't take the medicine now, I'll not live to tell any more tales!" he croaked. Methuselah stared at the desperate man and wondered if he and Noah had taken on too much. His panic grew when Obadiah fell to the floor, unconscious.

"I know you said a double measure would work faster, but this is ridiculous!" he exclaimed, leaning over the carpenter and feeling for a pulse. "This man's so sound asleep he's hardly breathing. He'll catch his death of cold if he stays here. We should carry him to bed before we're unable to do so."

"We'd all be wise to go to bed before receiving our doses," Noah suggested, as he staggered back into the room. "My wife's also sick and I want to be with her."

"A curse on my foolishness for picking those roots!" Methuselah growled. "I am sorry."

"No sorrier than Seraphina," Noah replied tersely. "I insist she be treated before things get any worse for her."

"You're right," Hophni agreed. Smiling to himself, he picked up the jar and followed his masters to their quarters.

"Here they come, My Lady!" Beulah exclaimed from her post at the window. "Now, draw your knees up and hold your belly like you're fit to burst. And try to look pale, Miss, or Hophni'll know something's not right."

"For goodness' sake, Beulah!" Seraphina scolded. "You're also supposed to be groaning and moaning, remember? One slip-up and Hophni will guess he's been outwitted."

"And well I know it, mistress," the old nurse replied solemnly. "It's not for nothing that I threw my dinner away. The rogue might do something we haven't bargained for. I want to be in a fit state to thwart him."

"I hadn't thought of that," Seraphina conceded. "But come quickly, Beulah! I hear footsteps! Lie beside me and don't forget to look like you're in pain."

"Fear not, My Lady," Beulah grinned as she snuggled under the blankets. "I'm good at pretending when I put my mind to it."

Pushing open the door, Noah preceded the two men into the room and frowned at Beulah. He had seen the old lady keeping watch and could only hope Hophni had not. Hiding his irritation, he kissed Seraphina lightly on the forehead.

"Is Beulah also unwell?" he asked.

"She's more ill than I am," Seraphina whispered brokenly. "How will I manage without her?"

"Nobody's going to die, granddaughter," Methuselah remonstrated gently. "A double dose of Enos's medicine will put you both to sleep, but you'll wake up feeling as fit as ever."

"A double dose? But surely that's...?" Seraphina began to object, then gasped.

"Enough talking," Noah grumbled. "My wife can't take much more." Nodding, Hophni put his arm under Seraphina's head and helped her drink from the beaker. He then measured out another dose and gave it to Beulah.

"Your agony will soon be over," he said. Gripping the beaker with both hands, the old lady swallowed its contents, then flopped back against the pillows. Hophni smiled. His scheme was going much better than expected.

Even though Seraphina had taken some of Enos's stimulant just before Hophni entered the room, the effect of the extract was immediate. Knowing how much hinged on her staying awake, she was tempted to again put Enos's wooden bottle to her lips, but could not. The look in Hophni's eyes told her he would stop at nothing to achieve his own ends. She took a deep breath to slow her racing heart. *Please, dear Elohim[7], help me,* she cried silently. In an instant, her drowsiness lifted and she breathed a sigh of relief. She could now feign sleep without fear. Turning on her side, she closed her eyes.

Once satisfied Seraphina was asleep, Hophni turned to Noah.

"The mistress's resistance to the extract had me worried," he said.

"We'll probably all respond differently," Noah shrugged.

"True, but I'd hoped the extract would work on her as quickly as it did on Obadiah."

"Who wouldn't? The agony's killing!" Methuselah grumbled, but shook his head when Hophni offered him the beaker.

"I'm responsible for this mess and should be last to take the medicine," he said.

"Anyone could've made the same mistake," Noah chided. "Now stop arguing and swallow your dose. The others are waiting." Smiling wryly, the Patriarch[23] lifted the beaker to his lips, then handed it back with a grimace. Within minutes, he was snoring softly.

Her eyes barely open, Seraphina saw her husband swallow his dose of extract. She also saw the malice on Hophni's face as he watched and felt her resolve begin to crumble. Did the man intend to do something awful? Panic welled up inside her. Noah was too groggy to ward off an assault and she had neither the strength nor agility to defend him. If only Methuselah and Beulah were still awake! Desperate, she again prayed for God's intervention. The attack, when it came, was not what she expected. Outraged by Noah's rapid loss of consciousness, Hophni doused him with a pitcher of water.

"You'll not sleep until you hear what I have to say!" he snarled, grabbing Noah's beard and pulling him into a sitting position.

"W-what're you doing?" Noah mumbled as he tried focusing on his assailant. Hophni doubled over in mirth.

"I'm destroying you, that's what!" he laughed, prodding Noah in the chest. "What a fool you are, Noah! Methuselah's purgative may not have poisoned you all, but I have. I don't suppose Enos thought he was putting anyone at risk when he told me an undiluted dose of the extract is lethal. You'll soon fall into a sleep from which you'll not waken. Just think of it. You'll never see your wife again or get to know the child in her womb. Neither will you get to build God's Ark. I wonder what *He* will say about that. And while you're sleeping off eternity, I'll be using your fortune to start a new life. How wonderful it will be to not have to bow and scrape to the likes of you!"

"You'll never get away with it, Hophni!" Noah said hoarsely. "They'll find you, track you down."

"Not if they think I'm already dead. Oh yes, I've many a trick, Noah, but you'll never know what they are. You're dying even as we speak."

Laughing, Hophni pushed Noah back against the pillows. "Feast your eyes on all you hold dear. A few minutes more and you'll no longer be able to see Seraphina. Another few hours, and your heart will stop altogether. Think on these things while you lie there, dying."

"You're wrong, Hophni, so wrong," Noah slurred just before he fell into a death-like stupor.

As sleep overtook him, he silently prayed for Seraphina to remain calm. Any display of fear would put her in jeopardy.

CHAPTER 6
FALLEN PREY

You will always reap what you sow! Those who live
only to satisfy their own sinful desires will harvest the
consequences of decay and death.
Galatians 6:7b–8b

It was purely by God's grace that Seraphina kept her self-control. Her heart leapt when Hophni left the room, but she remained still until she could no longer hear his footsteps. Jumping out of bed, she forced a few drops of Enos's stimulant down Noah's throat.

"Wake up, husband!" she pleaded. But Noah's body was cold and unresponsive. Weeping, she combed her fingers through his dark mane of hair.

"Please, Elohim[7]!" she whispered.

Noah's eyes suddenly flickered open and he sat up, bewildered. Seraphina gently pushed him back down.

"Not so fast," she urged. "Enos said you'll feel awful, but it will soon pass."

Noah stroked her wet cheek with the back of his finger.

"I'm sorry you had to listen to Hophni's diatribe," he said.

"I thought he was going to do something violent, Noah!"

"So did I," he admitted, rising to put his arms around her. "We've got to stop him, Seraphina. Now, stand watch while I pour some of Enos's stimulant down Grandfather and Beulah. And, for goodness' sake, keep your head down!"

Seraphina settled herself by the window. She shuddered when she saw Hophni's silhouette in the lamp-lit doorway of the crew's sleeping quarters, a hundred or so paces away. What had started out as a devious scheme was now a nightmare!

Enos arrived at the giant redwood well before dark and began preparing for his long vigil. Years had elapsed since he had climbed such a large tree. He hoped he was still equal to the task.

Nobody would have known about the secluded spot had it not been for John. The lad had taken a payment to the mill two days ago, but Salassi had not been there to receive it. Unwilling to entrust the gold to anyone else, John had sat down and waited. The merchant had eventually returned in a high temper over Hophni's failure to turn up at their meeting place. He had become even more irate when he saw the youth. Refusing to do business at the mill, he had taken John to the giant redwood and insisted the lad keep his secret.

Feeling uneasy about the subterfuge, John had returned to camp and confided in Methuselah. Had the lad anticipated the Patriarch's[23] reaction, he probably would not have shared the information so freely. The thought of what Salassi might do when he realized he had been betrayed made the doctor shudder. He hated violence.

Having secured his hiding place, Enos swung to the ground and put his cheek against Boaz's soft muzzle. The dappled-grey horse nickered with pleasure.

"It's now your turn, old friend," Enos said, holding out a piece of sweet cane. Blowing softly, Boaz eagerly wrapped his tongue around the delicacy. Enos watched him eat, then stood back and pointed towards camp.

"Home, Boaz," he commanded. "Home now!" Startled, the horse tossed his head and neighed.

"Home, I said," Enos repeated, slapping the stallion's broad rump. Puzzled, Boaz stared at the doctor, then obediently headed back the way he had come.

Enos felt desperately alone when Boaz cantered out of sight. Methuselah's plot was becoming more complex by the minute and he feared they had taken on too much. Squatting, he unlatched Sheba's cage. The pigeon crooned with pleasure as he rubbed the back of her head.

"This will be your most important job yet, girl," he said after he had tied the linen scroll to her ankle. "Now, fly home, Sheba. Home to Lamech!" He threw the bird into the air and watched as she circled twice before heading west. She was soon no more than a speck in the sky.

Enos had not told Methuselah and Noah about his decision to send for help. His masters were confident of a victorious outcome, whereas he believed the risk of defeat was great. Hopefully, Lamech would feel the same as he and do something about it.

Sighing, Enos climbed back into the tree. He would not be needed before dawn but deemed it prudent to remain hidden until then. With nothing to do except eat and sleep, he was in for a long, lonely time of it.

"Where is he going?" Methuselah whispered.

"I'm not sure, but I'm beginning to have a good idea," Noah answered. Keeping to the shadows, the two men followed Hophni to the small graveyard and saw him stick his spade into the ground.

"He's not thinking of burying us, is he?" Methuselah said in alarm. Noah shook his head.

"That would take too much time and effort. I'd say he's about to dig a mock grave and mark it with his name."

"What on earth for?"

"What else but to account for his whereabouts? He thinks we'll be dead by dawn and that a search party will come looking for us. The problem is they won't find his body with ours. So he creates a false grave marked with his name to avoid raising suspicion. Anyone seeing it will presume we only just managed to bury him before succumbing to a fatal disease ourselves."

"If he can scheme up something like this, what else is he capable of?" Methuselah muttered as Hophni dumped a laden sack into the shallow grave. "We're in over our heads, Noah. We should nab our man before the situation gets out of hand."

"I'd agree if you weren't convinced Salassi is involved. Our safety lies in playing along until we've got both men where we want them."

Methuselah nodded soberly.

"You're right," he agreed as Hophni shovelled the dirt back into the hole and jammed a crude marker into the soft mound. The two men drew back into the shadows as he walked past. The expression on his torch-lit face made them shudder. They had just begun to follow when the sound they had been waiting for broke the silence. Hophni swung round in alarm, then grinned.

"Lost your rider, eh?" he said as he caught Boaz's trailing reins. "Not that I care, mind you. Come here, brute. We've work to do." The stallion submitted reluctantly, his ears flat against his skull.

"It worked!" Methuselah whispered excitedly. "Come on, I want to see what he does next."

Without further ado, the two men crept silently after their prey.

Noah had always been careless with keys. For this reason, he seldom carried them on his person. He did, however, hide them from prying eyes. It was with anger that he realized Hophni knew where he kept the key to his coffer.

"Perhaps I'm not so discreet, after all," he muttered.

"I'd say Hophni's been watching you for weeks to discover its whereabouts," Methuselah said. "He knows that smashing the chest open would make this look like the robbery it is. That's something he wants to avoid."

"But an empty coffer would raise the same suspicions, surely?"

46

"Not if Salassi claims you paid him up front. But hush. Hophni's just unlocked it. Look at him, Noah! Have you ever seen such greed?"

Hophni was mad with gold fever. His shrill laughter made the blood of the two men run cold. The rogue had already proved he would do anything to obtain the wealth he craved. They would be wise to remain hidden.

"My father claimed the love of money to be the root of all evil," Methuselah said sadly. "I now see he was right."

"Quiet!" Noah warned. "You're thinking your thoughts far too loudly."

"I doubt Hophni can hear anything above his gloating! But you're right. I must be careful."

They watched as Hophni tried lifting the coffer, but the combined weight of coinage and oak was too heavy. He impatiently cast his eyes around the wagon's dim interior, and grinned when he saw the saddlebag used to carry gold to Ben Salassi. He knew Noah had included several with their supplies and rose to look for them. Scarcely able to see by the flickering light of the guttering lamp, he tripped over a pile of goods and cursed. His eyes lit up when he saw they were the very things he was looking for. Grabbing a wooden scoop, he began shovelling coins into the first bag.

"What's he doing?" Methuselah asked in a whisper.

"Filling the saddlebags with my gold," Noah muttered. "A few minutes more, and he'll be fully loaded and on his way."

"You don't think he'll wait for dawn?"

"It will be to our advantage if he doesn't. Meanwhile, we should return to our beds. Hophni may want to check on us before he leaves."

"I suppose I'd do likewise," Methuselah said, "but it's going to be difficult to play dead."

"You don't have to. Enos told Hophni it can take up to twelve hours to die."

"And you're confident he won't delay his departure until then?"

"Would you?"

"Probably, but I'm a lot more level-headed than Hophni is right now," Methuselah answered dryly as he preceded Noah into the small room where Seraphina and Beulah were waiting.

Hophni never did check on his victims. Relieved, the small group watched him mount Boaz and leave camp.

"I'm surprised the rascal didn't take our cows as well as our horse," Beulah muttered.

"Come now, Beulah! He'd hardly be interested in our few animals when he believes he's got away with enough to buy herds of cattle," Methuselah said with a wag of his bony finger. "But we waste time with small talk. Dawn will be breaking in a few hours. We need to get some of Enos's stimulant down the others as soon as possible."

"You're right," Noah nodded. "We'll need their help if I've underestimated Salassi." Turning, he embraced Seraphina.

"Are you sure you understand what you and Beulah must do?" he asked. Seraphina grimaced. She wanted to accompany Noah, but he was adamant she stay.

"Please let me come!" she implored him again. "I promise I won't get in the way."

"No, Seraphina. Hophni's capable of murder. I don't know what I'd do if he hurt you."

"Have you thought how I would react if he hurt you?" she asked in dismay.

"Yes, I have," Noah answered sombrely, "but it's a risk I have to take." His remark distressed Seraphina even more, and Methuselah stepped forward to wrap his arms around her.

"You have nothing to fear, granddaughter. Elohim[7] has told Noah to build the Ark. He will keep him safe. Neither of you will die until you've done everything the Lord has commanded." Grateful for the comforting words, Seraphina clung to the Patriarch[23] before tearfully submitting to her husband's wishes.

"Thank you," Noah said, kissing her tenderly. Nodding, she gently pushed him out the door. Noah laid his hand against her wet cheek, then followed Methuselah to the crew's sleeping quarters.

Roused from their drugged sleep, the men listened to Noah in growing disbelief.

"Are you saying Hophni meant to murder us?" hot-tempered Ichabod exclaimed.

"Precisely," Methuselah answered.

"The rotten scoundrel! Just wait till I lay my hands on him!"

"Calm down, Ichabod!" Noah said sternly. "Nobody takes up arms until I say so. Understood?" The men reluctantly agreed.

"We'll soon have our man where we want him," Noah continued. "Meantime, we must join Enos before Hophni meets Salassi. You've taken many a walk through this forest, John. Is there a quicker route to the giant redwood?" The youth's eyes widened in surprise. It was not often his master consulted him.

"T-that there is, Sir," he stammered eagerly. "It's no more than a track, mind you."

"Can you lead us there in the dark?"

The lad hesitated for a moment, then nodded.

"My only worry is old Master," he said in his slow, deliberate way. "He may find the path too steep."

"Why, I'm as fit as I was 700 years ago!" Methuselah objected strongly.

"That's not altogether true," Noah said. "Perhaps you should consider staying behind. Seraphina and Beulah would be glad of your company."

"Stay, and miss out on catching Hophni? Not likely, Noah! The women are more than capable of looking after themselves."

"But what if you stumble and fall?" Noah objected. "We can't afford to be delayed."

"It could happen, I suppose," the old man conceded gruffly. "Very well. If I struggle, I promise to drop out and return to camp at first light. Agreed?"

"Only if you bring that stout walking stick you've been using lately," Noah grumbled. "Indeed, we all need to carry staffs. They'll serve as weapons if we need them."

"What'll you do when we find the rascal?" Jasper asked.

"I'm not sure," Noah answered solemnly. "But we will catch him. You have my word on it."

"Your word, eh?" Jasper grinned. "I reckon the stupid young fool will soon be sorry he ever tangled with you." The remark made Noah laugh.

"You're right, Jasper. Hophni *has* been a stupid young fool. But, come. We waste valuable minutes jesting. Organize the crew, and don't forget to bring water."

Within minutes, the men quietly fell in step behind John. True to his promise, Methuselah brought up the rear and prayed he would be able to keep up. He had not bargained for such a brisk pace.

CHAPTER 7
CHANGE OF HEART

The king's heart is like a stream of water directed by the
LORD; He turns it wherever He pleases.
Proverbs 21:1

Lamech stood on the flat roof of his home. The sun had just sunk below the horizon, casting Je'el into russet shadow. It was a time of day when he usually felt most at peace, but this evening he was troubled. It had been months since he had had word of Noah and he was disturbed more than he cared to admit. He deeply regretted their estrangement. Had he known then what he knew now, he would have acted differently.

Lost in thought, he did not see the approaching speck in the dusky sky and was startled when Sheba fluttered down beside him. He immediately recognized the bird and took her up in his arms. Descending the stairs, he shut himself in his room and removed the tightly rolled message from her ankle.

The brief communication was not what Lamech had hoped. While delighted with Seraphina's pregnancy, Hophni's duplicity made him irate. Like Enos, he feared Noah's scheme would fail without his help and knew he must act quickly. Running his hands through his hair, he screwed his eyes shut in an effort to concentrate. With no wagons or livestock to slow him down, he could cover the distance to Ben Salassi's estates far quicker than Noah had. Even so, he would need a change of horses if he was to make good time. One of his buyers farmed on the direct route to the Aldargs and should be willing to hire out fresh mounts.

Throwing open the door, Lamech called for his steward and instructed him to put two dozen men on his finest ponies.

"Also saddle a horse for me," he added. "We'll be riding hard for most of the night, so each man must bring enough food and water for the journey. I'll meet you in the yard when you're done." The steward's eyes flickered in surprise. It was not like his master to be so decisive.

"What of the mistress, Sir?" he asked quietly.

50

"Tell her I've gone to join my son in the Aldargs and expect to be away for some time." The steward touched his fingers to his forehead and hastened to obey. Lamech saw the sympathy in the man's eyes as he withdrew and sighed. The servants despised Miriamne for her bitter tongue. But even more offensive was her infidelity, now too blatant for him to refute. He scowled. So much time wasted, with nothing but sorrow to show for it!

Rising to his feet, he unlocked his coffer and removed three bags of gold. He did not expect the hiring of fresh mounts to cost so much, but did not want to risk taking less. He had allowed too many things to stand between him and his family of late. He dipped his pen into the inkwell and quickly replied to Enos's note. He would have liked to have sent it immediately, but Sheba would not be fit to fly for several hours yet.

The quarter moon provided enough light to ride by, and they covered a good distance before the ponies began to flag. Reining in his mare, Lamech took his bearings. He had ridden this route often enough to know they were about a mil[17] from Aaron Solomon's farm – beyond which lay the Aldargs and the narrow track leading to Ben Salassi's estate. Negotiating it would not be easy if their fresh mounts were untried.

He was, of course, assuming Solomon would be prepared to hire out his horses. The man had always been amenable in the past, but Lamech feared this was no longer the case. Many of his customers had defected since his son's call to build the Ark.

Lamech was surprised to find Aaron Solomon had changed the main thrust of his business from stud to hire. Not only did the horse dealer have stock available at a fair price, he also agreed to stable Lamech's animals at no extra charge. The generous offer was more than Lamech had hoped for. He wondered if he was being duped.

"You rank among the best when it comes to breeding horses, Aaron. What made you change?" he asked.

"Don't really know. The idea came out of the blue, just like that." Laughing, Aaron Solomon clicked his fingers for emphasis.

"Fancy me thinking of such a thing, Lamech! I was horrified to begin with. But the more I thought about it, the more I liked it. I now wish I'd diversified earlier. Hiring out horses brings more money for less work. And, at my age, it's time to relax a little. I also get to meet folk this way. It's lonely here, with the wife and children gone."

The horse dealer's sentiment did little to arouse Lamech's sympathy. Were it not for the man's gross infidelity, his wife would still be alive and his children in his fields! Even so, Sadie Solomon's suicide had hit her husband hard, resulting in him taking a vow of celibacy that had not been broken since her death. But the man's change of heart had come too late to heal the rift between him and his sons. Ashamed and angry, they saw their father's reformation as a hypocritical bid to expunge his guilt and refused to have anything more to do with him. Lamech did not blame them. His own lust-filled infatuation with Miriamne had hurt Noah as much as Solomon's adultery had hurt his family. Hopefully, the gap in their relationship would be bridged.

"I do understand your loneliness," he said quietly.

"Marriage not going well?"

Lamech scowled. It was clear from Solomon's expression that he was aware of Miriamne's misconduct.

"Had I heeded the warnings and not married Miriamne in the first place, our lives would not be in the mess they are today," he said. "But I digress. We've a long ride ahead."

"So you have," Aaron Solomon agreed. "Your horses are ready. I've chosen good, sturdy mounts that know these foothills well."

Within minutes, Lamech and his men were back on the road, their way lit by the torches Solomon insisted they carry.

"You'll need them now the moon's beginning to wane," he had said. "The piles of loose scree in these foothills are treacherous." Lamech was grateful he had taken the horse dealer's advice. They would have stumbled often had their way not been lit. Turning in the saddle, he looked at the line of dancing torches and smiled. It was fascinating how much light a single flame could generate. *Another one of God's miracles*, he mused, then gave himself a shake. He wasn't usually so sentimental, but tonight's experience proved without doubt that God had gone before him to meet his needs.

Although excited by the miracle, Lamech was also troubled. Why would the Sovereign Lord move on behalf of one and not another? His face darkened momentarily. Remembering Orpah's suffering and death usually made him so angry that he forced himself to forget. But tonight was different. Sighing, he closed his eyes to prolong the peace he felt. He now knew God caused all things to work together for good and would one day answer his questions. Meanwhile, there was much to do. Reining in his horse, he withdrew Sheba from the cage tied to his saddle.

"Fly, Sheba. Fly to Enos," he said as he lifted the pigeon into the air.

Dawn was just beginning to break when Enos realized he was not alone. Cupping his hands to his mouth, he gave a long, low whistle and grinned when Sheba fluttered down into his lap. The pigeon was exhausted and he hoped the return flight had not taken too heavy a toll on her. Holding the bird against his chest, he removed the message she carried and sighed with relief when he read it. Closing his eyes, he slept at last.

He awoke just over an hour later to the sound of furtive movement in the bush below.

"Are you there, Mister Enos, Sir?" John softly asked as he peered up into the giant redwood.

"That I am," Enos answered, kneading his aching limbs. "And stiff as a board, too. I'll be glad to be back on solid ground."

"You're not like me, then," the youth grinned as he clumsily helped the doctor down. "My mother said I should've been born a monkey."

"Not so, John. If you were anything except who you are, you'd lose the joy of acting like what you are not." The boy stared at him with such puzzlement that Enos could not help laughing out loud. Wiping tears from his eyes, he placed his hands on the narrow shoulders and looked into the ingenuous blue eyes. He had come to love John like a son and knew he would be lonely without him.

"You're special, John. Don't change, ever. People like me need you." Not knowing how to respond, John merely nodded. Few showed such kindness to a simpleton.

"We'd better get going, Sir," he said. "Old Master's not too good."

"Methuselah? What's wrong with him?"

"He's gone and collapsed, Sir. The way we've come was too much for him, I'm thinking."

"Well, what're we waiting for, then?" Enos said briskly. "Come, hide the rope and help me cover our tracks. We can't afford to be careless now." Once satisfied the glade was cleared of all evidence of their presence, they quickly retreated into the forest.

"Thank God you're here," Noah said, pulling Enos into the small circle. Methuselah lay on the forest floor, his head pillowed in Jasper's lap. The Patriarch's[23] pallor was ashen and he clutched feebly at his chest.

"I told him not to come, but he would not listen," Noah muttered in frustration.

"Yes, it's my fault," Methuselah whispered through blue-tinged lips. "So sorry."

"Quiet!" Enos admonished. "You're using up too much strength." Closing his fingers around Methuselah's wrist, he sat still for several seconds.

"Well, it's nothing that can't be fixed," he said, as he felt the slow but regular pulse. "But it could've been worse had you pushed yourself any harder."

"What's wrong with him?" Jasper asked.

"Your master's heart isn't beating as fast as it should. I'll give him a stimulant to ease his distress, but he must rest if he's to regain his strength."

"You waste time with small talk," Methuselah rasped. "I can't breathe, for goodness' sake!"

Enos reached for his bag, then groaned. Hophni had it!

"Are you looking for this, Sir?" Obert asked, holding out the worn satchel. "Hophni left it behind and I brought it along, just in case." Enos gratefully took it from him.

"Well done!" he said warmly. "Your good sense will serve your master well this day."

To Enos's relief, the contents of his bag remained largely undisturbed and he quickly spooned some red lavender[24] down the Patriarch's[23] throat. Within seconds, Methuselah's breathing stabilized and the colour began returning to his cheeks.

"You'll have to stay here until you're fit to travel," Enos instructed as he re-covered his patient with Noah's homespun mantle.

"But why? I'm as good as new!" the old man exploded.

"So you think, but I doubt you'd be able to walk more than a pace or two without keeling over," the doctor answered dryly. Stubborn as ever, Methuselah attempted to rise, but got no further than a crouch when his world started spinning. Groaning, he fell back and rubbed angrily at his eyes.

"Oh God, I feel so useless!" he complained impatiently. He then glared at the silent group. "Well, don't just stand there! Any more time wasted and Hophni will have done his business and hightailed it out of here!"

Noah, however, felt uneasy about leaving his grandfather alone in the woods.

"Perhaps we should back down," he suggested quietly to Enos. The doctor was horrified.

"No, Noah! We must see this through or run the risk of Salassi hunting us down to complete what Hophni began. As for Methuselah, no one will come looking for him here. Have Jasper stay with him, if you like. The foreman knows the forest as well as young John does."

"You're right, I suppose," Noah conceded. "But can we afford to be down two men when Salassi's crew outnumbers us three to one? We'll not fare well if the situation becomes violent." Enos saw the worry in Noah's eyes and knew it was time to tell him about Lamech.

"You've less to fear than you think," he said. "I sent a message to your father, asking him for help."

Noah stared at Enos in disbelief.

"My father? How is he going to help?"

"Only God knows, Sir, but he's replied to say he's on his way."

"Lamech? Coming here?" Methuselah exclaimed. "Now there's a miracle I never thought to see this side of Heaven! I tell you this, Noah. Your father never does anything by halves once he's made his mind up. He'll bring as many men as he's able."

"Even so, I doubt they'll arrive in time," Noah muttered gloomily.

"They will," Methuselah declared.

"I hope so," Noah answered, turning on his heel. "Come, men, it's time to move out."

Methuselah and Jasper silently watched their departure.

"I hope they'll be alright," Jasper whispered.

"Elohim[7] has said that nothing will stand against my grandson. The promises of the Lord never fail," Methuselah replied quietly.

"Even so, Sir, those rogues are too cunning for my liking."

"Perhaps, but the Lord will give Noah the wisdom he needs to outwit them. What we must do is pray for God's will to be accomplished." Jasper's face split into a toothless grin. Praying was one thing the old carpenter could do well.

Chapter 8
Divide and Conquer

Any kingdom at war with itself is doomed. A city or home
divided against itself is doomed.
Matthew 12:25b

Hophni grabbed the saddle horn and cursed. It was the third time in as many minutes that the horse had stumbled. Convinced the beast was trying to unseat him, he lashed out with his whip, but Boaz merely snorted and plodded on. Hophni reined in the stallion and stared in frustration at the lightening sky. Salassi's men would be up and about well before he reached the mill. What if they noticed his gold-laden bags and asked questions? Unwilling to take that risk, he kicked his mount into a reluctant trot and headed for the giant redwood instead.

Enos had just retrieved his rope from the old badger hole when he heard the sound of approaching hoofbeats. Gesturing for silence, he cupped his hand around his ear.

"What do you hear?" Noah whispered.

"A horse big enough to be Boaz, and only a mil[17] or so away," the doctor replied.

"Then Hophni's coming here without Salassi. I wonder why?"

"Could be they're riding two up," Jasper suggested.

"Granted, but my feeling is that Hophni's had a change of plan. Whatever his reason, we can't risk being seen. Quickly, hide yourselves!" Crouching behind a fallen tree, Noah and his men watched Hophni circle the glade before dismounting beside the old badger hole.

"Nobody will think of looking here," they heard him say.

The exertion of stashing the heavy saddlebags soon had the villain pouring with sweat. When he was done, he wiped his forehead and covered the hole with bramble. He then climbed back into the saddle and left without a backward glance. As the hoofbeats retreated into the distance, Noah came out of hiding to retrieve what was his.

"Let me help you, Sir," John offered, scrambling into the hole ahead of his master. "Those bags are too heavy for one."

"You're right, they're heavy," Noah answered grimly. "Here, lad, pass them up quickly. We've no time to lose and there's something important I want you to do." John's face glowed. Nobody had ever entrusted him with so much in one day.

"W-what job, Sir?" he stammered as he hauled himself out of the badger hole.

"I know you've been to the mill only once, John, but you've a good eye and probably know its layout better than I do. Did you get to know any of Salassi's men while you were there?"

"I got talking to one of them, Sir. He was complaining something terrible about his master. I didn't say anything, though. I was too scared of stirring up trouble."

"Rightly so, John, but we're going to have to make trouble for Ben Salassi today. He and Hophni have done much harm and must be stopped. Now, you're to find the man you spoke to and this is what you must tell him." John's eyes grew wide as he listened to his master's instructions.

"But will they heed a boy like me?" he asked when Noah concluded.

"They'd be foolish not to."

"But … but what if you're wrong, Sir?"

"Then I'll deal with it later. Now go, and make sure you're not seen by Hophni or Salassi."

"I'll do my best, Sir," John called over his shoulder as he set off at an awkward lope.

John cautiously approached the outskirts of the lumberyard and hid behind a cord of logs. Inching his head upwards, he saw Boaz loosely tethered outside the timber merchant's shed. The door suddenly swung open and the lad ducked back out of sight as Salassi strode angrily from the building with Hophni. The two men were still in sharp disagreement when they rode into the forest a few minutes later.

Coming out of hiding, John walked nervously across the yard towards the surly foreman.

"What do you want, boy?" the man growled.

"I-I'm looking for Palti, Sir," John stammered, respectfully touching his fingers to his forehead. "My … my master sent me with a message for him." The foreman snorted at the lad's slow, impaired speech.

"He's over there, in the storehouse," he drawled, "sitting with his feet up and acting like God Almighty, now the boss isn't here. A little bit of learning and he thinks he's better than the rest of us. Bah! His sweat stinks just like mine when he chooses to work!" The foreman laughed, but his sarcasm fell flat beneath John's innocent stare.

"You're an idiot!" he mocked, waving the lad on. "Go see Palti, then, and good riddance!"

John pushed open the storeroom door and was surprised to discover the foreman had spoken truly. Startled by the unexpected intrusion, Palti swung his legs off the table, then snickered.

"You?" he said, casually resuming the task of cleaning his nails with a dirty knife. "Funny how the boss is out whenever you arrive, but he's always here for Hophni. They've just gone off in a high temper about something."

"A-and that's why I've come, Mister Palti," John said urgently. "I-I know what they're up to."

"You do? Well, tell me, then! I'm all ears."

Palti's face was dark with rage by the time John had finished.

"Are you certain, boy?" he asked aggressively. John nodded slowly, deliberately.

"W-why else would they meet in secret, Sir?"

"How much did you say Noah paid last time?"

"F-fifty gold shekels[28] it was, for ten cords of timber."

"Only ten cords? Are you sure, lad?"

"As sure as I've a nose on my face," John answered adamantly. Palti rose angrily to his feet.

"Then five shekels[28] per cord Salassi's been charging, and telling us he was only receiving a tenth of that!" he exclaimed. "He's likely been doing it for years, too, creaming the profits that should've gone towards increasing our wages."

Throwing open the shutters, Palti bellowed for the foreman.

"Look sharp, Nabal," he said. "I want the mill stopped and the men assembled." The man looked dubious. Work was only brought to a standstill for the most important of reasons.

"Don't just stand there," Palti snarled. "We've a lot at stake!"

Nabal's eyes darkened. He disliked being ordered around but knew from Palti's expression that something serious was wrong. Nodding, he raised the alarm with three strikes of the gong. Within minutes, the men were grouped in the yard.

"I've called this meeting to tell you we've been working for a thief," Palti declared. "Salassi claims he charges half a shekel[28] per cord of timber, right? John here says Noah's been paying five."

"But you keep the records!" a logger named Micah protested. "Surely you know how much gold comes in?" Palti shook his head.

"In all my years here, I've never seen a buyer's contract or the coins that change hands. If what John says is true, then Salassi's been giving me false figures and pocketing the rest. But enough is enough! It's time to demand our fair share, plus that increase in wages he's been withholding."

"You mean us against him?" Nabal grinned.

"Yes, I do."

Frightened of the consequences, Luz, the axe grinder, angrily shook his fist.

"The boss will dismiss us if we stand against him," he cried. "What will I do then? I've a wife and six children, for God's sake!"

"Don't worry, Luz. Salassi won't be in any fit state to dictate terms once we're done with him," Palti replied smugly. "John here has told me about his secret place. We'll catch him red-handed if we're quick about it. So saddle the horses, Andrew. We need to get moving."

"But we've not enough ponies to seat us all, Sir!" the stable boy objected.

"Then ride two to a horse," Palti answered tersely. "Those without mounts must follow as fast as they can. Our numbers are our strength."

"D-don't forget Boaz," John haltingly reminded him. Palti looked at the enormous draught animal and nodded reluctantly. He disliked horses and rode only when necessary.

CHAPTER 9
COUNTER-ATTACK

*Do not be afraid! Don't be discouraged by this mighty
army, for the battle is not yours, but God's.*
2 Chronicles 20:15b

S alassi almost exploded with anger when Hophni dismounted at the giant redwood and uncovered the badger hole. Never had he dealt with such an idiot!

"The gold's *here*?" he spluttered. Misinterpreting Salassi's rage for fear, Hophni grinned.

"You worry too much, Ben," he said as he slid into the deep recess. "The only things occupying this hole are six gold-stuffed saddlebags, and I need your help hauling them out." Scowling, Salassi dismounted and braced himself for the first laden bag. Its weight was grimly satisfying and he eagerly reached for the next one. Soon all six were above ground.

"We've no time to split the gold coin for coin," Salassi said, rubbing the dirt off his hands, "so I suggest we simply take three bags each. They weigh more or less the same."

"It would also make sense for me to keep your horse," Hophni agreed as he hoisted his takings onto his saddle.

"You're welcome to her, Hophni, but she's not half as strong as the brute you rode in on."

"True, but the mare's less conspicuous. You can keep Boaz in exchange. He's a good animal, but stubborn."

"He's also expensive. Are you sure you want to part with him?"

"Of course I am," Hophni replied, giving Salassi a good-natured slap on the shoulder. "Now, I must be going. I've a good distance to cover by nightfall. You'll sort out the logging camp, won't you?"

"With pleasure. I can't wait to feast my eyes on Methuselah's rotting flesh."

"Macabre thought!"

"It's my nature," Salassi grinned as he strapped his share of gold to his saddle. One of the bags suddenly tore and he stared in horror at the dirt pouring from the gaping hole.

"What in hell's going on?" he shouted, tipping the contents of the saddlebag on the ground.

"God, no!" Hophni cried. "I swear all six bags were full of gold! Someone must've seen me hide them and done a switch."

"Check them then, but I promise I'll kill you with my bare hands if this is a trick." Terrified by the threat, Hophni reached for the saddlebags and emptied each one. To his dismay, all were filled with rubble.

"This is not my doing, Ben," he protested.

"Don't take me for a fool, man! You would have left me high and dry had my bag not burst!"

Hophni nervously backed away, but the older man was quick as a cat.

"Please, Ben! Hear me out!" Hophni croaked as Salassi locked his hands around his throat.

"This had better be good, lad, or else," Salassi warned, loosening his grip slightly.

"I know you're angry, Ben, but it's not like you think. I'd never deceive you – not when you've forty men to chase me down."

"Hah! You know they'd sooner see me dead!"

"Not when their jobs are at risk. One word from you and they'd hang me without blinking. But I swear I haven't cheated you, Ben. Please, believe me!" The timber merchant stared long and hard at his victim, then nodded.

"Alright, I believe you," he growled, releasing his hold. "But then who in hell's taken the gold? All my men were accounted for this morning, and the logging camp crew is at death's door – or so you tell me."

"You couldn't be more wrong!"

The disembodied voice made the hair of the thieves stand on end. Panic stricken, Hophni swung round, but the glade was empty. He turned to question Salassi, only to find his partner in crime was even more afraid than he.

"You believe in ghosts?" Hophni asked sceptically. Salassi clenched his hands.

"It's hard not to when the voice I hear belongs to one who is as good as dead," he answered.

"I'm neither dead nor dying," Noah declared, as he emerged with his men from behind the fallen tree.

"You!" Hophni cried in disbelief. "But how?"

"You'll figure it out in the end," Noah answered grimly. "What a fool you've been, Hophni. You, too, Salassi. Today we've seen enough to put the two of you away for a long time."

"Never!" Salassi shouted. "My men won't let you ride out of here alive."

"I doubt they'll support you now," Noah said wryly. "But you'll find that out for yourself if that's the sound of hoofbeats I hear."

"That'll be them, come to save me," Salassi gloated.

"They're coming to indict you, Ben, not save you."

"What do you mean?"

"You'll know soon enough," Noah said as John rode into the clearing, followed by the millhands. Salassi's belligerence changed to consternation when he saw their anger.

"What in hell have you told them?" he demanded.

"That you've been swindling them."

"That's not true!"

"Then how do you explain why the youngster brought you fifty shekels[28] for the last batch of wood, but you only gave me five to bank?" Palti sneered.

"You can't prove the lad gave me fifty shekels[28]," Salassi replied aggressively.

"Yes, he can," Noah interjected. "He has the boy's word for it as well as mine."

"Oh, yes, the word of God's Prophet!" Salassi mocked. "But you weren't with John when he brought the gold. What's to stop him hoarding some for himself?"

"Nothing except who he is, Ben. Look at him, all of you, and tell me if you think a boy like this is capable of lying and cheating." As one, the men turned and stared at the simple, tow-headed youth.

"Well, what do you have to say for yourself, boy?" Palti asked impatiently.

"A-all I did was give Mister Salassi the gold, like Master Noah told me to," John stammered, nervously wringing his hands. "Paid it to him right here, I did. H-he said he didn't like keeping money at the mill because he couldn't trust anybody. But I know where he hides it, Sir. I've seen him do it."

Salassi's eyes flickered.

"Don't talk nonsense, boy!" he growled.

"B-but it's *true*, Mister Salassi, Sir," John insisted. "That day I came to the mill, you forgot to give me your mark of receipt. S-so I came back for it and saw you hiding the gold."

"You're talking rubbish, you halfwit!" Salassi objected.

"We'll soon find out, won't we?" Palti said sternly. "Come, lad, show us where Salassi hides his gold." Smiling, John pointed at a gnarled fig tree a hundred or so paces away.

"It's in the hollow of that tree," he said. "See. Mister Salassi's worn a path right to it."

"That's a lie!" Salassi raged. Dismounting, Nabal grabbed his employer's arm and cruelly twisted it behind his back.

"That remains to be seen," he said.

The fire in Salassi's eyes died and he shuddered. For years he had feared this day would come. Now it was here.

Strangler vines had drained the giant fig tree of life-giving sap and now served as buttresses for the hollowed-out trunk. Dragging Salassi after him, Nabal pushed his way through the narrow fissure of an entrance and cursed when he stubbed his toe.

"There's something here," he said, peering into the gloom. "Has anyone a lamp?"

"Isn't there one inside?" Noah suggested. "Salassi must've used a light when he came here."

"Well?" Nabal asked, remorselessly twisting his employer's arm. Gasping in pain, the timber merchant groped for his tinderbox and lit a small lamp. Feeble though the light was, it clearly revealed the two locked coffers and rickety chair that filled most of the hollowed-out space.

"It looks like you've made yourself a nice little counting house, Ben," Noah said. "That's assuming these chests contain what I think they do. We'd better take a look, hadn't we?" Still rubbing his sore arm, Salassi swung round and glared at Noah.

"You've no right!" he shouted.

"We have every right, Ben. You know how strict the law is when it comes to paying a tithe of your profits to your workers. Admit it. You've been caught cheating your men out of their fair wages and nothing you say can prove otherwise. So how about letting us see what's in those coffers?"

Knowing he was beaten, the timber merchant sullenly unlocked the chests.

Salassi's underpaid men were stunned to see such a vast quantity of gold. Interspersed among the thousands of coins were priceless gems.

"I remember Methuselah telling me about these," Noah said, holding up a string of pearls.

"I served my time for them," the timber merchant said morosely.

"So you did, but they're not worth a thing to you now, Ben. An accomplished thief would have cashed in on them years ago."

"What's done is done," Salassi sneered. "Jail's as good a place as any to start again."

"True, but if any of your workers or their dependents has died because you were underpaying them, you may incur the death penalty instead." Salassi looked in dread at his irate men. To his shame, he did not even know if they had families to support.

"Our boss owes us plenty if this heap of gold is anything to go by," Nabal taunted. "Him and his black heart. I say we hang him!" Alarmed by the threat, Palti drew Nabal aside.

"Lay one finger on Salassi and we'll be up for murder!" he hissed.

"And who'd be there to tell?" Nabal growled.

"Them, of course!" Palti answered, jerking his head in Noah's direction. "You're wrong if you think they'll tolerate another injustice this day!"

"Injustice?" Nabal roared. "Injustice, I'll be damned! We'd only be doing to Salassi what he deserves! As for you," he said, addressing Noah, "we'll not allow you to stop us, will we, lads?" The millhands eagerly responded by brandishing their weapons. Palti's blood ran cold.

"You can't be serious?" he said.

"We're dead serious," Nabal snarled. "Don't know about you, Palti, but I'm sick of being poor – and all because of Salassi's greed. It's time, now, for revenge. So decide. Are you with us or not?"

Palti turned his back in disgust, and Nabal unsheathed his own knife with a laugh of triumph. Hophni stared at the naked blade. His life was in just as much danger as Salassi's unless he did something about it.

"Wait!" he cried. "Don't kill anybody – not yet! There's more!"

"More what?" Nabal demanded, pressing the tip of his dagger against Hophni's neck.

"There's m-more gold," Hophni stammered. "Six saddlebags full. I hid them down this hole, but Noah must've seen me and exchanged the gold for rubble while I was gone." Flinging Hophni from him, Nabal turned to Noah.

"Well?" he demanded. "Where is it?"

"You'll not get a shekel[28] from me without a fight," Noah said.

"You think you can threaten us with sticks, old man?" Nabal goaded.

"Not with sticks, but in the power of Almighty God, who will not fail us," Noah declared.

Nabal rolled his eyes, then spat.

"All your talk about God makes me sick!" he roared, lunging wildly at Noah. "Defend yourselves like men or be damned." Noah quickly sidestepped and drove his fist into Nabal's chest, but with little effect. The man merely grunted and began circling him like a cat toying with a mouse. Spurred on by their foreman, the millhands hastened to also enter the fray and, in so doing, forgot to secure their captives. Hophni and Salassi stared wide-eyed at one another, then ran for their lives.

"We should've taken the horses!" Hophni panted, his lungs burning for air.

"And attract Nabal's attention? Not likely," Salassi replied, as he raced through the forest with Hophni on his heels. So intent were the two men on their flight that they did not see the dark-clad riders until the last minute. Skidding to a halt, Hophni looked up at their leader and groaned.

"Not you!" he cried.

"You know this man?" Salassi asked hoarsely. Hophni nodded.

"He's Noah's father," he muttered.

"You obviously didn't count on me being here," Lamech said with a thin smile. "And don't try escaping. We'll soon run you to ground." Hophni stared at the men surrounding them and nodded. He was not prepared to risk losing his life as well as his riches and freedom.

"Well decided," Lamech said. "Now, where is Noah?"

"He's back there, fighting Salassi's men," Hophni answered sullenly.

"So, it's started. You'd better pray Noah survives today, Hophni, or it will not bode well for either of you."

Noah soon realized he was no match for his adversary.

"Where's your God now?" Nabal goaded, slashing cruelly with his knife. Grunting, Noah thrust Nabal's dagger aside. His body ached with exhaustion and his eyes burned with sweat. Another few minutes, and he would be done for.

"Yes, Elohim[7], where are you?" he shouted in desperation. Enraged by the cry, Nabal lunged at his victim's throat, then froze as if he had been turned to stone. Noah stared in amazement at the still, cruel face and reached out to touch it, but there was no response. A great, throbbing light began filling the glade, and he shook with fear when he realized that all except he had been struck motionless by the Shekinah[29] Glory of God. Falling to his knees, he hid his face from the all-seeing One.

There is much I have called you to do, Noah, the Voice like no other said. *Things that are beyond anything you can imagine. Fear not, for I am with you and will never forsake you. When you walk through the fire, you will not be burned. Neither will the waters drown you. Thousands may fall around you, but I will keep you safe. I am your shelter by day and by night, the glory and the lifter of your head, your sword and your shield. Through me, and me alone, you will accomplish my call on your life. Do you understand this?*

"I do, Lord, but there are times when I forget – like now."

That is because my ways and my thoughts are so much higher than yours.

"Then teach me Your ways, oh Elohim[7]! Give me a heart to remember Your promises!"

Well spoken, Son of Lamech. This battle is not yours but mine. Now rise. Your salvation is at hand.

The light suddenly faded and the skirmish resumed as though it had never stopped. Noah leapt to his feet to ward off Nabal, but was knocked over by John. He felt the knife slash his robe as he fell and knew the accident had saved him. Furious at being deprived of his quarry, Nabal drove his blade into John's chest. The agonizing scream startled the fighting men and they lowered their weapons to stare at the lad writhing on the ground.

"Not John!" Enos exploded as he turned on Nabal. "I'll kill you with my own hands, I swear I will!"

"Time for that later," Obert said, grabbing the doctor by the arm. "The boy needs you."

"Not for much longer," Nabal snarled. "No one gets in my way without paying for it. Finish the little monster off, Luz. I'm busy with Noah." But nobody moved and the silence was broken only by John's groans. Angry at being disobeyed, Nabal lashed out with a fist that sent Luz sprawling.

"What're you waiting for?" he demanded.

"You shouldn't have gone for the boy," Luz answered, wiping his bleeding lip with the back of his hand. "He's not like us. The Lord will curse us for raising a hand against him."

"Oppose me, and I swear you'll regret it!" Nabal growled.

"You're a fool, Nabal," Palti said. "We're in for trouble if the boy dies." There were several murmurs of agreement and Nabal looked with disdain at the motley group.

"Cowards!" he accused.

"They're merely being prudent, and you'd be wise to do the same. Stand down, now." Recognizing the voice, Noah eagerly turned to greet his father.

"I never thought I'd see the day!" he exclaimed with relief.

"That makes two of us," Methuselah chuckled as he emerged from the forest with Hophni and Salassi in tow.

"Well, we're here, now, and fully armed, too," Lamech said as he watched Jasper prod the two tightly bound felons forward. "Sorry we didn't arrive before anyone got hurt. How's John?"

"It's a bad wound, but not fatal," Enos replied grimly.

"The lad took the blow intended for me," Noah said sadly. Dismounting, Lamech squeezed his son's shoulder.

"God always uses the innocents in ways we cannot foresee," he consoled. Noah nodded.

"Thank you for coming, Father," he said warmly. He then turned to his men.

"Bind Nabal also," he ordered. "He'll be charged with attempted murder." Nabal lashed out wildly, but was soon overpowered by Lamech's men and bound. Noah had the three captives roped together for the journey back to the logging camp, then turned to address the mill workers.

"Taking the law into your own hands is illegal, even when your grievance is valid," he said. "You must come with us until a penalty has been meted out." The men silently remounted their ponies and waited while Enos finished dressing John's wound.

"Carry the lad carefully," the doctor told Obadiah and Matthias. "He's lost much blood. It will not go well if he starts bleeding again."

The group was soon wending their way solemnly through the forest. Little did Noah realize how much impact the events of the day would have on his life.

CHAPTER 10
JUSTICE WITH MERCY

... if you have been merciful, then God's mercy toward
you will win out over His judgment against you.
James 2:13b

The camp well had once been prone to such heavy flooding that it had been necessary to dig an overflow tunnel just below its lip. The recess had been dry for months and provided a good hiding place for Seraphina and Beulah.

Expecting to be holed up for some time, the women had been startled when a large group of horsemen had ridden into camp soon after they had entered the tunnel. Fearing the worst, they had crept deeper into the shadows and lain in silence until they heard Lamech's call.

"We're down here, in the well!" Seraphina had shouted, crawling to the tunnel's entrance and waving frantically. Alerted by her cry, Lamech had ridden up to the well and dismounted.

"Are you alright?" he had asked, clutching at her hand.

"Beulah and I are fine. It's the others you need to be concerned about. They left a little while ago to meet Enos at the giant redwood. You'll come straight to it if you follow the track out of here and keep bearing left." Lamech had immediately swung into the saddle.

"We're on our way, Seraphina. But whatever you do, daughter, remain hidden until we come back for you. Do you understand?" She had nodded impatiently.

"Delay no longer, Father. It's Noah who needs you now."

"As does my grandchild," he had replied with a crooked smile.

"You know?" she had asked. Lamech had thrown back his head and laughed.

"Even if Enos hadn't told me, I'd be blind to not notice you're pregnant!" Seraphina's peal of laughter had been drowned by the thunder of hooves as the men left at a fast canter. Relieved and exhausted, she had snuggled up to Beulah, her baby's heart beating against her hand as she slept.

Although more than three hours had elapsed, Seraphina felt like she had only been asleep for a few minutes when Beulah woke her.

"I hear horses, My Lady, lots of them!" the old lady said. Rubbing her eyes, Seraphina crawled to the tunnel entrance and looked straight up into the face of her husband.

"Noah!" she cried, grasping his hands. Noah silently hauled her out of the well and held her tight. Sensing something was wrong, she pulled away.

"What is it?" she asked. He shook his head.

"God saved my life today, Seraphina, but at great cost. It's John, I'm afraid. He's badly hurt." Seraphina's eyes clouded with worry.

"Will he live?"

"Yes, but he'll take a long time to recover."

"I'm so sorry, Noah."

"No sorrier than I," he said. "The good news is that we have achieved our goal, with Lamech's help." Seraphina smiled.

"He found you, then?"

"Yes, he did," Noah answered. "It was good to be told you were alright."

"You won't be feeling good for much longer if you don't get me out of here," Beulah grumbled from below. They looked down into the nurse's dirt-streaked face and laughed.

"We'll have you out of there in no time at all," Seraphina grinned. She watched Noah struggle to heave the stout old lady out of the narrow tunnel, and wondered how she would have managed had he not come back. Turning, she saw Methuselah and raised her hand in greeting.

"All's well, granddaughter," he assured her from across the yard. "A few legalities to sort out and we'll soon be back to doing what God has called us to do."

Hophni spat in disgust – much to Seraphina's horror. He and two men she did not know had been tightly bound together. The better dressed of the two was undoubtedly Ben Salassi, but it was the cruel eyes of the other that made her shudder.

"What's bothering you, Seraphina?" Noah asked.

"I'm just wishing all this was over," she replied wistfully.

"It soon will be. I promise."

Seraphina prayed her husband was right.

It was decided to hold court in the logging camp yard, with Lamech's men standing guard over the prisoners. Methuselah took his place behind the bench and opened the proceedings by appointing Lamech and Noah to be his assessors[2]. Clearing his throat, he solemnly addressed those on trial.

"With so much evidence against you, and no witnesses to testify, you are in no position to argue your case," he stated.

"Who says?" Nabal demanded. "This isn't a proper court! Your ruling won't hold water."

"You're wrong," Methuselah replied. "I am a legally appointed judge, with authority to call for and preside over a trial whenever the need arises. You will find my rulings just and fair."

"Bah!" Nabal cursed, turning to face the others. "Can't you see it's all a trick, to put our necks in the noose without a fuss?"

"No, Nabal!" Luz objected. "You're on trial for attempted murder, not us! We'll not risk our lives by siding with you, will we, lads?" There was a roar of agreement and Methuselah impatiently called for order. Cowed by the white-haired man with the blazing eyes, the men fell silent.

"We all despise what Nabal has done," Methuselah said quietly. "But I will not condemn anyone to death when God has told Noah to build an Ark of refuge for the living. Vengeance belongs to the Most High. He is merciful when sinners turn to Him for forgiveness." He looked at the accused men from under his bushy eyebrows and wondered if any understood what he was saying. He hoped so, for their sakes.

"So, with God's mercy in mind," he continued, "I call Hophni to stand and face this court." Hophni stepped forward with a boldness he did not feel.

"Do you have anything to say in your defence?" Methuselah asked. Hophni sullenly shook his head.

"So be it. I charge you, Hophni, son of Obed, with attempted murder, aiding and abetting the theft of 40,100 gold shekels[28], and wilful damage of property and equipment. How do you plead?"

"You know how I plead," Hophni retorted. Lamech rose angrily to his feet.

"You will address Methuselah with the respect due his position," he commanded. "A public confession is a legal requirement. To refuse to comply is contempt of court and would be taken into account when passing sentence."

Methuselah looked at his son with renewed appreciation. It had been years since Lamech had been so forceful.

"I repeat the question," he said after Lamech had resumed his seat. "How do you plead?" Hophni clasped his trembling hands behind his back. He had not realized how difficult confessing would be. Squaring his shoulders, he looked up and felt sick to his stomach. The compassion in Methuselah's eyes was more than he could bear!

"I'm guilty," he admitted through clenched teeth.

"In response to your admission of guilt, Hophni, this court sentences you to fifteen years in Eretz penal colony, where you will serve the poor and the dying. It is our hope that such service will help you turn from your wicked ways."

"I don't need help," Hophni sneered.

"Everyone needs help, Hophni," Noah said sadly. Hophni merely shrugged but he was, in reality, terrified of going to jail. Perhaps death would have been preferable after all.

Salassi was convinced he had come to the end of his road. Not only did the evidence indict him as a thief, further investigation revealed he was responsible for the deaths of a woman and child. Had he been paying fair wages, Malachi would have been able to afford a midwife. Another court would probably have sentenced him to the gallows, but Methuselah had said he would execute no one. Even so, Salassi knew he would be imprisoned for life – which was in many ways worse than death.

"You have heard the charges," Methuselah said, interrupting his thoughts. "How do you plead?" Salassi looked up into the Patriarch's[23] eyes and sighed.

"I'm guilty," he replied wearily. Nodding, Methuselah continued.

"Ben Salassi, in response to your admission of guilt this court sentences you to twenty years in Eretz penal colony, where you will serve the dying and those giving birth to new life.

"Furthermore, you are to sign over your business to your workers, as compensation for the wages you have defrauded them of. You are to also restore all stolen items in your possession to their rightful owners. Whatever is left after restitution has been made will be held in trust for you until you are released. If you die while in prison, your possessions will be given to a nominee of your choice. Now, have you any questions?"

"Why is my sentence so light?" Salassi asked suspiciously. Methuselah leaned forward on his elbows and looked intently at the perplexed man.

"A life sentence would have driven you insane, Ben," he answered quietly. "That is not the intention of this court. Our desire is to help you become a better man than you are today."

"Don't expect too much, Methuselah," Salassi grumbled. "I've not done much repenting before. It's too late to start now."

"It's never too late, Ben. At least think about it."

Salassi narrowly eyed the Patriarch[23], then nodded.

"I'll do that," he said. To his surprise, he meant it.

Something inside Nabal snapped when he was called to the bench and he ran towards the river, knocking two men down in his flight.

"Obert! Matthias! Stop that man!" Noah shouted as he sprang to his feet and ran after the fugitive. But Nabal had already reached the jetty and turned to taunt his pursuers.

70

"You'll be running forever if you run now," Noah warned. "Be a man and atone for your crime."

"And end up being trapped like a bird in a cage? No, Noah! I'll never let you catch me. I run like a deer and swim like a fish, even with my hands tied!" To prove his point, the felon leapt onto the raft of logs extending almost to the opposite bank of the Tigris and was halfway across within seconds. A cracking sound suddenly rent the air. Nabal stared at the widening gap beneath him, then plunged helplessly into the river.

"Give up, Nabal," Noah said, stooping to grab the convict's collar. "There're at least ten logs between you and land." Snarling, Nabal swam beyond Noah's reach.

"I swim underwater as well as I do above it," he retorted. "And even if I don't reach the other side before I'm out of air, I'd rather drown than be taken!"

"Don't be a fool!" Noah cried. But it was too late. Nabal was already beneath the water.

"Quickly! To the other side!" Noah ordered Obert and Matthias. "We run faster than he can swim." The men leapt across the breach, but their progress was impeded when more of the lashings binding the logs snapped. The raft was rapidly drifting apart, now. It was with dismay that they saw Nabal resurface several paces ahead of them.

"What did I tell you?" he gloated as he made his way towards the bank. Exasperated, Noah turned to Obert.

"Get the others and be quick about it. I want this man caught." The words were barely spoken when the water around Nabal began to swirl violently. The men watched spellbound as the convict's head disappeared beneath the surface, then bobbed back up.

"Wha-what's happening?" Nabal cried before being sucked under again. It was several seconds before he resurfaced, his face pinched with fear.

"For God's sake, save me!" he gasped. Noah fell to his stomach and grabbed Nabal's hair, but the strong current snatched the man away. Scrambling to his feet, he threw off his robe.

"No, Sir! You'll drown in this whirlpool!" Matthias cried, wrapping his arms around his master. Noah felt sick with helplessness as he watched the raging vortex suck its victim under for the last time. Drowning was such an awful death.

Within minutes, the river was once again calm, and Noah stared at the spot where Nabal had disappeared. He knew what he had seen had nothing to do with nature.

"I should've hobbled him," he said ruefully.

"You can't blame yourself, Sir," Matthias answered quietly. "Nabal would have made a break for it sooner or later, and not cared who he hurt doing it."

"You're right, I suppose," Noah conceded sadly, "and now he's facing the consequences of his bad choice. You and Jasper are to look for his body as soon as you've resecured these logs. Nabal's entitled to a decent burial, if nothing else."

Turning his back on the river, Noah returned with heavy feet to the logging camp. He hoped the rest of the court proceedings would go smoothly. Another tragedy would be hard to stomach.

The camp was in an uproar when Noah returned.

"The men think Nabal's death is the act of an angry God," Methuselah explained quietly. "But we know Elohim[7] is loving and merciful. He would not have dealt with Nabal so severely unless it was for the good of all."

"People who don't revere God struggle to understand His love and mercy," Noah responded.

"Then how do we settle this dispute without compromising the truth?" Lamech asked.

"Certainly not by preaching," Noah said. "The men need to know what actually happened. May I?" Methuselah nodded and Noah rose to his feet.

"Quiet!" he thundered above the din. The men stared at him, then fell into sullen silence.

"You're right in thinking Nabal's death was an act of God," Noah declared. "What you don't realize is that Nabal wanted it that way. He said he'd rather drown than be taken captive and God granted his request. It's as simple as that."

"But we've all said foolish things," Luz cried. "Yet God didn't strike us dead because of our words. Why now?" Many in the group loudly demanded an answer, and Noah again raised his hand for silence.

"Only the Lord knows," he replied. "Elohim[7] has said He will destroy the Earth with a flood. Perhaps Nabal's tongue sealed his fate earlier than expected. But that is speculation. We're all accountable to God for our actions. He shows mercy to those who take responsibility for them. You've participated in a fracas that resulted in the serious wounding of a boy. It would, therefore, be prudent to calm down and allow this court to proceed."

As Noah concluded, Palti asked for permission to speak to the millhands.

"Nabal got what was coming to him, and all because he refused to obey the law," he said. "Listen to what Methuselah has to say. He hasn't passed an unfair sentence yet. We can always object if we disagree with him."

"Palti's right," Lamech interjected. "Anyone disagreeing with their sentence has the right to appeal. The case would then be retried, with another judge presiding."

"Then why didn't Hophni and Salassi appeal?" Luz asked.

"They probably knew a retrial would result in a heavier sentence," Methuselah answered dryly. He then turned to Palti.

"I commend you," he smiled. "Your work fellows would not be on trial today had they heeded you from the outset."

"Even so, Sir, I knew what kind of man Nabal was and should've ordered him to remain at the mill, out of harm's way. I therefore insist I stand trial with the others." Methuselah saw the man was in earnest and reluctantly conceded to his request. Clearing his throat, he ordered the millhands to rise and face the court with Palti.

"I charge you all with violently disturbing the peace," he said. "Those pleading guilty must raise their hands." The admission of guilt was unanimous.

"So be it," Methuselah continued. "I herewith fine each of you two gold shekels[28], as compensation to John for the injury inflicted on him by Nabal. In addition, the mill – which now belongs to each of you equally – is to be managed by Lamech until you have proved yourselves capable of running it. Now, are there any questions regarding your sentence?"

"Two gold shekels[28] is a lot of money," Luz grumbled.

"No more than John deserves!" Palti exclaimed. "Lord in Heaven, Luz! You're sounding just as greedy as Nabal was." Luz's eyes burned with anger, but he held his tongue. Andrew, the young groom, hesitantly raised his hand.

"I think you've given us a good deal, Sir," he said with glistening eyes. "I've an ailing mother who would have died of grief had you not been so merciful."

"I agree with the lad," another spoke up. "You *have* been merciful." There were several more murmurs of approval.

"I could've been harsher, but to what purpose?" Methuselah said. "However, any further trouble will result in your sentence being reviewed. Do you understand?" The millhands nodded. They knew they had been given a reprieve and were determined to not jeopardize it.

Methuselah concluded the court by setting his seal to the judgements. He then dismissed the millhands with an instruction to pay what they owed by month-end. Hophni and Salassi would be escorted to the penal colony on the morrow.

Jasper found the corpse in a small backwater the day after the trial. The terror-contorted face made him shudder. He wondered what Nabal had seen before the river swallowed him.

"This is no fitting thing to see in your condition, My Lady!" Beulah exclaimed when she stripped the sheet away from the body to prepare it for burial. Seraphina did not argue. Being near the dead man chilled her to the core. For hours she sat on the jetty, staring into the Tigris. Nabal was to be buried in the mock grave Hophni had dug, but she would never go near it. Just knowing he was gone was enough. But, as day followed day, the lechery she had seen in Nabal's eyes continued to haunt her. He had not done anything but lust after her in his mind. Yet she felt so dirty! So offended!

Exasperated, she rested against her pillows and placed her hand on her belly. She wanted her heart to be upright for the birth of this child, but knew that was impossible while she harboured such resentment.

"I suppose the first step lies in wanting to forgive Nabal – even if my motives are selfish," she murmured. "But do I want to?" Folding her hands, she took a deep breath.

"Heavenly Father," she whispered, "I don't know how to deal with my hatred. Please help me!"

Lost for words, she sat in silence and felt calm for the first time in days. As the quietness enveloped her, she saw how small her struggle was in comparison to Elohim's[7] great mercy. She had seen the Lord's justice. He now wanted her to experience His sorrow, to know His heart. Forgiving Nabal could not change his fate. But it would cleanse her of the defilement she felt.

Her eyes brimmed with tears. She had been so busy fighting her feelings that she had not realized what the Lord wanted, or why. She needed forgiveness as much as Nabal did. Struggling off the bed, she fell to her knees.

"Dear Elohim[7]," she prayed, "please forgive me. I will do what You want. All I ask is that You make it real to me."

She closed her eyes and proceeded to forgive Nabal – haltingly at first, then with joy as the burden on her heart lifted. Raising her hands, she gave a great shout of praise, then gasped in pain. Prayer forgotten, she staggered to the door.

"Beulah!" she cried. "Come quickly, and bring Enos with you!" She watched the stout nurse waddle across the yard, then stumbled back to bed as another contraction overtook her. *Oh God!* she silently cried. The pain was more than she could bear!

The room was suddenly filled with the sweetest of smells. Seraphina screwed her eyes shut against the agony and breathed in God's presence. How good it was to know He was with her.

PART 2

THE ARK
2275–2164 BC

*It was by faith that Noah built an Ark to save his family
from the Flood. He obeyed God, who warned him about
something that had never happened before. By his faith
he condemned the rest of the world and was made right in
God's sight.*
Hebrews 11:7

CHAPTER 11
WITHDRAWN AGREEMENT

The wise look ahead to see what is coming, but fools
deceive themselves.
Proverbs 14:8

Seraphina walked beside the lumbering wagon and wondered where the time had gone. It seemed like only yesterday that Enos had placed her baby into her arms. The agony of the difficult birth had been instantly forgotten when she had gazed into the infant's eyes for the first time. Never had she felt so needed, so loved.

She would always think of Shem's birth as a turning point in their lives. In an act of goodwill, the millhands had lowered the cost of cypress, and Noah had set his seal to the new agreement moments before her first contraction. The memory would have made her smile were she not so concerned about John. The wound inflicted by Nabal was worse than originally thought and it was unlikely the lad would recover. Yet, despite his failing health, John remained cheerful.

"Don't waste time worrying about me," he told her. "What we need to do now is pray for Master Noah."

Seraphina could not argue. They would soon be back in Je'el, and she knew folk would be more opposed to Noah than ever. While her husband might be willing to withstand such hot disfavour, she doubted his men would. Unlike Jasper and John, who had been believers for some time, and Lamech, who had recently returned to the faith, Noah's work crew remained unconverted. Indeed, they would probably have quit working for Noah long ago were it not for the bid they had made on his workshop. The time to sell had come, but she did not think the men would allow them ongoing use of the premises after the sale went through. The risk of a severe loss of custom and liquidation was too great.

She sighed. If only they had remained at the logging camp, where life had been that much simpler! But Noah had been adamant they return to the city.

"Elohim's[7] real call on my life is to preach repentance," he had said, stroking her face. "The crowds won't come to us, dear heart. We've got to go to them."

Noah was right, of course, but she wasn't looking forward to returning to Je'el. Hopefully, he was already there, waiting for her. He, together with Obert and Matthias, had taken on the task of floating the remaining logs downriver and should have arrived days ago.

The tired party pulled up at the city gates just before sunset and were relieved to find Noah awaiting their arrival. Bone-weary from tending her fractious baby for most of the day, Seraphina could scarcely contain her tears when Noah leapt up beside her.

"You're exhausted," he said, kissing the dark shadows beneath her eyes. "It's time to get you home and asleep." The thought of sleeping in a real bed again made Seraphina's eyelids droop, but her desire for rest diminished as they entered Je'el. The sullen gatekeepers and empty streets were reminiscent of the day they had left seventeen months earlier, and she could sense the resentment of the unfriendly eyes behind their darkened shutters. Feeling her tension, Noah put his arm around her.

"I know it's hard," he murmured, "but I can do nothing about it except give up." Startled, Seraphina sat bolt upright and looked at him closely.

"You *can't* do that!" she exclaimed.

"Don't worry, I won't!" he chuckled, patting her arm. "Elohim's[7] brought us too far for me to retreat now, and I trust He will undertake for what I cannot. The tragedy is that most folk continue to refuse my message of God's great love and mercy, little realizing they don't stand against me, but against the Almighty Himself."

Seraphina felt her eyes prickle. How much rejection the Lord suffered from the people He had made for His pleasure!

"Home at last," Noah said, interrupting her thoughts. Securing the reins, he climbed down from the high wagon seat and reached for her.

"You enjoy being pampered, don't you?" he teased when she flopped into his arms.

"Only when I'm beyond myself," Seraphina mumbled. "I've missed you, Noah. Three weeks is too long to be apart!"

"I've missed you, too, dear heart. But enough small talk. You're desperate for rest."

"I must first get Shem. He's asleep in the wagon."

"Stop fussing! The baby's safe with Beulah. All you need worry about is getting to bed before you collapse." Too tired to resist, Seraphina sighed as Noah carried her through the house and laid her down on their enormous feather bed. She was sound asleep within seconds.

Seraphina awoke the following morning to find Noah's side of the bed cold. She was not surprised she had overslept. The journey had been long and tedious. Even so, her fatigue was uncharacteristic, as was her queasiness over the past several days. Her difficulty in holding down food had resulted in a loss of appetite that was cause for concern. She needed to be strong if she was to continue nursing Shem.

As she stood retching over the basin, she realized she was probably pregnant. Although she had not experienced nausea during her first pregnancy, she had been prone to the same exhaustion she felt now. Closing her eyes, she did a quick calculation and grinned. She had been so preoccupied with returning home that she had not noticed her cycle was late. *Dear Lord!* she mused. *Can I possibly be having another child so soon?* The thought made her laugh. She may have entered motherhood late in life, but Elohim[7] had made her as fruitful as a girl! Shouting for joy, she ran to the kitchen to share her good news.

Noah was both overjoyed and anxious when he heard Seraphina was expecting their second child. Shem's difficult birth had aged her considerably.

"Don't look so upset," she teased. "I've been told it's easier the second time round."

"I can't help but be concerned, Seraphina," Noah replied soberly. "I'll soon be working long hours. How am I going to take proper care of you?"

"For goodness' sake, Noah!" she answered irritably. "God will make a way for us to do all we have to – including having another baby. Our lives are in His hands. Worrying about what we can't change or influence is a waste of energy."

"I suppose you're right," he conceded.

"You know I am!" she answered sharply. "If you're anxious about this baby because of what I went through with Shem, then let me remind you that the Prophecy talks about us *and* our sons. Children are Elohim's[7] gift, Noah. We should praise Him for this child, not fret."

"But the pain you went through last time ..." he objected lamely.

"Hush, dear husband. I'd go through that agony a thousand times over just for the joy of bringing forth our children. But enough said. The sickness is upon me again!" Holding her hand to her mouth, Seraphina ran from the room. Noah began to follow, then held back. He had never had a strong stomach!

"Please, God, keep her safe," he prayed. He stood with bowed head for several minutes. There was so much he admired in his wife. She might never learn to use a hammer and chisel, but her determination, courage and focus were as valuable a tool as any in bringing the Ark to completion.

Smiling, he helped himself to some porridge. He had hoped to share breakfast with Seraphina but doubted she would be up to eating until later. It was unfortunate. He needed to be at the workshop within the hour.

Although Noah had expected his workforce to disagree to a legally binding proviso in the terms of sale, he had not anticipated their contempt.

"I refuse to sell unless you agree," he insisted. The angry men glared at him.

"You're bluffing!" Obed challenged. "You can't even cover the cost of looking after your family, let alone the expenses of building the Ark. Accept our offer before we change our minds. You'll not find one better."

Obed had become bitterly vindictive and unreasonable since Hophni's imprisonment. Frustrated, Noah turned to his grandfather. It was customary for a Patriarch[23] to arbitrate in such matters, but Methuselah was speechless with rage. It fell to Lamech to speak in his stead.

"I do have a proposal to make," he said quietly, "but the three of us need to discuss it first." Noah ushered the two men into the cutting shed and closed the door.

"Well?" Methuselah grumbled. "Spit out what you've got to say!" But Lamech refused to be rushed and it was several seconds before he spoke.

"You need an alternative to selling the business, Noah," he said gravely. "By rejecting the proviso granting you ongoing access to the workshop and premises, your men are also refusing you the use of equipment and tools – without which you will come to a standstill. You could try dropping your price in a bid to sway them, but I doubt that would work. Apart from the expense of replacing your tools and equipment, where else would you find an affordable site on which to build the Ark? My advice is that you withdraw your offer of sale."

"But I've already agreed to sell and am a man of my word," Noah objected.

"Your verbal agreement is binding only insofar as the bidding party honours their side of the bargain," Lamech pointed out. "Your men originally agreed to allow you continued use of the workshop after the sale went through. The majority have since withdrawn that option. You now have the moral right to cancel the sale altogether."

"Perhaps, but cancelling the sale does nothing to fill my empty coffers!" Noah retorted.

"Which brings me to my proposal. I've given the matter much thought and suggest we lease our family home on a hundred-year grant." Methuselah and Noah could not believe their ears. The idea of strangers occupying the large house was unthinkable.

"It's the only viable solution to our problem," Lamech insisted. "While my vineyards are adequate to provide for our everyday needs, they don't generate sufficient profit to cover the cost of completing the Ark. A long-term lease, on the other hand, would provide more than enough for both. I've already had a handsome offer for such a lease, provided you're in agreement."

"A handsome offer from whom?" Noah asked.

"None other than Miriamne's lover," Lamech answered bitterly. His farce of a marriage had crumbled months ago, but the thought of his ex-wife in another's arms was as intolerable as ever.

"I swore that woman would never get the house. Now you're giving it to her on a platter!" Methuselah growled.

"I hardly think so," Lamech said wryly. "Phineas outstrips Miriamne for shrewdness. He will probably abandon her to the streets before year-end."

"Which is when she'll come crawling back to you," Methuselah said caustically.

"No, she won't. Our divorce came through yesterday."

While Noah and Methuselah knew Lamech had not shared Miriamne's bed in a long time, they had not realized the couple had decided to make the split permanent.

"So! You finally came to your senses," Noah smiled. Lamech shook his head indignantly.

"I may've been a fool to marry the wench in the first place, but I take my vows seriously, Noah. Miriamne asked for a divorce, not I. She claims Phineas loves her. Little does she realize he's toying with her affections."

"She's only reaping what she's sown," Methuselah said. "I don't know if you were right in granting her a divorce, though. You know how much Elohim[7] hates it."

"How could I not? She's been living in disgrace for so long. Who's to say Phineas won't make an honest woman of her?"

"Perhaps," the old man agreed reluctantly, "but we digress. Your idea of leasing the house on a long-term basis is sound in theory, but what if the lessee defaults on payment?"

"Phineas has agreed to pay for the lease in one lump sum."

"Are you certain?" Noah asked. Lamech nodded firmly.

"His banker assures me the gold's available as soon as we've finalized the lease agreement."

"This new development will not make my men happy," Noah remarked dryly.

"Then don't tell them about it," Methuselah said. "All they need to know is that they can purchase the business if they sign over to you a right of access to the premises and equipment. It's unlikely they'll agree to your terms. But even if they do, I think we should still put the family home up for a long-term lease. The Flood will reduce it to worthless rubble, anyway. Why hold on to something that has no eternal value?"

Noah had never considered his inheritance being washed away like sand on the riverbank. How temporal life was, and how important God's call on his life! His men would feel let down by his decision, but they had left him with no alternative. The Ark must be built.

Obed was livid with rage.

"I'll have you for this," he snarled. "You see if I don't!"

"Easy on, Obed," Jethro, the chief sawyer, admonished. "You'll lose us the sale if you take on so!"

"You know nothing, fool!" Obed barked. "What do you think will happen if we let Noah build his Ark on our wharf?" Offended, Jethro turned his back on the record keeper. Obed grimaced. He had to control his anger if he was to retain the respect of the crew.

"Can't you see nobody wants anything to do with Noah?" he continued more moderately. "Giving in to him would cost us most of our trade, if not all. Think again, lads. The business is worth nothing if we allow him the use of it."

Despite Obed's persuasiveness, the men were undecided and the tension in the room mounted. Realizing their presence made matters worse, Noah and his kin retreated back into the cutting shed.

"There's surely not going to be another uproar!" Lamech groaned as he shut the door.

"You can't blame them for feeling upset," Noah replied. "What would you do in their place?"

"Knowing my temper, I'd hate to think!" Methuselah laughed. "Sadly, everything Obed's told them is true. They *would* lose most of their trade by associating with you."

"I never thought folk would be so bigoted," Noah said.

"We haven't seen the half of it yet," the old man answered solemnly. "You've no choice but to cancel the sale, Noah. Soften the blow by telling them you'll retain them on full pay."

"Do you think they'll stay on?"

"Some may. Most probably won't. They might demand severance pay you can ill afford, but they're only entitled to it if they're laid off unjustly. So be on your guard against any provocation. And take care to treat them with respect. The troublemakers will soon tire of the game and resign."

"It's hard to be so calculating," Noah objected. "I feel I owe my men so much more."

"We can't always obey our feelings, Noah. Neither can we carry the world on our shoulders. That's God's job. You knew building the Ark wouldn't be easy. This is just another hiccup that has to be dealt with before we can go any further."

It was with a heavy heart that Noah returned to the workshop to confront his crew.

"You took your time," Obed said defiantly. "Whatever your scheme, Noah, it won't work. We're not buying if you insist on having ongoing access to the shop. That's our final word on it."

Obed's belligerence grated on Noah like sandstone, and he turned to the rest of the men for confirmation.

"Are you all in agreement?" he asked, searching their faces. "Or is this just Obed talking?" Jasper stepped forward with a look of apology on his seamed face.

"I don't agree with Obed, Sir. But the others do. Not that they're happy about forcing your hand, mind you. Will you really refuse to sell if you can't use the workshop?"

"Yes, I will." A shocked murmur rippled through the group of disgruntled men.

"You leave me with no alternative," Noah said. "I cannot sell the business unless I'm allowed unlimited access to the premises and equipment. And that's *my* final word on it." Obed's mouth dropped open in disbelief.

"You have to sell!" he yelled.

"No longer," Noah informed him. "God's provision has come through another source. I will soon have more than my entire business is worth. I will also be in a position to retain all of you on full pay, should you decide to stay on."

"You're out of your mind!" Obed shouted.

"Perhaps," Noah answered, "but at least I'm not dumping you."

"No, you're signing our death warrant instead," Jehu, the chief sawyer's assistant, cried.

"I know it will be difficult," Noah said, "but God will protect all who help build the Ark."

"Even if we don't believe in Him?" Jethro asked.

"Even then."

"Don't talk rubbish, Noah!" Obed interjected. "These men would be fools to stay, and you know it."

"Easy on, Obed!" Jethro exclaimed. "I have my wife and family to consider."

"Me, too," another shouted. Noah put his hand up for silence.

"The only one likely to get dismissed today will be Obed," he announced. He turned to the record keeper and stared hard into his implacable face before continuing. "Your behaviour is offensive, Obed. Unless I get an apology and a promise of submission to my authority, I'm dispensing with your services."

"Me apologize to you? Never!" Obed roared, his eyes filled with hate.

"Then you have no place here. Collect your things and leave. I'll have your wages delivered to you later today."

"You can't do this!"

"I can and have. Your belligerence is an obstruction to me, and a bad influence on the rest of the crew. You've been an excellent worker, Obed, and it's a pity to part on bad terms. But that is your choice, not mine. I've no more to say. You are dismissed."

"Damn you and your Ark," Obed spluttered as he stormed from the room.

"How lightly men curse Elohim[7] and His work," Methuselah murmured. Noah nodded sadly, then turned to address the men.

"I'm closing shop for the day," he informed them. "You're to go home and think about what I've said. Working for me will cost you dear, and I can do no more than pray for your safety. Those wanting to leave may do so at any time. Understood?"

"You've been more than fair, Sir," Matthias answered for them all, "but staying to work on the Ark is going to take some thinking through." Noah smiled. Despite Obed's vile behaviour, the meeting had ended on a positive note.

"Thank you," he concluded. "I look forward to hearing your decision."

"Well handled," Methuselah congratulated him after the men had filed out of the room.

"Even so, I doubt those without a belief in God will stay," Lamech said. "You know how much faith it takes to remain loyal to a mission like this."

"True," Noah answered. "But God can give anyone a heart for the work, even if they never come to know Him as we do." Lamech smiled wryly.

"I hardly think I qualify as being one of the faithful, Noah."

"Don't you?" Noah asked softly. "You may not realize it, Father, but your faith has grown much these past few months."

"So it has," Lamech conceded, "but I'm far from being home and dry."

"There you go again, tossing yourself on the rubbish heap when you think you've failed to come up to scratch," Methuselah said dourly. "Living up to human expectations is what limits you, Lamech. But Elohim[7] is so much bigger than that. Our confidence must be in Him and not ourselves if we're to get this Ark built."

"Amen to that," Noah said, placing his brawny hand over Methuselah's and looking expectantly at his father.

The warm invitation in Noah's eyes was unmistakable. It had been years since Lamech had had such a sense of belonging. Smiling with gratitude, he covered his son's hand with his own.

"Amen and amen," he agreed eagerly.

It was with regret that Noah watched two thirds of his men leave his yard for the last time.

"They weren't even willing to stay on until they'd found alternative employment," he said ruefully. "I suppose they thought working for me would jeopardize future prospects."

"Whatever their reasons, it's actually more than we bargained for," Lamech pointed out.

"So it is. But how will I cope with so few?"

"Those who've remained are those who really want to stay, Noah. It takes more than brawn to get a job well done. It also takes heart." Noah was not entirely convinced, however. The task of building the Ark would far exceed the capabilities of the small group. They would have to rely on God to strengthen their hands for the work. With that thought in mind, he strode across the yard to speak to the men.

"Thank you for staying," he said. "We may be few, but we can succeed if we function as a team with a vision."

"That we can, Sir," Jasper agreed, his eyes gleaming with excitement.

"How do the rest of you feel?" Noah asked. The men looked at each other and nodded. Pleased with their response, Noah rubbed his hands together. "Then let us start by harnessing Boaz and hauling the final batch of logs out of the river."

"I can help with that, Master."

Noah swung round in surprise.

"John!" he exclaimed. "What're you doing here?"

"I've come to work, Sir," the youth answered wanly.

"No, lad. You're not well," Noah objected.

"P-please, Sir. I beg you! I'm well enough to ride a horse and tow timber up the ramp."

"Do listen to him, Noah," Enos urged as he walked up to join the boy. "The exercise and encouragement of continuing to be part of the team will do him good."

"Very well," Noah agreed hesitantly, "but only if you promise to keep an eye on him."

John's face immediately lit up.

"Hey, Obert! Wait for me!" he called. The two men watched him eagerly cross the yard to the stables. The lad's joyful determination was an elixir to their souls, but his unsteady gait was worrying.

"He's not long for this world, is he, Enos?"

"Sadly no," the doctor replied. "Nabal's knife damaged his heart too seriously. While my herbs and potions do their work in keeping the lad alive, they can do nothing to stop his health from declining. I sometimes wish he was mature enough to understand just how ill he is, but perhaps it's fortunate he never will be. Children have a way of making the most of their infirmities."

"Even so, disease is a vile scourge," Noah said dolefully. "But tell me, Enos, what are your plans now?"

"I'd like to continue working with you, if I may. I know I've little experience, but it can't be that difficult to dress timber."

"A bit backbreaking, that's all," Noah answered dryly.

"Then it's about time I put some muscle onto this scrawny frame of mine, wouldn't you say?"

"You're serious, aren't you?"

"More serious than I've ever been about anything," Enos admitted. "Your mission to build the Ark attracts me like nothing else ever has. I'd like to be part of it."

"That's all very well, but engaging in another's vision is not enough. You must believe in it, too."

"That's just it. I do believe. Indeed, I want to discuss how I feel. Are you able to give me a few minutes of your time?"

"Of course," Noah said, ushering Enos into the workshop and closing the door. He wondered what the physician had to say that was so important. He had often prayed for his crew to acquire an intimate understanding of the Almighty. Had his prayers for this man at last been answered?

"For years I've doubted God's existence," Enos said bluntly. "That might shock you, but my doubts are reasonable. I've seen more pain and suffering than most folk do in a lifetime. Little wonder I've found it difficult to believe in a Creator. Even so, I've always known Someone is out there, watching, waiting for me to turn to Him. Like a father yearning for his son. But it was only when I met John that I began to respond.

"I don't really know what drew me to the lad in the first place. We had so little in common. Yet I was bitterly devastated when I realized he would never recover. One question kept going around and around in my mind: How could God allow this innocent boy to die so unfairly?

"But John has never questioned any of it. When I realized how much my cynicism upset him, I knew I had to get rid of it, for his sake. I'm not sure when I began to change, but I no longer feel angry or disillusioned. Neither do I doubt that God is holding me and guiding me. Helping me to bring hope to those I touch." Pausing, Enos looked up at Noah with tears in his eyes. "Do you understand what I'm trying to say?" he whispered.

Noah fondly squeezed the physician's shoulder.

"I know exactly what you mean, Enos," he said. "I also think you're a doctor in the truest sense of the word."

"But I want to do so much more than just doctoring," Enos replied. "That's why helping build the Ark is important to me."

"And grateful I am for it, Enos. You've a willing heart, and I strongly believe you'll reap the rewards of your labours soon." The unexpected praise made the doctor flush.

"I've done little to deserve a reward," he said.

"You have endured, my friend, and that is more than enough. But come. John has just hauled the first logs out of the river. It's time for your first lesson in debarking."

Armed with a pair of worn linen gloves, Enos followed Noah across the yard.

CHAPTER 12
THE LAMP OF GOD

... let us be thankful and please God by worshiping Him
with holy fear and awe. For our God is a consuming fire.
Hebrews 12:28b–29

Noah was delighted when Lamech and Methuselah moved into the workshop the day after leasing the family home. Both were experienced carpenters and took on the task of making the hundreds of treenails needed to fasten the Ark's stout planks together. The small but efficient crew had finished dressing the timber and were now in the process of laying the mammoth keel.

The citizenry of Je'el remained sullenly resistant to the building of the Ark. The dam of resentment finally broke at the end of the fourth month, when Noah was challenged by Obed and a group of stick-brandishing mobsters. The man was a caricature of his former self, with a body odour so powerful it almost made Noah gag. Mistaking the look of distaste for fear, Obed thrust out his chin and spat. Noah angrily raised his fist, then let it fall to his side. One blow and he would be no better than the embittered man before him!

"Get off my property," he demanded in a low voice. "You're trespassing."

"Trespassing?" Obed slurred drunkenly. "I'm not trespassing! I've come to take what's mine!"

"Nothing here is yours to take, Obed. Now, get off my land."

"Just try and make me, fool! Don't you understand we want you out? Out! Out! Out!" Noah drew his breath in sharply. Obed was beside himself and would incite his rowdy friends if left unchallenged.

"Quiet!" Noah roared. "Have you forgotten I am God's representative? Oppose me and you stand against the Most High Himself." Obed's eyes went round in mock horror and he laughed uproariously.

"Oh, Noah!" he cried in amusement. "You threaten us with words, but we get things done, don't we, lads? I swear you've dallied with me for the last time. Cain! Come!" At his command, a youth ran forward and threw a torch into a trough of caulking.

Expecting the resin content in the mix to burst into flame, Noah threw himself to the ground.

"Take cover!" he shouted. But there was no explosion, only silence. Noah lifted his head and stared at the flaming torch suspended in mid-air above the trough. Enos, who lay but a few paces from him, lifted his hands in praise. Any lingering doubts about God's sovereignty had finally been laid to rest.

Frightened out of their wits by the phenomenon, Obed and his mobsters turned to run, but the flame blocked their way.

"I'll wager the scoundrels didn't expect this to happen," Methuselah chuckled from the open doorway of the workshop.

"I wonder why Elohim[7] won't let them go," Noah murmured.

"Perhaps He wants you to preach to them first," Methuselah suggested.

"Hah! I've done that often enough and only got scorned for it."

"You'll not get much jeering today, Noah. Besides, their response is not your concern. Doing the will of God is."

"Very well, I'll preach. Hopefully they'll listen to what I have to say this time."

"Maybe. Maybe not. But what has happened this day will never be forgotten."

The news spread rapidly and hundreds flocked to see the torch that continued to burn like a beacon. Noah made the most of the opportunity and refused to stop preaching even for food or drink. By the eve of the seventh day, his self-imposed fast had begun to undermine his health.

"You must have some water," Methuselah pleaded, offering Noah his flask.

"How can I drink while the Lamp of God still burns?" Noah objected hoarsely. "No, Grandfather. I will do nothing but proclaim God's word until the light goes out." Frustrated, Methuselah drew up a stool and insisted his grandson sit down.

"Persuading you to drink is not my only concern, Noah," he chided. "What about the Ark? Work has come to a standstill while you preach, and the morale of the men is low. They went home hours ago without even raising a hammer today. We need your direction if we're to continue."

"I'm sorry, Grandfather. I can do nothing but preach right now. Can't you understand that?" Methuselah did indeed understand, but some things were not meant to be borne alone.

"Why don't you let me preach while you pray?" he offered. "It would give you time to rest and regain your voice." Noah's body ached with weariness. The thought of a few minutes' respite was irresistible.

"It would only be for a little while," he said, covering himself with his prayer shawl. But he was asleep before his head slumped down onto his forearm. Methuselah gently eased him to the ground, then stepped forward to speak. To his amazement, the torch gave one last flicker and dropped to the ground. Blinded by the dark, the crowd began to panic.

"Fear not," the Patriarch[23] assured them. "The moon is rising. You'll soon have enough light to find your way home."

Within minutes, the yard was deserted and the old man stood alone and disappointed. He had been so eager to preach, but that mantle was now Noah's to wear. Pride flooded his chest. It had been a privilege to watch his grandson grow into a man so determined to please Elohim[7].

A sharp breeze sprang up, making him shiver. He stooped to rouse Noah, but there was no response. Smiling, he ambled to the storeroom to fetch some blankets. It had been a while since he had slept under the stars, and he would probably be as stiff as a board by morning. But the joy of being with his grandson would far outweigh the discomfort.

Pulling the blankets up under his chin, Methuselah put his arm around Noah's shoulders. He then surrendered to the most peaceful sleep he had had in days.

Although the Lamp of God no longer burned, it soon became a legend that attracted crowds from far and wide. They watched and they waited, but the torch lay where it had fallen – a lifeless symbol of the Most High's power and glory.

"They worship that thing like it was the Sovereign Lord Himself," Noah grumbled one day. Methuselah nodded grimly.

"The spiritually blind often exalt the sign more than the Sign Giver," he said.

"Are you saying these folk place greater importance on the miracle than on the One who performed it?"

"It's worse than that, Noah. They've made it into an idol. You can preach all you like, but they'll not hear a word while that piece of wood remains. Get rid of it!"

"But the torch is what draws them!" Noah objected.

"It's a wicked generation that worships a sign, Noah. You must confront them with their idolatry or be damned. God has promised to protect you and make the way plain – but not at the cost of taking second place to an idol."

"I've never thought of it like that," Noah said.

"Well, now's the time to start."

Noah looked into the seamed old face and smiled.

"You're nobody's fool, are you, Grandfather?"

"The road to wisdom is fraught with many potholes," Methuselah answered. The dour comment made Noah laugh. Stepping forward, he picked up the charred torch and flung it into the Tigris. The horrified crowd surged forward to follow its progress, but froze when a disembodied hand rose from the water, brandishing the burnt-out relic. In an instant both disappeared, and the Lamp of God was no more.

The ensuing silence was deafening. Many people fainted, while others strained to focus on the spot where the torch had disappeared. The realization that it was gone forever gave rise to an uproar that made the sweat break out on Noah's forehead.

"Stay calm," Methuselah whispered. "Elohim's[7] hand is upon you for good, not for evil. He will keep you safe."

Although Noah had heard and lived by those words often, he found them hard to believe now. He put up his hands to defend himself against a brawny red-haired man, then stared in amazement when his assailant suddenly fell to the ground.

"My eyes!" the man cried. "My eyes! I can't see!"

"Me neither!" another yelled. "What's happening?" The air was soon rent with cries of alarm as the entire crowd was struck with blindness. Noah looked at Methuselah in astonishment.

"How can this be?" he asked hoarsely.

"The same thing happened to me the day the Ne'um[20] of God was given," Methuselah grinned. "Nothing is impossible to Elohim[7], Noah. I said He'd keep you safe and He has. It's the crowd who now need help. They'll hurt themselves if we don't put a stop to their frenzy." Without further ado, the Patriarch[23] stepped forward and clapped his hands.

"Silence!" he roared above the din of the frightened crowd. "Be still and listen! You've acted like fools and God has stricken you because of it. But the Lord is merciful, slow to anger and abounding in great love. He does not delight in afflicting you. He will restore your sight if you go home and repent of what you've done. But be warned: something worse than blindness will befall you if you ever raise a finger against Noah again. Do you understand?"

"Too right we do, Sir," a robust youth answered. "But how do we get home without eyes to see?"

"Hold hands and I'll have a couple of my men lead you," Noah said.

"Why would you do that when we've treated you so badly?" a shrivelled old woman asked. "You can preach to us all day and night now, and there's not a thing we can do to stop you."

"That is not God's way, aged mother," Noah answered. "He wants you to listen to me, but He'll not hold you against your will. And neither will I. Now go. I pray your affliction is short-lived and that you will return to listen to my message. It's more serious than you know."

He watched as Obert and Matthias escorted the crowd off his premises. Seeing so many people back to their homes would be quite a task, and he did not expect the two men to return before nightfall. Sighing, he turned his attention to his awestruck crew.

"Well, what're you staring at?" he asked. "It's time to get back to work."

To Noah's surprise, Obert and Matthias returned to the workshop within the hour, full of excitement at how God had healed the people along the way.

"It was incredible, Sir, how the Lord did it!" Matthias exclaimed. "Those most afraid were healed first, then the others."

"What do you mean by most afraid?" Noah asked.

"Well, it's like this, Sir," Obert proceeded to explain. "Many people were so scared they couldn't get away from here fast enough. Tripping over their own feet, they were. The old lady you spoke to was healed first. 'My eyes,' she cried. 'My eyes. I can see again!' I went and had a look, Sir. Sure enough, she could see clear as day."

"That's right, Sir!" Matthias interjected. "Then others started jumping up and down, saying their eyesight was back, too. A real jubilee it was, they were so excited!"

"Yes, a real jubilee until those troublemakers tried to stick their oar in!" Obert said bitterly. Methuselah looked up from what he was doing and raised his eyebrows.

"Troublemakers?" he asked.

"Yes, Sir. Obed's cronies, they were, saying they ought to do Master Noah in once and for all. Folk began to be persuaded, too, and we thought we were going to have to run for our lives. But the ones stirring up the others suddenly ran away, screeching and tearing at their hair like the Nephilim[19] were chasing them. It frightened the others terribly and they ran like demons were after them, too. I reckon they're all on their knees now, praying the same fate doesn't befall them."

"I strongly suspect you're right," Methuselah agreed dryly. Noah, however, was deeply saddened by the news and said nothing. Dismissing the two men, the Patriarch[23] drew his grandson aside.

"Your grief proves you have begun to share God's burden for the lost," he said softly. "Don't grow weary with hoping and praying for their salvation, Noah. As long as there is life, there is opportunity for repentance." Noah shrugged glumly.

"At times like these, I find that difficult to believe," he answered. The old man chuckled.

"It's never easy to give our all in the face of such resistance, Noah. But we have to if we're to attain God's highest calling on our lives. Everything the Lord does is generous. We must therefore live life as generously as He's given it."

"Agreed, but I seem to bumble along from one day to the next with little progress being made. It's discouraging."

"It may seem that way. Yet, as long as you're doing what Elohim[7] has told you to do, He will make up for your shortcomings with His strength and grace. You saw what He did today. Will He not undertake for you tomorrow as well?"

"Of course He will," Noah admitted. "It's just that I often feel so alone, so small in faith."

"As do we all. But we're not alone. God is always with us. We must continually ask Him for wisdom, instead of trying to do things in our own understanding. Learn to be at peace with His Lordship in your life, Noah. It's the only way to be truly content."

Noah turned to respond, but that faraway look was in his grandfather's eyes again. The Patriarch[23] was lapsing into his unseen world more often of late. It could not be long, now, before he left them altogether. The thought saddened Noah. He would miss the old man's input.

CHAPTER 13
DECEPTION

... in the last times some will turn away ...; they will
follow lying spirits and teachings that come from demons.
These teachers are hypocrites and liars. They pretend to
be religious, but their consciences are dead.
1 Timothy 4:1b–2

The miraculous disappearance of the torch attracted people as strongly as it repelled them. So great was the press of the crowd that progress on the Ark once again ground to a halt. Unable to do anything else, Noah preached day and night, but his words had little impact. With decadence more prevalent than ever, the temptation to abandon his calling became hard to resist

"You worry too much," Lamech said one morning, as he set aside some cypress offcuts. Unlike the rest of Noah's crew, he and Methuselah were able to continue working. The two men had filled three crates with treenails and had begun on a fourth. It was unlikely so many would be needed to complete the enormous boat, but it was prudent to cater for breakage.

"How can I not worry?" Noah grumbled. "It's been over six weeks since the men lifted a tool. The Ark will never get built with so many delays."

"True," Methuselah conceded. "But do you really think Elohim[7] wanted it built in the first place?" The terse remark was like salt to a wound.

"Of course He does! He told me so!" Noah exclaimed.

"I know He did, grandson. Even so, I believe God would change His mind if the majority of folk repented. That might be hard for you to swallow, but His heart is for mercy, not judgement. This delay in building the Ark is simply another chance for the lost to turn from their wickedness and be saved."

"But they're doing just the opposite!"

"The Lord is well aware of that and will one day repay," Lamech reminded him. "In the meantime, He remains as patient with these people as He was with me. And

He's calling us to do the same. It will soon be over one way or another, but everything must come to a conclusion in God's time, not ours."

Noah saw in his father's aging face the compassion he himself lacked.

"I'm being a dolt, aren't I?" he said ruefully.

"No more than usual," Lamech teased. "Jests aside, Noah, God has called you to this task because you're persistent enough to see it through."

"Sometimes I wonder," Noah replied, looking at the crowd.

"Well, don't!" Methuselah warned. "Idle thought profits nothing. Return to your preaching and, if you don't know what to say, ask Elohim[7] for wisdom. He'll give you a boldness that will make people sit up and listen – whether they want to or not."

Noah sighed with exhaustion. He had worked harder over the past few months than he had ever done and wondered how much more he could achieve before collapsing.

Oh God, he prayed silently, *I can't do this on my own. Please give me something that will stir them to the core.*

Fired with even greater zeal than usual, Noah's preaching drew a more positive response than ever before. Sadly, this was short-lived, but it was several days before he discovered the reason for the drastic decrease in the crowd.

"What's wrong?" Noah asked when John burst into the workshop one morning, extremely agitated.

"Oh, Sir!" the lad wailed, wringing his hands. "You've got the devil's own competing with you!"

"The devil's own? Surely not!" Noah said in an effort to calm the distraught boy. But John would not be comforted and hugged his knees to his chest until Enos arrived a few minutes later. To Noah's dismay, the doctor immediately confirmed John's report. He had been on his way to work when he heard the raised voice in the town square and stopped to listen.

"I couldn't believe my ears at first," he went on to say. "In short, Je'el has been wonderstruck by a false prophet, who says our freedom of choice justifies our every act, both good and bad. He has also denounced marriage in favour of promiscuity, and insists that uninhibited coupling will expand mankind into a force against which not even Almighty God can stand."

"That's heresy!" Noah exclaimed. "No one can thwart the Most High's power and authority!"

"Yet that's what this charlatan purports, and the crowd believes him," Enos stated flatly. Noah groaned. So much of what he had been told reminded him of the devil's deception in the Garden of Eden[35]. Would this false preacher lead this present age to an even worse downfall?

94

"How can people, who are made in the image of Elohim[7], believe such lies?" he cried.

"They believe because it makes them feel justified in living the way they do," Enos replied.

"But nobody can run away from a guilty conscience, Enos. Our knowledge of right and wrong is too deeply ingrained."

The doctor shook his head.

"I'm afraid these people desire the fleeting pleasures of sin more than they do righteousness, Noah. Even if their consciences weren't so seared towards God, I doubt they'd respond to whatever feelings of guilt they might have."

Despite the physician's sobering insight, Noah knew his call to preach had never been more urgent. And preach he would, regardless of whether he had an audience or not. Striding from the workshop, he lifted his arms and addressed the few who remained as though his heart would burst.

Although there was some renewed interest in Noah's preaching, the majority were swayed by the false doctrine and began indulging in unsurpassed licentiousness. Of particular concern were the young victims of sexual abuse. The City Fathers refused to take positive action, however, and the situation worsened like a festering sore.

Noah's one consolation was the folk who continued to drift down to the wharf to hear him. Fearful of victimization, most came after dark and he decided to only work on the Ark by day and preach at night. The new arrangement was a relief. It had been months since he had been able to dedicate so much time to the enormous boat. Even so, his small team had made fair progress and he did not know how he would manage without them. At least half his men had reached the end of their tether and wanted to quit. Replacing them would be impossible. Too many remembered what God could do when provoked!

His sombre thoughts were interrupted by an urgent shout. Startled, he turned to see Beulah running towards him and knew something was amiss.

"What is it?" he demanded.

"E-Enos!" the old lady gasped, doubling over to catch her breath. "We need Enos! The baby's coming, but there're complications I can do nothing about!"

"But the child's not yet due!" Noah exclaimed.

"I'm telling the truth, Sir. The baby's coming, but it's breeched! Seraphina's in great pain and needs Enos."

Alarmed, Noah spun round, almost knocking Enos off his feet. The doctor had seen the nurse's frenzy and crossed the yard to find out what was wrong.

"Don't worry, Noah," he said quietly. "I know what to do." He then turned to the stout old lady.

"I'll need your help, Beulah. Are you strong enough to join me as soon as you can?"

"I'll get one of the lads to fetch me a horse," she wheezed.

"Good woman," he said, patting her shoulder before heading for Noah's home at a quick trot. Despite his show of confidence, he was worried. Delivering a breech baby was seldom easy. Seraphina's age could give rise to further complications.

Noah watched Enos's rapid departure in a daze, then threw down his apron and followed. It was not customary for a man to watch a birthing, but his longing was too strong to deny.

Seraphina's condition was worse than Enos had feared. The breeched child had already begun to bear down, its tiny spine curving with each contraction. Neither mother nor infant could survive for much longer. He had to push the foetus back into the womb and turn it before the next contraction. Clearing his throat, he looked down into Seraphina's pale, strained face.

"We've little time, My Lady, so listen carefully. Your baby is wedged in the birth canal. You're going to have to relax if I'm to do what's necessary. I know that sounds impossible, but I will tell you how. Do you understand?"

"Is it really that serious?" she whispered brokenly.

"I fear so," Enos nodded. "Now, you are to take a couple of deep breaths and breathe out slowly. You must then take another deep breath and hold it until I tell you to exhale. This will help you relax long enough for me to turn the child. The procedure will take no more than a minute."

"A minute?" she asked in alarm.

"Most people can hold their breath for at least a minute or two, My Lady. But we waste precious time. We must get the baby into the right position soon. Now, breathe!" Seraphina closed her eyes and took the first deep breath, and the second. Then she took the third and held it.

"That's it," Enos said, pushing against the foetus. But it would not budge and it was several seconds before Seraphina's muscles relaxed enough for him to try again. The child moved slightly, but no further. Fearing he would not complete the procedure in time, he clenched his teeth and pushed harder against the tiny spine. To his relief, the baby popped free.

"We've done it!" he cried. "You can stop holding your breath now." He had only just turned the child when Seraphina began her final contraction.

"The worst is over, My Lady," he said, patting her. "Now, bear down as hard as you can. Your baby should be born without any further problems."

"I certainly hope so," Noah said from the doorway. Striding into the room, he held Seraphina as she brought forth their second son. His eyes swam as he looked into the infant's tiny face and compared his feelings of helplessness to the remarkable woman who had endured so much.

"God knows what would have happened had you not been here," he said to Enos.

"It's Beulah you should thank," the doctor replied as he washed his hands. "Many a mother and child are lost because of the pride of a midwife. Fortunately, Beulah asks for help when she needs it. It's a pity she wasn't here for the birth."

"A right pity!" Beulah cried as she waddled into the room. But there was a glint of fun in the faded old eyes and she grinned as she took the babe from Noah's arms.

"He's real tiny, but strong, too," she marvelled when the little hand gripped her finger. "What will you call him, Sir?"

"I've not a clue," Noah laughed. "It's my wife who chooses our children's names." Seraphina smiled wearily.

"I would like to call him Japheth[11]," she answered.

"Why, that's the name of my dead brother, God rest his soul!" Beulah exclaimed.

"Which is why I've chosen it," Seraphina said. "Your quick action saved the life of our son and I want to honour you for that." Beulah's eyes welled with tears.

"Anyone would have done what I did, My Lady!" she cried.

"Not anyone, Beulah, and you know it. Please, I want to do this – not just to thank you, but also because of what the name means. You forsook all to care for us when we were children. May this child become a great tribe that brings honour to your family name and to mine."

The old woman was now sobbing without restraint.

"I don't know what to say," she wailed.

"Then say nothing and be content," Noah said, wrapping his arms around her and smiling at his wife with gratitude. It had been years since he had thought about Beulah's young brother and the tragedy that had claimed his life. It was appropriate the lad be remembered with such affection.

CHAPTER 14
COMING OF AGE

We, too, wait anxiously for that day when God will give
us our full rights as His children...
Romans 8:23b

Noah hammered in the last treenail for the day and stood back to survey the bows of the ship. They had been hard at it for over ten years now, but were no more than an eighth of the way to completion. Despite his frustration, there was little he could do to speed up progress. Most of his crew had resigned years ago. Of the remaining few, only Enos and Jasper were able-bodied – the aging patriarchs[23] having become too frail to offer more than moral support, and the heavier tasks beyond John's failing health.

Sighing, Noah looked down to where Shem and Japheth were playing a game of tag. He had begun to teach his sons carpentry and had them help each day with the Ark's construction. Both boys were quick to learn and would be even more knowledgeable were it not for their enforced isolation. Venturing into the city was not safe for anyone working on the Ark, and Noah had long since relocated their home to the cutting shed yard. He had also modified the storeroom to house his diminished workforce.

Despite their humble living conditions, the small community was self-supporting. With plentiful harvests of fruit, vegetables and grain, and a steady supply of milk from their two cows, they fared better than most folk in Je'el. A vast number of farms had been abandoned by hundreds flocking to the cities in pursuit of the riches they had been falsely promised. It was dismaying to see the backbone of the world's wealth forsaken for a lie, but there was nothing the community could do to stop the flow of madness except pray.

While Noah worked on the Ark by day and preached by night, Seraphina turned their home into a hive of activity. Apart from her many household chores, she also attended to the children's education and had the rare gift of knowing how to mix work with pleasure. She had recently taken to tutoring the boys in the evenings and Noah would often arrive home to find his family burning the midnight oil.

Tonight, the time usually given over to lessons and preaching would be spent in celebrating Shem's coming of age. The transition from boyhood to manhood was a solemn occasion, at which the father publicly welcomed his son into the fellowship of men and pronounced him his heir. The ritual was then sealed with a Blood Covenant that could only be broken by death.

Noah remembered his own coming of age and the two bloody thumbprints endorsing the Covenant. It had been an awesome moment when his father had pressed his bleeding hand to his own. Lamech had shown such tenderness, such warmth. Sadly, his mother's death had cast a pall on their relationship, but no longer. Every promise he and his father had made to each other on that day long ago had at last been fulfilled. The realization made Noah smile and it was several seconds before he felt the impatient tugging at his sleeve.

"Abba[1]! Abba[1]!" Japheth shrilled. "What're you thinking?" Noah looked down at his youngest son and smiled.

"What am I thinking?" he asked, swinging the lad into the air and laughing when he squealed in delight. "I'm thinking it's time to call it quits and go help your mother. Right?"

"Right," Shem solemnly agreed in an effort to hide his excitement. Setting Japheth down, Noah ruffled his firstborn's hair and grinned. Shem's looks and mannerisms were so much like Methuselah's. Hopefully, the boy's coming of age would be a landmark towards acquiring a faith like the Patriarch's[23].

"Well, what're we waiting for?" he asked, putting an arm around each boy and leading the way to the house, where their mother patiently waited.

Seraphina stood back to survey the small group around her table. It had been necessary to hire the town hall for her coming of age, but force of circumstance prevented them from having such a big gathering for Shem. Even so, there was something extraordinary about tonight's ceremony that she had not experienced at her own. Watching her husband welcome their son into young manhood made her proud. The youth had grown up to be everything they had hoped for.

She listened attentively as the promises of the Covenant were exchanged, and wept when Noah opened his arms to receive the customary embrace. The young man clung to his father, then withdrew self-consciously.

"Does being an adult mean I can't do this anymore?" he asked in his half-broken voice.

"Of course it doesn't!" Noah exclaimed, pulling his son back into his arms. Shem grinned and hugged his father tightly – much to the delight of those present. Noah waited for the laughter to subside, then addressed the lad more soberly.

"Growing up doesn't mean leaving the tender things behind, Shem. Elohim[7] Himself declares His gentleness makes us great. What better example do we have of real manhood? A man of valour is not afraid to weep with compassion or to speak words of kindness. He knows a soft answer can turn away wrath and a timely embrace keeps relationships strong."

Pausing, Noah reached for the ceremonial knife. He had honed the blade just that afternoon, in the hope it would cause his son less pain than he himself remembered.

"What we're about to do is perhaps the greatest act of love a father and son can demonstrate towards each other," he said solemnly. "I want us to seal our Covenant in our blood, just as your grandfather and I did. I hope this is what you want, too." Shem looked fondly at the frail old man who seldom showed his feelings and saw the glow in his eyes. The sealing of the Covenant clearly held great meaning and honour for him.

"Yes, Father," he answered earnestly. "I want to do this more than anything." Smiling tenderly, Noah sliced his own thumb open from tip to base. He winced as the blood began to spurt, then quickly drew the blade in a horizontal cut across the top of Shem's thumb.

"We're almost done," he whispered when the lad gasped in pain. "Now come, join your hand with mine." Shem's bleeding was quickly staunched as Noah pressed his wounded thumb to his own. The two smiled at one another in a private moment of understanding.

"The vertical cut on my thumb symbolizes God's love for us. Whereas the horizontal cut on yours symbolizes the love we have for each other," Noah went on to explain. "This ritual is not just a mingling of our blood to set our seals to this Covenant. It is also an acknowledgement that Elohim[7] is our witness. He will hold us accountable for every promise we have made to each other. Do you understand?"

"Yes, Father, I do," Shem answered. Releasing his son's hand, Noah pulled the linen scroll towards him.

"Let's do this then," he said, firmly pressing his thumb to the bottom of the Covenant and waiting for his blood to soak into the fabric.

"Now come and place your mark on top of mine," he invited Shem. The youth eagerly obeyed and his eyes shone when his father gave him the right hand of fellowship. The two then turned to face their family and friends.

"It is done!" Noah proclaimed, holding up the Covenant for all to see. A lump formed in Seraphina's throat when she saw the bloody seal. The cross-like mark always moved her to tears.

It was after midnight before the ceremony came to a close, and Shem stood beside his father to wish their guests a good night. The past thirteen years had come and gone in the blink of an eye. Two summers hence and it would be Japheth's turn. Seraphina looked at her youngest son and smiled. Although different in temperament, the lad adored his brother. Hopefully, Shem's new status would not dampen their relationship.

As though reading her thoughts, Noah turned from the open doorway and pulled Japheth close.

"Why are you standing all alone?" he asked, draping his arm over the boy's shoulders. "You'll be doing this yourself in a couple of years. What better time to learn than now?" Japheth beamed with delight and wrapped his skinny arms around the big man's waist.

"Thank you, Abba[1]," he said in his high-pitched voice. "I was feeling lonely by myself."

"There's no need for that, lad," Methuselah said as he joined them. "We're here for you. Remember that."

"I'll remember," Japheth answered with a grin at his great-grandfather. Laughing, Methuselah affectionately embraced the youngsters before shuffling off to bed.

Seraphina wiped her eyes and silently thanked God for her two fine sons. She had hoped to have more children, but feared the stress she lived under had made her barren before her time. She had given up trying to maintain her rigorous lifestyle long ago, but Noah had not. He could not keep up such a pace for much longer, however. Aside from his lustreless hair and stooped shoulders, his eyes were sunken with exhaustion. The realization that he was growing old depressed her.

Noticing her mistress's mood, Beulah rose unsteadily from her chair and waddled across the room. The old lady was now riddled with rheumatism, but her senses were as sharp as ever.

"They make a pretty sight, don't they, My Lady?" she said. "Proud enough to burst is what you must be feeling."

Seraphina smiled.

"I am proud, very proud. And so should you be, too. You helped me raise them. They're good boys, but very different, don't you think?"

"As different as ink is to milk," the old lady chuckled. "At least Shem looks like his father. Japheth is another story altogether. I can't imagine *what* you were looking at when you conceived that child!" Seraphina laughed at the superstitious folklore, but had to admit there was truth in what the old lady said. With his pale skin and ice-blue eyes, Japheth did not resemble anyone in their ancestry. Yet his sunny nature made him very much her son.

"Have you considered having another child, My Lady?" Beulah asked shrewdly. Seraphina nodded wistfully.

"There are times when my longing to hold another baby hurts so much I feel like I'm in labour again. I was so sure I'd have more than two children, but that seems unlikely now, doesn't it?" Beulah clucked in sympathy.

"Babes aren't just the love creatures of men and women, My Lady. They're gifts from God Himself. If you want another baby, you should ask Him for one."

"I'd love to, Beulah, but what if He doesn't hear my prayer?"

"The Good Lord always listens," Beulah admonished sternly. "It's just that we're too busy to hear Him, or His answer isn't what we want to hear. Pray and trust Him, My Lady. Even if His answer is no, it will be for the best."

The old nurse's words made Seraphina feel ashamed. She had always made much of living by faith, but how small her own faith had been of late! She would pray and she would trust God to answer as He thought fit. Reaching out, she grasped Beulah's gnarled hand.

"You're right," she admitted. "I will pray for another child, and I'm asking you to pray with me. Will you do that?"

The old lady beamed toothlessly.

"Of course I will, My Lady!" she exclaimed joyously.

CHAPTER 15
HOPE NOT DEFERRED

Hope deferred makes the heart sick, but when dreams
come true, there is life and joy.
Proverbs 13:12

Four months after Shem's coming of age, Seraphina knew her request had been granted. She fondly recalled her husband's passion the night she had prayed for another child. They had talked for hours afterwards and she had dreaded the coming dawn that would put an end to their time of intimacy. To her surprise, Noah had spent the entire day with her – something he had not done for months. Work on the Ark had sidelined the Sabbath[25] day of rest, but those few beneficial hours had prompted Noah to reinstate it. The weekly break gave them all the opportunity to refuel their strength, without which they could not complete the boat or survive the Flood.

Her thoughts were forgotten when she felt the ripple across her stomach. Grinning, she crossed the yard to tell her husband the good news.

Noah was deeply moved when Seraphina told him she was pregnant. It had been years since her last flow.

"Just when we think we've got our lives mapped out, the Lord does something greater than ever!" he exclaimed. "I'd stopped believing we'd have another child."

"So had I until I felt the baby move," she admitted

"Has Enos examined you yet?" he asked. Seraphina shook her head.

"You don't think I've got it wrong, do you?" she said.

"Hardly, but it would be wise to have him keep an eye on you. You're not as young as you were."

"What impudence!" she laughed, slapping him on the shoulder. "But you're right. Where is Enos? I'll see him now." Noah's face fell.

"He's attending John, dear heart. I'm afraid the lad's taken a turn for the worse." Saddened, Seraphina flopped down on a chair.

"We knew it would happen sometime," Noah said gently. "He hasn't been able to move for days now."

"Do you think Enos will mind if I sit with the lad?" she asked tearfully.

"I don't think so. But what if seeing him so sick affects you or the baby?"

Seraphina shook her head firmly.

"This child comes straight from Elohim⁷, Noah. I doubt anything could harm him!"

"Then go and bring what comfort you can."

John was unconscious when Seraphina knelt by his bedside and held his hand.

"Even if I could revive him, it would only prolong the inevitable," Enos told her sadly. "The lad's suffered enough. It's time to let him go now."

Practical though the doctor's words were, Seraphina knew John's death would hit him hard. She wondered if he would be able to withstand the grief.

"Dear Enos. You have a way of saying the right words but it's not your heart talking, is it?"

Enos pressed his lips firmly together and shook his head.

"I've never been able to hide anything from you, have I?" he smiled wryly. "You're right. It's not my heart talking, but what I've said is true. John doesn't enjoy life anymore."

"You're still not letting your heart do the talking, Enos! What do *you* want for John?"

"You already know the answer to that," he replied bitterly.

"Very well, what would you do if John was healed, then?"

Enos's eyes grew misty.

"It's foolish, I suppose," he said, studying his hands, "but I dream of us doing things together. The sort of things a father does with his son. But it'll never happen now."

"What if John has the same dream?" she asked.

"Strange you should say that," Enos said in surprise. "He did express the same desire a few months back, before he became too ill to talk. It was very moving."

"Have you told him you share his longing?"

Enos shook his head.

"No, that would be too cruel," he answered.

"I don't think so," Seraphina disagreed. "Sometimes our dreams are all we have. John would be touched to know you yearn for the things he does. Do you think he can hear us?"

"I've heard of those who've been fully aware while unconscious," Enos mused. "But John's organs are beginning to fail now. I don't think he can hear us at all."

"What if you're wrong, Enos? What if John has heard every word? Don't you think it might stir up the faith you both need to ask God for a miracle?" The suggestion shocked Enos.

"I know what I'm talking about," Seraphina insisted, squeezing his hand. "Something similar has happened to me." She told him about her pregnancy, and how she had thought it impossible to conceive again. "Yet God heard my cry and gave me what I asked for," she declared. Enos shook his head sceptically.

"Wishing so hard for a child can bring on a false pregnancy," he warned.

"This is not false, Enos. I'm as sure of being pregnant as I've ever been, but I want you to examine me, anyway. That's why I'm here." Nodding, Enos ushered her into the curtained alcove at the far end of the room. The examination confirmed what Seraphina already knew.

"It really is a miracle, isn't it?" the doctor remarked.

"Yes, it is. If God can do this for me, might He not also grant your wish for John?"

"But what if He doesn't, My Lady?"

"That's His concern, not yours," she answered softly. "You'll never know if the Lord wants to give you the desire of your heart unless you ask Him for it."

"But I've never asked God for anything. Where would I start?"

"Would you like me to pray with you?" Seraphina offered, but Enos was reluctant. Nodding, she quietly withdrew and closed the door behind her. Her presence would simply hinder the work the Lord was about to do in the doctor's life.

Not knowing how to begin, Enos sat and stared at John for a long time. Much as he wanted the lad healed, he had been raised to believe all things came from God, and that it was wrong to seek divine intervention. He could no longer accept this concept, however. Not when it touched such a raw nerve.

After much travail, he came to the conclusion that disease did not originate with the Creator, but with the first man and woman, in the Garden of Eden. It had been their disobedience against God that had loosed the scourges of pain, sickness and death upon the world. Scourges that hurt the Lord as much as those they afflicted. Why, then, did He not heal those who repented of their waywardness more often? And why had He not healed this innocent boy who loved Him so much? There had to be a key. Something he could unlock to bring John back from the brink of death. Desperate, Enos clutched his head and cried for answers. There was so little time left! A few minutes more and the lad would be gone.

"I'm not sure you can hear me, John," he said hoarsely, "but I know God can. I don't want you to die, lad. Not yet. There's so much I want to share with you, so much I want us to do." Overcome, Enos buried his face in the bedclothes. John's breathing was so shallow, his face so lifeless.

"Dear God," he whispered brokenly, "please make this boy well." There was the tiniest flicker of movement as a tear escaped from under John's eyelashes. Then he was gone.

Enos knew he should enshroud John's body, but could not face it. Not yet. Needing to be alone, he crossed the yard to the cutting shed and closed the door. The heavy odours of pine tar and hemp made him sag.

"Why, God, why?" he cried, abandoning himself to his grief. He had believed so hard for John's healing, but now regretted praying. It would have been easier to just accept the inevitable.

He heard a flutter of wings but took little notice. Sheba often roosted among the shed's rafters. It was only when the room began to glow that he looked up and saw the luminescent Dove. Believing the Bird to be symbolic of John's departed spirit, he broke down and wept. A great peace suddenly surged within him – the peace of God's presence. Filled with renewed hope, he leapt to his feet and ran from the shed. But the boy lay just as he had left him.

"No!" he shouted, throwing himself across the bed. Waves of heat coursed through his body, making him shake violently.

"Dear God! What's happening to me?" he cried.

"Enos? Mister Enos? Are you alright, Sir?" Thinking he was going insane, Enos covered his ears, then gasped. The faintest of breaths had warmed his neck!

"John?" he whispered, raising his head to stare into the lively blue eyes.

"I'm back, Enos. I'm back!" the youth exclaimed. Overjoyed, Enos clung to the lad.

"Thank You, God!" he wept. "Thank You!" John held the physician until his trembling ceased, then gently pulled away.

"Come, now. It's your turn to rest," he urged. Enos nodded wearily.

"*L'chaim*[14], John," he said, as he tightly clasped the lad's hand. John smiled tenderly.

"Yes, Enos. To life, and to Elohim[7] Most High who has given it," he agreed, easing the exhausted doctor down onto the bed. Enos was sound asleep before his head touched the pillow.

Enos awoke to utter darkness. Startled, he reached out, but could feel nothing. He wondered if he had been taken back to the beginning of time, when the Earth was void of light and life. If so, why did he not feel frightened?

Hearing the faintest of sounds, he closed his eyes and listened. The song swelled, filling the emptiness with an ecstasy he wished could last forever. But the music quickly faded and his heart pounded in the silence. The Voice that broke the stillness made him drop to the floor like a stone. Never had he heard anything so glorious! So majestic! Suddenly, the Shekinah[29] Glory of the Most High flooded the void and Enos covered his head with his arms.

"Who am I, Lord, that You should come to me?" he cried, quaking with fear.

Fear not, Enos, the Lord answered. *I see the love you have for your adopted son. I have restored him to you so that you might learn to trust and obey me. Never again will the lad suffer. He will live out his days in fullness of joy until I bring him to myself. And, like Enoch of old, his going will happen in a way you least expect. Be ready for it.*

"H-how long, Lord?" Enos stammered.

John will remain for as long as it takes to complete my work in you. Do not resist that which I have destined for you both. It is for my glory and your comfort that I have given the boy back to you. The miracle of his healing will testify to my mercy and be for you a source of strength. Now go and live your life in accordance with my will. Fear not, for I am with you and will never leave nor forsake you. Fear not ... Fear not ...

The Voice became so soft that Enos could no longer hear it. Yet the words of the Holy One echoed in his soul, instilling in him a future and a hope. Sighing, he opened his eyes and smiled when he saw John sitting on the stool next to his bed.

"I was beginning to wonder when you'd rouse!" the lad exclaimed as he lifted a pot of broth from the brazier.

"What ... what time is it?" Enos asked, sitting up and scratching the back of his neck.

"The sun set a good six hours ago, Sir."

"That means I've been asleep for twelve!"

"More like thirty-six!" John corrected him. "The Sabbath[25] was the day before yesterday."

"Are you saying I've lost a whole day somewhere?"

John grinned and raised a spoonful of broth to Enos's lips.

"That I am, Sir." Enos sipped the hot soup, then eagerly took the bowl from John. If his appetite was anything to go by, it had been ages since he had eaten.

"You made short work of that meal," John said, taking the empty dish from him. "Would you like a refill?"

"That I would," Enos said. "My stomach feels like it's touching my backbone."

"Beulah thought it might and cooked a whole lot extra. There's also some bread and cheese." As the doctor gnawed at the crusty loaf, he noticed John had opened one of his scrolls and supposed the sketches held some interest for him.

"The pictures aren't as good as they could be, lad."

"Why, I think they're fine, Mister Enos, but it's not them I'm looking at." Enos smiled sadly. He knew how much John desired to read and write, but the boy's diseased brain rendered him incapable of doing so. The doctor had tried various techniques to help him overcome his disability, but with little success. John refused to be discouraged, however, and often sat for hours attempting to decipher words.

"Trying to read again, are you?" Enos asked.

"Not just trying, Sir," John claimed boldly. "I am reading."

"No, lad, you must be mistaken!"

"Not so, Mister Enos. I'll read something to you if you like." Enos's eyes widened as he listened. Apart from poor pronunciation, the youth's speech was no longer impaired and he read as though he had been doing it all his life.

"Can you imagine how I felt when I opened your scroll and could understand every word?" John said when he had finished. "I reckon God not only healed my body, He healed my mind as well! And it's not just the reading, Sir. I think differently, too. There were things I couldn't understand before, but now I do. I'm really excited, but also a bit worried. What if you don't like me so much now I'm different?"

"That will never happen, John. I'm grateful God has healed you beyond my expectations. Just promise you won't lose the joy you have in living. It's who you are."

"The Lord has already warned me that too much learning can rob a man of his joy. Don't worry, Sir. I'll make sure I don't fill my head with everything except God."

"Well said," Enos commended him warmly. "But come, rest now. You look worn out."

"I am tired," John acknowledged wanly. "I've been sitting here all this time, looking at your scroll. I was too excited to sleep when I discovered I could read it."

"Well, I think we both need rest. We've a lifetime to catch up on all we've missed out on so far."

"Yes, Sir," John said, snuggling down into the bed opposite and falling asleep at once. Enos watched the gentle rising and falling of the lad's chest for several minutes before closing his own eyes. Had it not been for the wonder of his earlier experience, he would have thought he was dreaming. But this was no dream. God had restored to him a life he swore to live to the full.

Seraphina's third pregnancy was difficult. Apart from a constant, aching discomfort, she experienced waves of heat that left her feeling exhausted. Beulah claimed the symptoms were normal in women her age, but Seraphina feared the worst when the child delayed his coming. What if there was more to this than the old lady thought? Setting her lips in a firm line, she crossed the yard to the doctor's quarters. It was time to confront him with her concerns.

"I've been so unwell, Enos. What if something's wrong?" she wailed. The doctor took her face firmly between his hands and gave her a gentle shake.

"Such anxiety will rob you of the strength you need for your baby's birth," he chided.

"But what if I'm right? What if there *is* something wrong with this child?"

"There's nothing to indicate this baby will be anything but normal, My Lady. And even if he isn't, would you love him any less than Shem and Japheth?"

Enos's words did not bring the comfort Seraphina desired, but she enjoyed a surprisingly good night's rest for the first time in weeks and awoke to her first contraction the following morning The curly-haired baby punched his way into the world just after dawn and bawled lustily when Enos examined him. Eager to part with his angry little charge, the doctor placed the infant in the crook of Seraphina's arm and watched him suckle.

"Well, he knows what he's about," Beulah chuckled.

"That he does," Enos agreed. "You'll not have any worries with this one, My Lady. He's sharp as an arrow and bound to grow up strong and active, too, if his appetite's anything to go by."

Enos's reassurance brought tears to Seraphina's eyes.

"What's wrong?" Noah asked with concern as the doctor left the room with Beulah.

"Nothing that a bit of rest won't cure," Seraphina smiled wearily. "But I can't even consider it until this little one stops feeding."

"We could've employed a wet nurse had things been different."

"Not when there's so much disease out there," Seraphina objected. Noah grimaced. The depravity within the city had indeed begun to take its toll on its inhabitants.

"Have you decided on a name for our new son yet?" he asked. Seraphina nodded slowly.

"I have, but you won't like it."

"Then the sooner you tell me, the better," he said dryly.

"Very well. The name I have decided on is Ham[10]," she answered. Noah frowned and Seraphina hurried to explain.

"I would never willingly choose this name for any of our children, Noah. But Elohim[7] has shown me this is what He wants our son to be called." Noah sighed heavily.

"You're right," he said. "I don't like it, but it would be foolish to resist what God has ordained. Perhaps this son is destined to be a prophet full of righteous indignation and anger, just like Methuselah has been in the past."

"Your grandfather still gets quite frightening when he stands for God," she said affectionately. "Do you really think Ham might grow up to be like him?"

"I don't think anyone can match the ferocity of Methuselah's faith, but I could be wrong. What Ham becomes will be his choice. Our responsibility is to train him up in the way he should go and pray he'll not depart from it."

Seraphina looked down at the now sleeping infant. Even in repose he was an agitated child. Sighing, she sank back onto the pillows.

"I fret too much," she grumbled. "And all because this little boy has worn me out with his impatience. I need to rest but would like to dedicate him to the Lord first." Nodding, Noah placed his hand on the baby's head.

"Thank You for this miracle child, Lord. Thank You for the gift of Ham. We dedicate him to You and pray for wisdom to bring him up in the love and knowledge of You. May he learn to honour You in all he does. Thank You for hearing our prayer. Amen."

Satisfied, Seraphina closed her eyes and drifted to sleep. Noah gently stroked her aging face and silky grey hair. Never had she been more beautiful. Smiling, he lifted their newborn from the crook of her arm and placed him in his crib. He then snuggled down next to his wife and held her while she slept.

CHAPTER 16
ASTONISHING NEWS

Don't let anyone think less of you because you are young.
Be an example to all...
1 Timothy 4:12a

It was a cold, blustery day. Seraphina paused from hanging the washing to wrap her shawl around her shoulders.

"Here, let me help you," Enos offered. She looked doubtfully at the physician's twisted hands. The effects of the crippling fever he had contracted just after Ham's birth had begun taking their toll. Yet, despite the debilitating disease, he had an enviable zest for life.

"Daydreaming again?" Enos teased. Stooped as the tall doctor had become, Seraphina smiled straight into his eyes.

"Not so much a dream as a desire, Enos. You've been a real inspiration to me."

"Oh? In what way?" he asked, reaching for a peg.

"Are you sure you can manage?" she said with concern.

"Not for long in this wind, but I'll get more done if we work while we talk. And don't change the subject, My Lady! You haven't answered my question."

Seraphina laughed self-consciously.

"It's your contentment that has us all amazed, Enos," she said with feeling. "There was so much you wanted to do with John after God raised him from the dead, only to be thwarted by this affliction you have. I don't think *I* could be so brave."

"I've the lad to thank for it," the doctor said easily. "When he was restored, I promised I would trust God in all circumstances and be grateful for what I have. I'm hoping the Lord will heal me this side of Heaven. But, even if He doesn't, it's unlikely John will be with us for much longer. There's little meaning to my life without him."

Seraphina's eyes brimmed with tears. She knew what the physician meant, for he had confided in her years ago.

"Are you sure?" she whispered. Enos nodded sadly.

"The lad's become restless and uncommunicative, like he no longer wants to be here," he said.

"Have you questioned him about it?" she asked.

"How can I, My Lady? I've never told him what God showed me concerning his future, but I suspect he knows. He has such a yearning for Heaven."

"I wish I could attribute *Ham's* restless spirit to such heavenly-mindedness," Seraphina said wistfully. "I swear that boy is hankering for things that have little to do with the Divine."

"Most youths tend towards a bit of carnality, Seraphina."

"I'm aware of the temptations pubescent boys experience," she retorted. "But Ham is different from how his brothers were at his age."

"Different? How?" Enos probed.

"In the way he talks, for a start. He knows things he could never have been taught here. He also looks at Noah and me in a way that belies his innocence. Where would he gain such worldly knowledge except on the streets? It scares me to think he's sneaking into the city. What if someone hurts him, Enos? What if he picks up a virulent disease?"

"I don't see how you can prevent the lad from being adventurous. Boys will be boys, and Ham is exceptionally bright. Has Noah explained to him the way of a man with a maid?"

"Yes, as soon as his voice began to deepen."

"Well, you know how he likes to learn everything firsthand, but I doubt he's done more than look."

Seraphina sighed with frustration.

"I don't suppose it's easy for him," she said.

"It's not easy for any of your boys. How old is Shem now? Twenty-nine?"

"Thirty," she answered.

"Which means Japheth is twenty-eight and Ham sixteen. Your sons might not say much, My Lady, but each of them is longing for a wife and family of their own. How will their desires be met if they remain in isolation here?"

"I don't know, Enos. But I do know the Prophecy includes them *and* their wives. So, what God has ordained will come to pass, even though the obstacles appear insurmountable."

"And I of all people should know that better than most!" Enos laughed. "You're right. God will make a way. But you do need to talk to Ham and find out what he's been up to. You may find he already has a girl."

"No! He's far too young!" Seraphina protested.

"Not necessarily. I know of men who've married young and proved to be good husbands. Rather that, than have him burn with lust."

"If Ham *has* got himself a girl, I hate to think what Noah's response will be," she grumbled. "I suppose the sooner I find out, the sooner we can face the music and dance."

"That's My Lady," Enos said, as she hitched up her skirt and crossed the yard to where Ham sat, whittling away at a piece of wood.

Ham welcomed his mother with a broad grin and casually tossed the carving to her.

"I hope you've something better for me to do," he said. "I'm bored stiff!"

"I thought you'd still be busy with your lessons," she answered, discarding the figurine.

"Don't be silly," he laughed. "The work you set was far too easy. I don't know why you force me to do it, Mother. You know I'd rather be building the Ark."

Seraphina sighed. Clever though Ham was, neatness was not his strong point. The thought of marking another rushed assignment was wearisome.

"If your work is as untidy as it was yesterday, I swear I'll make you redo it," she scolded.

"You wouldn't!" the lad exclaimed.

"Yes, I would," she replied sternly. "Neatness prepares you for a disciplined life later."

"Disciplined for *what*, Mother?" he asked in exasperation. "I've been prepared for nothing but the Flood, so the only drive I have is to work on the Ark. Besides, Father needs my help. We're not even halfway to completion. What if the Flood comes before we're finished?"

"I know how you feel, Ham. But we need to remember we've been called to survive the Flood and found a new civilization. It's therefore vital for us to be a people of learning, with skills we can pass down to our descendants."

Ham's amber eyes darkened with anger.

"Descendants?" he cried bitterly. "Please, Mother! What choice of women do we have while we live in isolation from everyone else? And how will we sire your grand-children without them? Apart from this, I'm also lonely. Can't you see that?"

"Lonely? You?" Seraphina asked in surprise. Despite his brashness, fun-loving Ham was well liked.

"Yes, me!" he answered bitterly. "I enjoy the company of men, but it's not the same as being with a woman. For goodness' sake, Mother! I'm no longer a boy!" Seraphina had no option but to agree. Already a head taller than Noah – and still growing – Ham had attained full manhood by the time he was fifteen.

"You're right," she admitted quietly. "So how do you suggest we solve our problem?" Ham heard the respect in his mother's voice and gave her a long, slow smile before answering.

"Let me and my brothers go find women for ourselves," he said.

"It's too dangerous," she demurred.

"So you keep saying, but what choice do we have? The likelihood of women coming to look for us here is next to none."

"You've already done it, haven't you? Gone into Je'el, I mean."

"Of course I've gone. Several times, in fact," he shrugged.

"Ham!"

"Don't worry! I haven't done anything inappropriate and I'm not likely to if she agrees."

"You've met somebody, then?" she enquired with a raised eyebrow. Ham nodded.

"You're not surprised?" he asked.

"I might've been had your behaviour not given you away."

"Have I been *that* obvious?"

"If how you've been looking at your father and me is anything to go by, then the answer is yes," she answered. The lad flushed.

"I'm sorry," he muttered. "It's just that the love you have for each other makes me desire Dinah even more. She's beautiful, Mother. I want her to live with us if you and father will allow it." Seraphina was sceptical. With little money to spare, their home had become shabby.

"I doubt Dinah will agree once she sees the house," she objected. Ham thought otherwise.

"Of course she will! She's already promised to marry me," he said. Seraphina gawked at her son.

"Don't you think you're a bit young for marriage?" she argued.

"There you go again!" he grumbled. "I know my own mind, Mother. Besides, if she lives here I won't need to sneak out every night to see her."

"Every night!" she exclaimed. Ham laughed at his mother's look of consternation.

"I don't suppose Father will be happy about it," he mused.

"I've no idea," Seraphina answered dryly. "We've never discussed this possibility."

"Will you break the news? You've a way with him that I don't."

"Not always, son. Perhaps it would be better if I spoke to Lamech first."

"Good idea," Ham said, embracing her. "Grandfather will know just what to do."

"I hope so, for your sake," she answered. "Now, off with you. If your lesson's not up to scratch by the time I return, I'll have your hide!"

"I'm at your command, My Lady," Ham said, sweeping the ground in a mock bow.

Seraphina laughed, but deep down she was worried. Her youngest might look like a man, but he was still a boy at heart. Would he be able to cope with the responsibilities of marriage? Sighing, she crossed the yard to the house and Lamech.

Lamech was mending a torn blanket when he heard footsteps outside his door. The light tread made him smile.

"Is that you, daughter?" he called.

"Yes, Father," Seraphina answered as she entered his room.

"What a pleasant surprise," Lamech said, snapping off the yarn and threading the needle into the woollen cloth. Having become too frail and blind to assist with building the Ark, he had taken on the family's sewing. He was amazingly deft at it and attributed his ability to a heightened sense of touch.

Seraphina seldom had time to spend with the old man during the day, and was glad he was able to fill the hours with something so useful. Hopefully, Ham's news would not upset him too much. There had always been a special bond between Lamech and his youngest grandson. He would be perturbed to think the boy was about to repeat the mistake he had made in marrying Miriamne.

"You have a heavy heart, Seraphina," Lamech said, breaking into her thoughts.

"Not so much heavy as confused," she answered, sitting down opposite him.

"And you're hoping I'm wise enough to unravel the tangle." Seraphina laughed at the gentle humour.

"I don't think anyone can untangle this except God Himself," she said. "I need help with breaking some astonishing news to Noah." Lamech nodded knowingly.

"I don't suppose it has anything to do with Ham?" he asked.

"How did you guess?"

"How could I not? That boy's been as restless as a mule with its head stuck in a bucket. What has he done this time?"

"I'm not sure you'll like it," she hedged.

"Try me." Seraphina looked doubtfully at her father-in-law, then took a deep breath.

"Ham wants to get married," she blurted. The news brought tears to Lamech's rheumy eyes.

"Oh, my dear!" he said, squeezing her hand. "Ham and I have always been close, but I never realized just how alike we are."

"Alike? Don't be silly, Father! You and he are as different as sweet is to sour."

"That's where you're wrong," he corrected her gently. "We may look different, but deep down we have many similarities. Indeed, this news makes me feel like I'm seeing a reflection of myself. Do you know I was only fourteen when I met Noah's mother? People laughed and said we were too young to feel so deeply, but our love was real. I begged Methuselah to let me wed her, but he refused and I was too afraid to resist him. And so – much against her wishes and mine – Orpah was given to another!

"No one could stop us loving each other, though, and we secretly kept in touch. I finally wed her many years later, after her husband died. Had I known how little time we would have together, I would not have let anything stand in the way of our love. Giving in to my father is one of my deepest regrets. His, too, I might add.

"Now, Ham might be making the wrong choice, Seraphina, but we're in no position to judge until we've met the girl. Even then, the decision is his. All we can do is pray for a favourable outcome. Whatever you do, don't browbeat the lad. Ham's more rebellious than I ever was. He'll not take to it kindly."

"After what you've shared, I'm prepared to accept Ham's decision. But what about Noah? The older he gets, the more like Methuselah he becomes."

"You misjudge my father, Seraphina. He acted in my best interests at the time, albeit in a foolish way. I hated his interference, but doubt I would have come to faith in Elohim[7] without it. But I digress. Do you want me to talk to Noah?"

"Do you think he'll listen?"

"Not to begin with, but he will in the end. Noah adored his mother. The realization that he could've had more time with her had we married early will not be lost on him. But enough said. Go and tell your husband I need to see him urgently." Relieved to have the matter taken out of her hands, Seraphina gave Lamech a warm hug and rushed outside to find Noah.

Noah was incredulous.

"You can't be serious!" he thundered.

"Calm yourself, Noah, or you'll lose control of the situation altogether!" Lamech said sternly. Noah glared at his father.

"I wouldn't be so angry were it not for Ham's insolence," he muttered into his beard. Lamech frowned.

"The lad's not being insolent, Noah. He's merely trying to establish his place in a community where he's by far the youngest. His coming of age was over three years ago now. Yet you continue to treat him like a child. He has been deceitful, yes, but only because he sought a solution to a serious dilemma – the answer to which I believe he has found. After all, I was only fourteen when I met your mother."

"Even so, it's unlikely you were as immature as Ham."

"Few sons imagine their fathers as ever being confused and afraid. But I was then. Had I been half as courageous as Ham, things might've been different for us. Let the lad make his own decision, Noah, then stand by him insofar as you can."

"But marriage? Why not a time of friendship first?"

"A good idea if you allow Dinah to stay here to avoid Ham sneaking out to see her," Lamech answered. "I know we've little space, but I'm willing to bunk down in the storeroom and let her use my room for as long as she needs it." Noah shook his head. The snug little nook had been Beulah's until she had died of heart failure the winter before last. Moving Lamech into it shortly afterwards had been a sensible arrangement Noah was reluctant to change. The old man was no longer capable of walking unaided.

"No, Father," he protested. "I'd rather move the boys instead. Their room is large enough to accommodate a couple, should Ham and Dinah marry."

Lamech laughed good-humouredly.

"*You've* changed your tune!" he declared. Noah shrugged.

"We all know Ham seldom backs down once his mind's made up," he answered. "Better to prepare for the inevitable than to resist it. But I've talked long enough. It's time to call Ham. Will you sit in on our discussion, Father, and bring your wisdom to the table?" Lamech eagerly agreed.

"Are you planning on anyone else being present?" he asked.

"Not until we've reached an agreement. I suppose Shem and Japheth will get their own ideas about finding wives after this. I swear it would be much easier if God just brought the girls to our doorstep."

"Good point. Have you asked Him to?"

The question took Noah by surprise.

"Er … no," he answered guiltily.

"How often we forget that we live, move and have our being in God," Lamech reminded him. Noah grimaced.

"So you keep saying!" he muttered as he left the room to call Ham. Smiling to himself, Lamech tried resuming his mending, but could not concentrate. It had been a long time since he had yearned for Orpah. Life would have been simpler and sweeter had he listened to his heart in those early years. Not that it did any good crying about it now. Hopefully, Ham would be wiser.

Ham was delighted with the proposal and could barely wait to tell Dinah.

"You're not thinking of going now, surely?" Seraphina asked, alarmed. "Wait for nightfall, when the danger will not be so great."

"Your mother's right, son," Noah said. "Indeed, I think I should accompany you."

Seraphina felt the colour drain from her face.

"Please not you, Noah. You're too easily recognizable," she pleaded. Ham agreed with her.

"It's easier for one to walk unnoticed through the streets than it is for two," he pointed out.

"Perhaps, but I don't think you'll go unnoticed when you escort Dinah back here," Methuselah remarked in his age-raspy voice.

"Your great-grandfather is right," Noah said. "It's important to think of Dinah's safety, if not your own. I insist one of your brothers goes with you."

"And I suppose you've decided that one should be me!" Shem shouted. Noah stared at his eldest in surprise.

"You're angry," he stated.

"Of course I'm angry! Japheth and I have always obeyed you because it was the right thing to do. Ham, on the other hand, has broken every rule. Yet you invariably let him off lightly! You would have whipped me had I sneaked off in the dead of night to find myself a wife."

"You're right. I probably would have a few years ago, but not now," Noah said. "Time and experience have smoothed my rough edges and given Ham an easier time of it. Sometimes too easy, I admit. But, in this instance, your brother's waywardness has pinpointed a need I should have addressed before now. From now on, I promise to daily ask God to bring you the women He has called to be your wives. More I cannot vouch for. But know this. The Lord *will* make a way for each of you to fulfil your destiny. What you've got to do is take it."

"Amen," Lamech agreed eagerly. "And remember, the so-called golden opportunities in this world aren't always ideal. It was a long time before I realized God's open doors usually come with more peace than excitement. Had I understood that principle when I was younger, I would not have made the blunder of a lifetime. It happened long ago, just before my fifteenth birthday …"

Methuselah's eyes filled with tears as he listened. For years he had rued the rash decision that had almost destroyed his oldest son. To have God redeem it in such a miraculous way was overwhelming.

CHAPTER 17
DINAH

He will not crush those who are weak or quench the
smallest hope. He will bring full justice to all who have
been wronged.
Isaiah 42:3

Despite Lamech's story, Shem resented accompanying his brother into the city that night. The stench of the backwater alley leading to Dinah's home was overpowering, and he impatiently tapped his foot while he waited. Ham had disappeared into the shadows, with a promise to return quickly. But the moon was now rising. They could afford to delay no longer. Pressing his hand against the mouldy wall, Shem inched his way along the pitted path. He would have fallen had Ham not emerged out of the dark and caught him by the wrist.

"Careful! You don't want to fall into *that*," the lad hissed. Looking down, Shem saw the oozing cesspool beneath the piles of refuse. The thought of sinking into the fetid slime made him gag.

"What have you been doing that's taken so long?" he demanded angrily.

"What else but persuading Dinah. It's a big step, her coming to live with us."

"Point taken, but where *is* she?"

"Packing her bags, of course," Ham grinned.

"Her *bags*! How're we supposed to walk through the streets unnoticed if we're burdened down with bags?"

"You'll not be burdened down, I assure you!" The cold voice made Shem shiver. Looking up, he stared at the woman standing haughtily in the light of an open doorway. Although striking in appearance, the fine lines around her eyes and mouth revealed she was well into her second century – a fact Shem found bitterly amusing. There had to be more on offer here than good looks alone. Why else would Ham be so besotted with her?

Shem's disturbing train of thought made him flush. Such thinking made him little better than the heathen! Nodding curtly, he reached for Dinah's one shabby bag and led the way home.

Despite their difference in age, Ham and Dinah were devoted to each other. Seraphina was delighted when Noah announced their betrothal. She had been looking forward to preparing a marriage feast since becoming a mother. It would be the last formal request Ham would make of her before taking his vows.

Although it was not customary for the bride to be involved in wedding preparations, force of circumstance made it awkward to exclude Dinah. Seraphina was chagrined to discover the woman was more talented than she and ended up deferring to her in everything except the bridal robe. The fabric Dinah had chosen was too gaudy and Seraphina insisted on discarding it in favour of something more appropriate. The incident was dismissed but not forgotten. Dinah's resentment hung heavily between the two women for months.

As Seraphina stitched the hem of the gown on the eve of the wedding, she wondered if Dinah was still a virgin. She recalled her own joy at giving herself pure and unblemished to Noah. Their faithfulness to one another had been a mainstay in their marriage. Hopefully, the love Ham and his bride shared would be just as firm.

Dinah struggled to regain her composure, then wept anew. If only she could forget that awful night, when her innocence had been stolen! But the pain of it lingered deep down inside, making her throat burn and her skin prickle with fear. She had endured much rejection from others. Could she withstand it from one she loved so much? Closing her eyes, she once again tried to shut out the memory, but could not.

Her father's rage at finding her naked and whimpering in her own blood still made her shudder. Although she had been little more than a child then, her extraordinary beauty had led him to believe the worst. She had begged for mercy. He had taken the whip to her instead. The lashes had rained down, leaving her conscious of nothing except his disgust. When he was done, he had tossed her into the street, where she would have perished had Abigail not nursed her back to health.

Dinah had initially been afraid of the misshapen wretch, but not for long. The old lady's resourcefulness had taught her how to survive without stooping to prostitution. Indeed, Dinah had refused to have anything to do with men before meeting Ham and had insisted on a chaste betrothal. Now they were married and her husband would expect more than she had given so far. Would he still love her when he discovered she was defiled?

Although she had only once seen the brute who had raped her, he was a silent accuser standing between her and the fulfilment of her dreams. Tears again sprang to

120

her eyes and she angrily blinked them away. Self-pity would be her downfall if she was not careful! Pulling the comb one last time through her hair, she nervously walked out of her closet into Ham's arms.

Their lovemaking was filled with a sweetness Dinah had never known. She had been sure Ham would notice her broken virginity, but the look on his face afterwards bespoke of nothing but satisfaction. A mingled sensation of joy and deep regret overcame her and she clung to him fiercely. Her dirty secret would not remain hidden forever but she could not reveal it. Not yet. Closing her eyes, she felt the warmth of her husband's love and began to cry.

CHAPTER 18
BREAKING TIES

And everyone who has given up houses or brothers or
sisters or father or mother or children or property, for my
sake, will receive a hundred times as much in return...
Matthew 19:29

waking to the strident call of a robin, Noah stretched languidly and got up. Seraphina was still fast asleep, her face in repose as sweet as a girl's. She usually rose late on the Sabbath[25], and he had taken on the task of serving her breakfast in bed. Humming to himself, he dressed and went through to the kitchen. His heart sank when he saw the three men seated at his table. Their garb and the packs at their feet said they were prepared for a journey. While he had been expecting John and Enos to leave for some time, Jasper had never expressed any such desire. Noah sighed heavily. He relied on the old carpenter for much and wondered what he would do without him.

Misinterpreting Noah's expression, Enos hurried to explain.

"I know there's still much to be done on the Ark," he said, "but it's time for John to go and I'd like to accompany him. I hope to return, but there's little I can manage now, anyway. My ability to forage for herbs is failing."

Noah was aware of the doctor's dead-of-night escapades into the forest, but had refrained from interfering. Enos's medicinal potions were necessary for the wellbeing of the small community. Sadly, the physician was now as stooped as an old tree and needed to retire.

"There's no need to apologize," Noah smiled, gently squeezing Enos's gnarled hand. "Go with my blessing and enjoy the time you and John have left." He then turned to Jasper, whose faded eyes were wet with tears.

"Sorry I am to be doing this to you, Sir," the old man said hoarsely. "But the more I pray about it, the more I know it's the Lord telling me to go. I have a sister I need to find. She was so wicked that my father chased her from the house when she was barely grown. I tried helping her, but she had a temper as ugly as a spitting cat, with nails to match. Last I heard, she was practising witchcraft on Ararat."

"Ararat? The twin mountains north-eastward of Yahrevan?" Noah asked.

"The very ones," Jasper confirmed. "Some say the taller is haunted. There were several murders up there some years back that had the finger of Jesse[12] on them. Or so I've been told."

"Is that her name?"

"Yes. Not that she's ever lived up to it, mind you. That's why I've got to find her, Master. She needs someone to help her turn to God for salvation. The Flood will be upon us just now and she'll be lost forever if I don't do something soon." Jasper was, by this time, weeping in earnest.

"Then you've no choice but to go, old friend," Noah said kindly.

"I will return, I swear it," Jasper promised. Noah nodded, but knew it was unlikely. Old age had taken its toll on the carpenter.

"Whatever the outcome, Jasper, don't consider coming back until you've done all you can for Jesse. Understood?"

"Thank you, Sir," Jasper beamed. Noah affectionately shook his foreman's hand, then addressed the practical aspects of the departure of the three men.

"It's dangerous out there. How do you plan to get out of Je'el undetected?" he asked.

"On the barge, Master Noah, Sir," John grinned. "It's easy. Enos and I have done it before."

"John's right, Noah," Enos confirmed. "The barge is moored a mere two berths from our own and is the simplest way of getting out of here – particularly on a Sabbath[25] morning, when folk are still recovering from the previous night's orgy."

"And how do you manage to travel on the barge unnoticed?"

"We hide in the empty wine barrels," John elaborated. "The boatman takes them downriver every Sabbath[25] and leaves them on the vintner's wharf for a refill. Nobody's around until the following day, so we're able to climb out and escape to the woods without anyone seeing us."

"You *hide* in those smelly barrels!" Noah exclaimed. John laughed.

"The stink's easily washed out with a little water, Sir!"

"Stinking is one thing. Getting drunk on the fumes is another," Enos said sourly. "Heaven knows how anyone survives the stuff!"

"Its stench has undoubtedly corroded whatever brains the imbibers once had," Noah said wryly. "Jests aside, you have my blessing. All I ask is that you be cautious."

"Thank you, Noah," Enos said warmly. "I promise we'll be careful."

"That we will, Sir," Jasper agreed. "The Lord bless you for caring for us so well."

There was no need to say more. The men had become close over the years and would always value their friendship. After embracing Noah, the three made their way down to the jetty and slipped into the Tigris for the short swim to the barge.

Apart from Enos's painful joints, the scheme went off without a hitch and the trio emerged from the woods a little after midday. It was late afternoon before they arrived at the crossroads a few mil[17] north of Je'el. Enos sank down on the milstone and wiped sweat out of his eyes. It had been a long time since he had walked such a distance.

"I never thought anything could be so hard," he panted.

"Maybe we should make you a crutch," John suggested. Enos laughed in frustration.

"No, lad. I don't have the strength for one. You'll just have to put up with my snail's pace."

"What if I carry you part-way?" Jasper offered. The doctor shook his head and held up his hand to forestay further argument.

"Finding your sister is more important, Jasper," he said. "Indeed, we'd be travelling with you if my legs weren't in danger of collapsing on that excuse of a track." Jasper looked to where Enos was pointing. The journey to Ararat was difficult at best, but would be even more arduous on the barely discernible path. He would have to cut his farewells short if he was to cover much more ground that day. Slinging his pack over his shoulder, he smiled sadly.

"Well then," he said, "I suppose this is the parting of the ways."

"It's only temporary, Jasper," Enos consoled. "We'll meet again in Heaven one day."

"Can you imagine what a glorious moment that will be?" John exclaimed.

"Now, that's a hard thing you're asking me to do, lad," Jasper chuckled. "Just think of it. Perfect bodies! No broken teeth or wrinkles! Do you think we'll recognize each other?"

"I'm sure of it," Enos enthused. "I'm praying we'll see your Jesse there, too, *and* know her." The comment raised the gooseflesh on Jasper's arms.

"Now, wouldn't that be wonderful?" he said softly.

"It would," Enos agreed, "so what're you waiting for?"

Jasper grinned and grabbed his companions in a bear hug.

"The Lord bless and keep you both," he said over his shoulder as he began his long trek. John and Enos watched the old man stride away into the distance, then rose and began to slowly make their own way north.

The two men camped in a small glade a quarter mil[17] or so off the road. John quietly prepared dinner while Enos soaked up the warmth of the crackling fire. After eating in silence, they reminisced for hours about the past but their thoughts were very much on the future. Neither knew what to expect, yet were certain it would be over by morning. Unable to stay awake any longer, Enos dozed off. He awoke some time later to the realization that he was alone. Hearing a cry, he struggled to his feet and stumbled to the edge of the clearing.

"John!" he cried. "Where are you?"

"I'm here," the young man answered. "Come quickly, Enos!" The doctor staggered forwards, then gasped. A brilliant shaft of light had pierced the *shamayim*[27], capturing John in its glow. The two friends hugged and laughed together. Then the lad was gone. Enos fell to his knees and moaned softly.

"The Lord gives and the Lord takes away. Blessed be the Name of the Lord," he whispered.

He touched the spot where John had stood seconds before and felt the warmth seep into his body, like sweet oil. The relief from pain was instantaneous. It had been years since he had been able to flex his fingers! Speechless with gratitude, he lay down on the mossy forest floor and drifted to sleep.

It was mid-afternoon when Ben Hazar found the corpse. Although many years had elapsed, he immediately recognized the doctor and thought it a pity the man should end his days so crippled.

"Who is he, Uncle?" his niece asked, dismounting from her pony to kneel beside the body.

"Someone from that time in my life I don't like to talk about," he answered sadly. "Looks like his heart failed."

"Are you sure?" she said, running her hands over Enos's smooth face. "He seems so peaceful."

"Yes, well, the heart sometimes stops when a person's asleep. It couldn't have gone on for much longer, not with him crippled like this. We'll have to bury him, but not here. The last I heard, he was still working for Noah. It would be a kindness to bury him there."

"Noah? You mean the Prophet we're going to see?"

"The very one," he confirmed.

"Have we far to go?"

"No more than twelve, thirteen mil[17]. I was hoping to be in Je'el before nightfall, but this will delay us. Here, girl, help me wrap him in my blanket. We'll tie him to your pony and you can ride with me." Hadassah did as she was bid and they were soon on their way again. She looked over her shoulder at the shrouded figure and sighed. She had seen much death in her young life, but each new case filled her with an even greater longing for such wastefulness to end.

CHAPTER 19
HADASSAH

A worthy wife is her husband's joy and crown...
Proverbs 12:4a

Upset by the departure of his three friends, Noah concluded his message earlier than usual that night. He was too despondent, too half-hearted to continue. The crowd was disgruntled by his mood and dispersed in a high temper, leaving the dockside as dark and empty as he felt. Noah sighed heavily and slumped down onto a bench. This was no good! No good at all! He had to take himself in hand.

Ben Hazar reined in and stared at the hunched figure. Had he not known otherwise, he would have mistaken the shaggy, white-haired preacher for Methuselah.

"Noah?" he said quietly. Noah raised his head in surprise. He had not heard the approaching horseman and thought his visitor must be drunk or ignorant to have come thus far. It had been years since anyone had dared to cross the boundary stones to his property. Curious, he squinted up at the rider, then leapt to his feet.

"You?" he growled.

"Is this how you greet an old friend?" Ben Hazar gently mocked as he dismounted.

"You were never a friend of mine," Noah said sourly.

"And little wonder. I played you dirty and got what I deserved for it. But I've come to regard you and Methuselah as friends, whether you like it or not. You men helped me see the light of God, both in prison and out of it. I swore I'd live uprightly after I served my time. I've stuck to my word, for the girl's sake."

Looking past Ben Hazar, Noah saw the young woman in the shadows and nodded a greeting.

"My brother and sister-in-law abandoned their daughter. I've cared for her ever since," Hazar explained. "She was a mere girl then, but has always loved God and taught me much about faith. We heard about your preaching from a friend and decided to come and listen for ourselves. Indeed, we'd like to stay and help build the Ark, if you're agreeable."

Despite the old embezzler's plausibility, Noah was wary of inviting him into their midst.

"Working for me has never been popular," he answered grimly. "Neither is it safe. Folk will brand you as a traitor. And what they'd do to your niece if they got hold of her is unspeakable."

"Jail has taught me to be no man's fool, Noah. I know that anyone working for you ends up being a prisoner here or dies out there. Hadassah and I are willing to make that sacrifice. Besides, you can't afford to refuse my offer. I've heard how shorthanded you are." Noah laughed bitterly. There was no denying he was desperate for more hands on the job.

"That's an understatement!" he exclaimed. "Three of my men left yesterday morning."

"I don't suppose one of them was Enos?" Hazar asked gruffly.

"You suppose correctly," Noah admitted.

"Then I'm afraid he didn't get very far. We found him dead in the woods and have brought his body back for burial."

Noah felt his eyes prickle. Although he had known the doctor would never return, he had not expected his journey to be so brief. Drawing back the shroud, he stared at the unlined face.

"I've never seen Enos so at peace," he murmured. "Was John with him?" Hazar frowned.

"You mean the lad Nabal so cruelly wounded? I heard the youngster died years ago."

"It's a long story," Noah answered. "You obviously didn't see him, then?"

"No, I didn't. But we did find two bundles of clothing a few paces from where Enos's body was."

Noah sighed.

"Thank you for your kindness," he said. "We seldom receive such gestures now. Here, let me help you stable your horses. Then we'll go inside for dinner. You and your niece must be famished."

"Shouldn't we first bury Enos?" Hazar suggested. "His flesh has already begun to decay."

"Our friend's body was merely a shell to contain his spirit and soul. There'll be time enough to do what we must after we've eaten." The remark made Hazar chuckle.

"Already you've said something I've never given thought to," he said. Nodding, Noah went on to elaborate his point.

"So much time is wasted on venerating the dead that we forget the Almighty is God of the living. Our bodies die and return to the dust from which they were made. But that *real* part of us – the spirit that comes from God – is eternal and will one day be judged by Elohim[7]. Those who've trusted in Him will enjoy His everlasting blessing and mercy. Those who have not will suffer eternal torment. That's why I spend every day doing what I do."

The two men looked up at the dimly silhouetted ribs of the enormous boat. Much work still needed to be done, and there were times when Noah believed the task was impossible. Ben's arrival was a strong reminder that he was not alone, and never had been.

"Thank you for coming, Salassi," he said with feeling. The old alias took Ben Hazar by surprise. He had forgotten Noah was unaware of his true identity.

"I am Ben Salassi no longer," he said with a shake of his head. "That title belongs to a time I don't care to remember. My real name is Ben Hazar."

"Ben Hazar it is then," Noah smiled. "I must say, your transformation will gladden Methuselah's heart." Ben Hazar's eyes widened in surprise.

"He can't still be alive, surely?" he exclaimed. Noah grinned.

"He's become frail and seldom speaks, but is very much alive."

"And undoubtedly still praying for my salvation," Hazar said dryly.

"Undoubtedly," Noah laughed as he picked up the guttering lamp and led the way to the stable. Hazar took up the horses' reins and gratefully followed. It had been years since he had been able to find permanent employment, or a place where he and Hadassah could settle. Now, for the first time in his life, he felt as though they had arrived home to stay.

Hadassah's joyful spirit was like a breath of fresh air – particularly for Dinah. Seraphina was glad the two women had bonded so well. She had always believed she would never get on with her daughter-in-law. Hadassah's friendship, however, had softened their relationship somewhat.

Although a reasonable housekeeper, Hadassah preferred being outdoors and spent hours helping with the Ark. Tall and as strong as most men, she worked barefoot in a smock and breeches.

"Why so shocked?" she laughed when Seraphina disapproved of her attire. "Girding up my loins would be far more immodest!" Seraphina had to concede the point. The young woman actually looked rather fetching in her practical garb. A fact that had not gone unnoticed by her oldest son!

Hadassah was acutely aware of Shem's eyes on her and knew it was time to stop pretending. This strong, quiet man had quickly won her heart, but the memory of her parents' bitter marriage made her cautious. For weeks she had watched and waited, but no more. Her longing was too intense, her love too deep. Lifting a plank to her shoulder, she crossed the yard.

"Can you help me with this, Shem?" she asked.

Shem felt his heart hammer loudly in his chest. Desire for this woman had burned in him from the moment they had met, but he had been reticent to express his feelings too soon.

"Shem?" she pressed when he did not answer. Shem flushed.

"Sorry. My mind was elsewhere," he apologized as he took the board from her. "Let's fit this, then take a walk before dinner. We're just about finished work for the day, anyway."

Hadassah eagerly agreed.

"It's a pity we're confined to the yard," she said. "A stroll through the woods would have been nice."

"You know it's not safe," he reminded her.

"It's still a pity," she smiled.

After fitting the shelf, they walked to the end of the jetty and sat side by side, intensely aware of each other. Hadassah felt the late afternoon breeze on her hot face and inhaled deeply. She longed to tell Shem how she felt but did not know where to start. Sighing, she leant forward to trail her fingers in the water. The weathered boards suddenly gave way and she clutched at Shem's hand.

"Some of these timbers are rotten," he said as he pulled her away from the edge, "but we haven't enough wood to replace them." Hadassah was painfully conscious of Shem's fingers on hers and did not reply. Feeling embarrassed, he let go of her hand.

"I'm sorry," he murmured. Hadassah vigorously shook her head.

"Not at all," she answered softly. "Indeed, I'm glad you saved me from falling in."

They sat for several minutes in awkward silence. Hadassah knew Shem wanted to hold her, but was afraid she would reject him. She had to tell him how she felt. Now, while the time was right. But the warmth in his eyes overcame her. Speechless, she raised her face to his and shivered when their lips met. Never had she known anything so sweet, so fulfilling!

"I love you so much," he whispered as he embraced her.

"I love you, too," she confessed. "Have done from the start."

"You've never once shown it," he accused gently.

"Only because I feared we'd end up like my parents. Their marriage meant nothing beyond the nuptial bed."

"My feelings for you are far more than just that!" Shem protested strongly. To his surprise, Hadassah began to cry.

"What's this?" he asked, wiping her face with his finger.

"Tears of relief, I think," she answered with a sniff. "I never thought God would give me someone as good as you, Shem. I love you and always will. And I know you'll love me, too, even when my face begins to age and my waist to thicken."

"And all these wonderful muscles of mine begin to sag," he added with a grin. She threw her head back and laughed.

"Even then," she spluttered, before continuing on a more sober note. "After what I experienced with my family, I did not think it possible to have a marriage based on friendship and mutual respect. Then I came here and saw how wrong I was. The love Noah and Seraphina have for each other is what I've been looking for all my life."

"Ah, my parents," Shem said. "They are amazing."

"They're only as amazing as they allow God to make them," Hadassah pointed out. "That's what I want for us, Shem. But my faith is small and I stumble badly."

"As do I," he admitted. "Yet God sees our desires. He will enable us to become all He wants us to be. As for basing marriage on friendship, my parents waited over 400 years before they wed."

"You're not serious!" she exclaimed incredulously.

"Yes, I am. They were such good friends that it was some time before they realized their affection ran deeper than familial love."

"How delightful!" Hadassah laughed, clapping her hands. "But I doubt I can wait that long!"

"Is that a proposal?" he teased. Hadassah blushed.

"You *do* want to marry me, don't you?" she asked.

"I've never been surer of anything," he answered, planting a firm kiss on her lips. Hadassah gazed into the honest eyes she loved so well and smiled.

"I'm so glad. I don't know what I would have done had you said otherwise."

"There's no fear of that," he promised, tilting her chin to kiss her again. "And if you leave me, I'm coming with you." She grinned at his gentle humour and laid her head on his chest. They sat in silence for several minutes, watching the sun sink below the horizon.

"Mother will insist on a time of betrothal," he said after a while.

"I'll agree provided it's not 400 years' worth!" Hadassah teased. Shem groaned.

"I don't think she'll make us wait longer than it takes her to sew your robe and prepare a worthy bridal feast," he said. "She never had much chance with Dinah."

"She'll not have much chance with us either if you carry on kissing me so fervently!" Amused by her candour, Shem sat back and laughed uproariously.

"It's the truth! And don't say you feel any different!" Hadassah exclaimed. "Seriously, Shem, we *must* exercise self-control if we're to have no regrets. I want to begin our marriage fresh and clean. Surely you desire the same?"

"You know I do," he replied, holding out his hand. She grasped it tightly.

"Here's to friendship, love and marriage," he said, pulling her to her feet.

"To friendship, love and marriage," she agreed.

They then walked hand in hand to the house to share their good news with the family.

The announcement was met with great excitement, especially by Hazar who had longed to see his niece suitably settled.

"I could not have chosen a better match," he beamed as he squeezed Hadassah tightly.

"We must start planning for your wedding," Seraphina declared with a clap of her hands. "You want to get married soon, I think."

"Is there anything to be gained from waiting longer than needed?" Shem asked.

"I'd say get married tomorrow, but your mother would never agree," Noah boomed.

"How can they get married without anything prepared?" Seraphina protested.

"Mother's right," Ham said unexpectedly. "I would never have been so impatient had I known how fine Dinah would look in her bridal robe. She was worth waiting for."

Hadassah had seen Dinah's gown and knew Ham had not overstated his wife's beauty. She doubted she would ever look as lovely, but did not mind as long as she was pleasing to Shem. She eagerly turned to share her thoughts with Dinah, but was surprised to discover the older woman had left the room unexcused. Knowing how much of a stickler Dinah was for protocol, Hadassah sensed something was amiss and quietly drew Shem aside.

"I'm going to find Dinah," she told him.

"Good idea," he said. "Mother will get upset if she notices she's missing." Hadassah grimaced. The truce between mother and daughter-in-law was fragile at best. Excusing herself, she walked down the narrow passage and repeatedly knocked on Dinah's door, but there was no answer. Feeling uneasy, she lifted the latch and entered the room. To her dismay, Dinah was slumped over the bed, clumps of hair protruding from her balled-up fists. Hadassah quickly shut the door behind her and embraced the weeping woman.

"Dinah! Whatever is the matter?" she cried. Dinah looked at her with dark, hollow eyes and twisted her head from side to side.

"You'd despise me if you knew," she sobbed.

"Never!" Hadassah protested.

"Oh yes, you would, and so would Ham!"

"Ham loves you far too deeply for that, and so do I. Talk to me, Dinah. Tell me what's wrong."

Dinah shook her head vehemently.

"I'm not sure I *can* tell you," she said. "It hurts too much."

"You'll never know unless you try. Nothing you say will make me love you less. I promise."

"That's easy to say in ignorance," Dinah said sullenly.

"Then tell me!" Hadassah pleaded. "Whatever you've done can't possibly be greater than God's forgiveness."

"I realize that, but will you and the others be so forgiving once you know my secret? It's been years since I've belonged to a family, Hadassah. What if I'm rejected now?"

"We'd never reject you over something that causes so much pain, Dinah. Come now. You need to let go of this hurt once and for all. And what better way to do that than by unburdening yourself to one you can trust?"

Unable to withstand the kindness in Hadassah's pale green eyes, Dinah began to haltingly reveal her dark secret. Hadassah felt her heart constrict with pain as the story of Dinah's loss unfolded. Her friend's face bore such a look of guilt, such a longing for the innocence she and Shem shared.

"I'm so sorry!" Hadassah cried when Dinah was done.

"No sorrier than I, Hadassah. What really bothers me is that Ham said nothing about it on our wedding night. What if Noah didn't tell him what to expect? Surely that would make my deception even greater?"

"You should tell Ham, Dinah, for your own peace of mind." The admonition made Dinah pale.

"No!" she wailed. "I will not, and you must promise you won't either. I can't risk losing my husband. He's my life."

"As you are his, Dinah. Indeed, he will love you even more if you tell him the truth."

"You're a fool to believe that," Dinah answered sharply. "Ham's extremely selfish. He would be ashamed of me if he knew."

"You underestimate your husband, Dinah. He knows you're a warm, caring person beneath that hard shell you wear. It's a pity you don't allow the rest of the family to see your gentler qualities. You'd get on better with Seraphina if you did."

"Do you really think so?" Dinah asked. "I respect my mother-in-law but am also afraid of her. She would turn me out if she knew."

"No, she wouldn't!" Hadassah insisted. "She longs to love you as a daughter, Dinah. But you won't be able to let her until your secret is laid to rest. The longer you hang on to it, the more it'll cripple you."

"Perhaps, but I don't have the courage to open up. Not yet."

"Do you feel better for having told me?" Hadassah asked. Dinah smiled wearily.

"Yes, I do," she admitted, "but I never expected you to be so sympathetic."

"It's hard to understand what a victim of rape feels. But I can love you through it. And that's exactly what the others would do if they knew, particularly Ham."

"But what if they don't, Hadassah? You know how people can change when confronted with something like this. I'd hate it if Ham loved me out of sheer pity. I want him to love me for myself."

"He already does."

"But would he if he knew? Please, Hadassah! You've got to keep my secret." Hadassah sighed with frustration.

"Very well, but only if you agree to join in tonight's celebration. Seraphina's planning a gargantuan feast and needs your help. I know the two of you don't get along too well, but she actually misses you when you're not around."

"Seraphina miss me?" Dinah hooted, as she ran a comb through her hair. "Now that would be a real miracle!" Hadassah giggled at her friend's rare attempt at a jest.

"It's impossible to stay depressed when you're around," Dinah grinned. She then squared her shoulders and preceded Hadassah from the room. The celebration was already well underway and would be for hours to come. Noah had declared the following day a Sabbath[25].

The couple married five months later. Contrary to her assumption, Hadassah was a glowing bride and there was not a dry eye present when she took her place beside Shem.

Japheth watched the ceremony with deep longing. The bond between him and his older brother had always been strong. He would miss the hours of companionship that would now be Hadassah's, and wondered if he would ever set *his* seal to a marriage covenant. He yearned for a wife, but believed his fair skin and blue eyes were repugnant to women.

Although somewhat odd in appearance, Japheth had two great qualities – self-discipline and the desire to serve. There were times when Seraphina found the latter frustrating.

"You'll turn your brothers into idle good-for-nothings!" she would protest with a wag of her finger.

"You worry too much, Mother," he would answer with a broad grin. Unable to stay cross with Japheth for long, she would march off in a huff, shaking her head and bewailing his soft-heartedness. When he had offered to serve at Hadassah's bridal feast, she had objected strongly.

"How can you suggest such a thing?" she had demanded, hands on hips. "You're supposed to be an honoured guest at your brother's wedding, not a servant!" But Japheth had firmly stood his ground.

"You can't expect Ben Hazar to do it, Mother. He has as much right as you and Father to sit at the bride's table."

"As do you, son," she had wailed.

"Agreed," he had conceded. "But I'll also be the only person standing idle at the wedding. It therefore makes sense for me to serve. You know I enjoy this sort of thing, anyway, so why fuss?

"I fuss because you're always doing things for others and missing out on so many privileges."

"But that's who I am, Mother, so just let me get on with it."

Seraphina had known it would be pointless to protest further.

"You're a good, warm-hearted man, Japheth. I appreciate you more than words can say," she had said with affection.

Smiling at the memory, Japheth looked across the room at his mother and felt his throat tighten. Her hair, hanging down her back like a girl's, was now completely white and her face was lined with age. Yet the dignity with which she bore herself transformed her into the most beautiful of women.

At the conclusion of the ceremony, Japheth slipped into the kitchen and returned with two heaped platters of food. Noah immediately called for silence and bowed his head to pray.

"Wait!" Seraphina interrupted as she moved to make room on the bench beside her. "I want Japheth to sit here, where he belongs. He may have a servant's heart, but he is our son."

"Amen to that," Shem agreed, stretching across the table to clasp his brother's hand. Grinning, Japheth enthusiastically took his place at the bride's table.

CHAPTER 20
UNFORESEEN COMPLICATION

For the Lord grants wisdom! From His mouth come
knowledge and understanding.
Proverbs 2:6

The weather had been unseasonably hot for weeks. Noah wiped the sweat from his face and took a swig from his flask. The tepid water made him grimace. Drinking straight from the Tigris would have been more refreshing, but the river was now too polluted to risk it. He looked in satisfaction at the Ark towering above him. Another month or so, and he and his family could relax and wait for whatever came next. Contemplating the future beyond that point was beyond him. The volume of water needed to float such an enormous vessel was incalculable. Sighing, he raised his flask to take another swallow, but paused when he heard Ben Hazar's shout.

"You sound worried," Noah said as he joined him on the scaffold.

"You will be also. Look at this."

Noah groaned when he saw the cracked caulking.

"It can't be!" he exclaimed. "We watered that section for months to avoid this very thing."

"It clearly wasn't enough," Hazar said. "The caulking's pulled away from the timber in several places. She'll leak faster than you'll be able to bale her out if you don't repair it."

"But why after all this time is it breaking like this?" Noah asked wearily.

"I'd say the hot weather's evaporated the moisture out of the caulking, causing it to shrink and crack like dried mud. A pity we weren't able to float the Ark. We could've kept the timber constantly wet then." Noah shook his head in frustration. To be thwarted now was bitterly disappointing.

"How are we to fix the Ark without taking it apart altogether?" he grumbled.

"I do have a suggestion," Hazar answered.

"Go on – I'm listening."

Hazar smiled and hunched his shoulders.

135

"Before committing yourself, you need to know that what I have in mind can only be found in the woods. We wouldn't need to go far to get it. Five … six mil[17]. No more."

"An enormous distance when the world out there regards us as the enemy," Noah baulked.

"True, but the chances of being accosted are slim. Few venture beyond the city walls now."

"I don't like it, Ben."

"There's nothing to fear," Hazar insisted. "The Most High has proved that He is greater than wicked men. You're born to complete the Ark, Noah. The Lord will not allow anything to stand in your way now."

Noah laughed wryly.

"I preach faith and repentance, yet have to be reminded of what a mighty God we serve!" he exclaimed.

"It happens," Hazar said kindly. "Now, what say we slip away at dawn tomorrow?"

"Dawn! No, Hazar. It would be safer to go after dark."

"Perhaps, but I need good light to find what I'll be looking for." Left with no alternative, Noah could only hope Ben's solution would prove sound. He was too exhausted to handle much more.

"Dawn it is, then," he sighed.

The sky had just begun to lighten when Noah crept out of the house to find Hazar awaiting him.

"You're bright and early, Ben," he said.

"I couldn't sleep," Hazar answered dolefully. "For all my mulling, I'm none the wiser this morning. My idea is based purely on hearsay, but a long shot is better than none."

"I agree," Noah said. "But enough talk. I'm hoping to be back before we're missed. My wife knows nothing about this."

"Do you think it wise to leave her in ignorance?"

"Building the Ark has been hard enough on her. Why add another burden before we have to?"

"I suppose you're right. But even if my idea does work, it's the Almighty who will protect you against the onslaught of the Flood, not the Ark."

Noah chuckled.

"There was a time when I thought you'd never trust God," he said. "How wrong I was! You have greatly encouraged me, my friend." Hazar flushed with pleasure.

"No more than you've encouraged me," he said.

"Thank you, Ben," Noah smiled. "Now, we must press on or be discovered. Lead the way. I'm in your hands."

Grinning, Hazar hoisted his bag onto his shoulder and cautiously unlatched the back gate. The section of city wall bordering Noah's property had long since crumbled and the men slipped quietly through the breach into the forest beyond.

Hazar cut a V-shaped notch into the trunk of a small tree and held a clay flask beneath it.

"This is chicle[4] sap," he explained as the milky fluid trickled into the container. "It looks like that of a fig tree, but is sweeter, and can be made into a palatable gum when cooked. I've used it before and found it to be an effective thirst quencher."

"And how will this gum solve the problem of our cracked caulking?" Noah asked dubiously.

"I once heard a story about a barrel of pine tar springing a leak. The hole was sealed with a piece of chewed gum until it could be repaired the following day. By which time the tar had permeated the gum and transformed it into a plug that could only be prised off with a chisel. I don't know of any other instances where gum has been used thus, but it's worth a try."

"But what if the gum simply cracks up like the caulking once it's completely dry?"

"The gum is extremely sticky and pliable when chewed, so the likelihood of that happening is minimal," Hazar answered confidently. "I'm no apothecary, Noah, but I believe we can make this work with a little experimentation."

"Perhaps Elohim[7] reunited us for this reason," Noah mused.

"Well, He's already brought us together for the purpose of my salvation, so why not yours, too?" Hazar said, corking the flask and covering the notch with wet clay. "There's also Hadassah. She found the husband of her dreams here."

"They are happy, aren't they?"

"Very. What more could an old rogue like me ask for, eh?" Hazar boasted as he led the way home.

Noah walked into the kitchen to find Seraphina rekindling the wood stove. Seeing his wife still warm and fluffy from sleep had never lost its charm and he savoured her scent as they embraced.

"You're up earlier than usual," he said, rubbing his chin against the top of her head.

"Only because you woke me when you got out of bed," she grumbled. "I thought you'd roused early to pray until I saw you leave with Ben. Knowing he's never up before dawn except in an emergency made me worry. So I got up to await your return."

"I didn't mean to make you anxious," Noah apologized lamely. Seraphina's face crumpled.

"You're never secretive unless something's wrong. So what is it, Noah?" she demanded.

"There's no need to be angry," he said. She stared at him, then let her arms fall to her sides.

"I'm not angry. I'm frustrated," she answered quietly. "I know you often keep your own counsel because I tend to fuss. But how am I to pray if you don't tell me what's going on?"

"You're right, I should've told you," he conceded. "But it can sometimes be hard for a man to admit failure." Hearing the defeat in her husband's voice, Seraphina placed her hand on his.

"What's happened?" she asked. Sighing, Noah pulled her down beside him.

"You'd better sit," he said. "This could take a while."

Seraphina's tendency to panic belied an inner strength that never ceased to amaze Noah. Although disappointed by the setback, she immediately called for Hazar to discuss his theory.

"You need to understand this may not be the way to go," he said when he had finished. "I've no idea how long the chicle[4] should be boiled, or what to do when it's cooled."

"So you don't know if cooking thickens it or not?" she asked.

"No, I don't. I've only seen the gum once it's set. It's quite hard then, but softens when chewed."

Uncorking the flask, Seraphina poured a little of the sap into a cup and sampled it.

"It's quite nice, but not as sticky as I thought it would be," she said, licking her finger clean.

"It's the set gum that becomes sticky when you chew it," Hazar reminded her. "Our saliva does it – or so I'm told."

"We're going to need a lot of spit, then, to get this repair job done," Seraphina concluded dryly. "I'm also assuming we'll need much more chicle[4] than what we have here."

"That we will, dear lady. I admit I never thought of how much chewing we would have to do when I came up with the scheme."

"What if we use an alternative to saliva?" she suggested.

"What alternative is there?" Hazar asked.

"I'm thinking of tree hibiscus[31] fruit. They look like small hard-skinned apples, but their flesh is slimy. My husband and I used to eat them a lot when we were children – much to Lamech's disgust." Noah grinned at the memory.

"It's what you called them that made Father's toenails curl," he reminded her. Seraphina laughed and slapped him on the shoulder.

"Well, how else would you describe them?"

138

"Don't tempt me, wife! I only ate them because I didn't want to be outdone by a girl. Fortunately, our children aren't quite so adventurous. But you're right, Seraphina. Their flesh would be an excellent substitute. What do you think, Ben?"

"Anything would be preferable to chewing our heads off. How do you plan to add the fruit to the chicle[4]?"

"Well, the gum probably needs both saliva and body heat to become sticky," Seraphina said. "I therefore suggest we add the fruit to the pot while the chicle's[4] still warm. Do you agree?"

"In principle, yes," Noah answered. "My only concern is whether or not our tree hibiscus[31] has any fruit on it."

"It has plenty," she answered.

"Then let's split the chicle[4] into equal measures and experiment. When we've developed a mix most likely to work, we'll try it out. You get the stuff on the boil, Seraphina, while we pick the fruit."

Seraphina eagerly stoked up the fire, then put the first measure of chicle[4] into a pot and began to slowly bring it to the boil.

By the end of the week, Noah was ready to abandon the idea altogether. Nothing Seraphina did would turn the chicle[4] and fruit mix into a sticky enough gum.

"We've no choice but to pull the Ark apart and repair it," he muttered.

"You can't do that, Father!" Ham groaned.

"Do you think I want to?" Noah growled. "I've been working on this project a lot longer than you, my lad. I refuse to give up because of flawed caulking."

"I'm afraid I agree with Ham," Hazar interjected. Noah resented being contradicted but had the good sense to wait for an explanation.

"I've thought long and hard about this, Noah," Hazar continued. "Dismantling would damage most of the treenails holding the boat together and render them useless. With so few left in stock, and insufficient timber on hand to make new ones, it isn't an option."

"Wouldn't it be possible to chop down the trees in our yard for that purpose?" Japheth asked.

"That's something I hadn't thought of," Hazar answered.

"Unfortunately, none of them have a good enough grain," Lamech pointed out. "It's important the treenails are of a similar wood to what has been used to build the Ark. Anything less would be like trying to patch a linen apron with silk."

"Why don't we simply go back to our original idea of chewing the gum and applying it to the cracks in the caulking?" Methuselah suggested in his raspy voice.

"Ben and I tried that yesterday, but it doesn't work," Noah told him. "The gum becomes hard as rock once dry, but splits when hit with a hammer. If such a small tool can break it, there's little chance of it withstanding the Flood. The final surface coating of pitch may be sufficient to keep the caulking intact, of course, but I'm not prepared to risk it."

"Have you tried stirring pine tar into the mix?" Hadassah asked.

"It doesn't seem to matter one way or the other," Noah replied glumly. "The end result is not durable enough."

"Perhaps the fruit and chicle[4] have to weigh the same in order to create an unbreakable bond," Dinah mused. "Maybe we also need to do things the other way round."

"What do you mean?" Noah asked.

"Instead of stirring the cold hibiscus[31] into the warm gum, why don't we cook the fruit and add the gum to it before it has set?"

"You've made a valid point, Dinah, especially in regard to the ingredients weighing *omer*[22] for *omer*[22]," Seraphina said. "Too much or too little of one or the other would cause the final mix to be too soft or too brittle. Well done for thinking of it, daughter." The compliment took Dinah by surprise.

"You're too gracious, Mother," she said quietly.

"Credit should always be given where it's due," Seraphina answered gruffly. "Now come, girl! Let's give your idea a try. The sooner we find a solution, the better."

Dinah eagerly began cutting away the fibrous peel of the uncooked fruit. Hopefully, her concept would succeed.

Noah awoke the following morning to find Seraphina lying wide-eyed beside him. He could tell she was upset and tenderly ran his finger across her cheek.

"Does it bother you that Dinah was right?" he asked. She shook her head.

"I'm glad she was, Noah. What annoys me is that I keep on misjudging her. I want to understand her better, but she keeps to herself, like she has something to hide."

"She'd probably open up if you were gentler with her," he suggested. Seraphina nodded.

"I'd like to be," she said, "but we continually clash no matter how hard I try."

"Elohim[7] often uses people to smooth our rough edges. Take Ham, for instance. He would have probably turned into a rogue were it not for Dinah."

A cry suddenly ran through the house like a shockwave. Conversation forgotten, Noah and Seraphina rushed to the kitchen, where they found Hadassah agog with excitement.

"I rose early to prepare breakfast, but got involved with this instead," the young woman explained, holding up the pot of fruit they had cooked the previous night. Noah and Seraphina stared at her blankly.

"Can't you see?" Hadassah laughed. "Allowing this pot of fruit to cool down completely has resulted in it becoming like the set gum in texture. But that's not all.

Mix equal quantities of the cold fruit with the set gum, and look what happens!" Noah took the pliable, grey lump from her and grinned. Unlike Dinah's tacky mix, this rolled cleanly between the fingers.

"Do you think it'll work as effectively?" Seraphina asked.

"It'll make our job that much easier if it does," Noah answered. "Prepare three lots for me, dear heart. We'll put them to the test once they're hard."

The samples lay hardening under the hot sun, while the family passed the day in fun and games. By late afternoon, Noah could wait no longer.

"I don't suppose they will set much firmer," he said, bringing his hammer down on the first sample. He repeatedly struck the hardened epoxy, but it remained undamaged and firmly bonded to the caulking beneath. Wiping the sweat from his eyes, he nodded with satisfaction.

"It's time to celebrate and render thanks to Hadassah," he declared.

"And also to Dinah, without whose input we would have given up," Seraphina reminded him.

"Hear! Hear!" Ham shouted, lifting his wife above his head. Dinah stiffened at their applause, then began to laugh like a girl. The warm acceptance of those she loved made her heart feel lighter than it had been in years.

The following day was spent in repairing one small section of the Ark, then calculating how much chicle[4] was needed to complete the job. Noah was dismayed when Hazar told him they required at least three talents'[32] worth.

"Would we be able to obtain so much from a handful of trees, Ben?" he asked.

"Yes, but only over a month or so. Fortunately, there's an enormous grove of them a few mil[17] beyond where I took you before. All the chicle[4] we need could be tapped over two days."

"Even so, transporting such a load will be a problem," Noah pointed out.

"Not if your sons help," Hazar remarked. Noah shook his head.

"I'll not leave the women and patriarchs[23] unprotected," he said.

"We could use your remaining draughthorse."

"And be as conspicuous as a lamp in a dark room? I think not!"

"You're right," Hazar chuckled. "An unpleasant confrontation would be the last thing we need! But there is another option. While I was at Eretz, I defended a fellow prisoner against some rogues. He was released long before I was, but never forgot that single act of kindness, and briefly took me in after I'd served my time. We've been friends ever since."

"You obviously esteem him highly," Noah said,

"He and his wife are like family, Noah. They've been hankering to repay me in full. I think the time has come to accept their offer. Haggai lives in the woods not far from here, and is a well-known drayman in the district. He can easily transport the chicle[4] without raising suspicion."

"Let's hope he's willing, then. I'm assuming you can get word to him?"

"I visit him quite often, actually," Hazar answered cockily. "Usually on a moonless night, when there's scarcely a soul afoot in the forest."

"Moon or not, we'll need to pay your friend a visit tonight."

"We?" Hazar asked dubiously. Noah nodded.

"Haggai may owe you the favour, Ben, but it is I who will ask him for it. Come. Let's tell the others what we're planning."

Within minutes, everyone was seated around the kitchen table. Seraphina's chest tightened when she heard Hazar's plan, but she remained silent. The men had no alternative but to venture into the forest again. All she could do was pray for their safety.

Not only were Haggai and Adah willing to help, they also provided fifty flasks, complete with webbing and belts.

"We'll use the belt to fasten the flask just below the tapping notch, and leave it to fill while we repeat the procedure on the next tree," Hazar said with satisfaction. "That will enable us to extract chicle[4] from several plants at once."

"And save us a lot of time," Noah added. Hazar agreed.

"With five of us on the job, I estimate we'll be done and back home within thirteen hours."

"A better prospect than the two days we originally planned for," Noah said dryly. "Who's our fifth helper, by the way?"

"My son, Isaac," Haggai answered, pointing to the youth at his feet. "He's only thirteen, but strong and clever."

"Shouldn't he be at *bet midrash*[3]?" Noah asked. Haggai grimaced.

"I pulled him out of Je'el's house of study after he got flogged for something he didn't do. It reminded me too much of prison. Besides, it's a lawless system we have, teaching our children things that aren't good for them. My wife tutors the boy for an hour in the evenings. The lad's safer for it, and happier, too." Noah nodded in sympathy. He had heard how wicked schools had become and was grateful his own sons lived such sheltered lives.

"You know I'll pay you as well as I'm able," he promised.

"No, Sir," Adah objected. "We don't do God's work for tender."

"Perhaps not, dear lady, but Elohim[7] is no man's debtor."

"Forgive her," Haggai said with embarrassment. "She waxes as spiritual as Hazar here. But she's right in telling you to keep your gold. It would profit us little and deny me the pleasure of paying Ben what I owe. The Ark means much to him. It would ease my mind to see him right."

"It's the Lord's work you're helping us with, Haggai. He will honour you for it," Noah responded warmly. "Indeed, He would bless you beyond what you can imagine if you yielded your life to Him. Do it now, before it's too late."

Haggai shrugged uncomfortably.

"I've heard it all before, Sir. God knows, Adah is always at me to change my attitude, but it's hard after what I've seen. I've too many questions and none yet answered. Now, concerning this job; we need to set a time and place where we can meet."

Noah sighed heavily at the man's reluctance and saw that Ben Hazar was just as concerned for his friend. But nothing they said could persuade Haggai to change his mind.

The following day, Seraphina anxiously watched her husband leave with Ben Hazar in the early hours of the morning. Bowing her head, she silently prayed for their safety. At least the men would find it easier to harvest three talents[32] of chicle[4] than to pick the same quantity of fruit. They had spent hours stripping their tree bare, but had not collected nearly enough. *No matter*, she thought, arching her aching back. There were plenty of hibiscus[31] trees just beyond the breach in the city wall. The rest of their foraging could be done when nobody was about.

Sighing, she returned to her daughters in the kitchen and took up one of the scoops Shem had fashioned. It made the job of separating the quartered fruit from its hard skin easier. She was surprised when her sons pitched in to help a few minutes later. It was refreshing to have them wake before dawn.

"We thought we'd make an early start at picking fruit," Shem said as Seraphina served breakfast. "Rather that than working in the heat of day."

"Good idea," she agreed. "We'll join you as soon as we've cleaned up."

"No, Mother," Japheth protested. "We'd rather have you women stay here and cook the stuff. You need to free up your pots for when Father returns with the chicle[4]."

"I hadn't thought of that," Seraphina said. "Very well. You go pick while we carry on here. We'll come for the next batch when we're ready for it."

"That won't be necessary," Ham mumbled between spoonfuls of porridge. "We'll bring the fruit to you every half-hour or so."

Seraphina proudly watched her sons leave the yard a few minutes later. They were seldom so decisive and it had been a relief to defer to their sound judgment. Perhaps she should consult them more often in future. Smiling, she closed the door and silently resumed her task.

Night had just begun to fall when Seraphina set aside the final batch of boiled fruit. Flushed with exhaustion, she left the cleaning of the kitchen to her daughters and anxiously peered through the breach in the city wall. It was over fifteen hours since Noah and Ben had left.

Hearing the creaking of lumbering wheels in the distance, she retreated into the shadows. The seldom-used road was carpeted with fallen leaves and she would never have heard the approaching dray otherwise. She thought it must be Haggai returning with her husband and Hazar, but could see no sign of Noah in the fading light. Fear clutched at her stomach. What if something was amiss?

Seraphina's nervousness grew when the driver pulled up and peered at her. His face was partially hidden in the dark folds of his cowl and she did not know if she was looking at friend or foe. The drayman suddenly leapt to the ground and she screamed. Her cry startled the horses and brought her children running.

"Mother! Where are you?" Hadassah called as she threw the house door open.

"I'm at the wall," Seraphina shouted. She then took a deep breath to calm herself, and emerged from the shadows to confront the stranger.

"Please, mistress," the man implored as he quieted his frenzied animals. "I have been sent by Noah and Ben to drop off a load of chicle[4]." Stepping forward, Seraphina looked up into his clear eyes and felt her anxiety dissolve.

"It's alright," she said, pushing aside the cudgel Ham waved in Haggai's face. "This man is sent by Noah and speaks peace."

Having allayed her family's fears, she turned her attention back to the drayman.

"Now, friend, what news do you bring of Noah and Ben Hazar?"

"They're well, My Lady," Haggai hastened to assure her. "At least they were when I left them to come here. We'd just finished loading the chicle[4] when we heard folk approaching and had to hide. It's good we did. They stopped to refresh themselves mere paces from where we'd been working. We lay low for a while, then Noah told me to slip away without him and Ben. He said they would follow as soon as it was safe to do so. My trade enabled us to leave without arousing suspicion. We three are often seen together, transporting wares."

Seraphina peered up at the woman and child huddled behind the wagon seat.

"My wife, Adah, and son, Isaac," Haggai said proudly.

"Noah told me you'd be helping," she said. "Thank you. It can't have been easy. But come. We must relieve you of the chicle[4] and let you return to the safety of your own home."

Once they were finished offloading, Seraphina turned to the drayman and shook his hand.

"*Shalom*[26], Haggai. God keep you all safe," she said gratefully.

"Thank you, My Lady," he answered. "And don't worry about Noah and Ben. They're sure to arrive soon." Turning the horses, Haggai headed back the way he had come. Seraphina leant wearily against the remains of the wall and watched the dray disappear into the deepening shadows. She could feel her fears for Noah resurfacing and closed her eyes.

"Oh Lord," she prayed, "let me know he's safe – please!" Looking up, she saw the faint glimmer of stars in the darkening *shamayim*[27] and was immediately filled with peace. The One who kept the heavens and everything in them from falling would keep her husband from harm.

It was several hours later when Seraphina awoke to feel Noah's arms around her.

"I'm sorry," he apologized, kissing the tip of her nose. "You must've been worried sick."

"I was until Elohim[7] put my mind at rest," she admitted, snuggling against him.

"More like He answered your prayers and kept us safe," Noah said grimly. "It was awful, Seraphina. You would have panicked had Haggai told you all." She stared at him wide-eyed.

"It couldn't have been that bad, surely?"

"It was worse than bad, dear heart. We saw men and Nephilim[19] indulge in an orgy so horrendous it made me gag. We initially thought their prime victim was an ape. It was only when the creature looked up that I recognized him. Oh God, Seraphina! I would never wish such torment on anyone."

"It was Obed, wasn't it?" she asked quietly. Noah closed his eyes and nodded.

"I know he brought his insanity upon himself, Seraphina, but for years I've prayed he would cry to God for mercy. I obviously hoped for too much."

"How can you hope for less when it comes to the souls of men and women?"

"Even so, it's like grasping at straws. Most people prefer choosing evil over good. Take Hophni, for instance – dressed like a warlock and urging his companions to smash his demented father to the ground! How Obed managed to get away was a miracle that gave Haggai a chance to make his own escape. Ben and I decided to stay behind. We wanted to find Obed and at least give him a decent burial if all else failed. He was badly wounded."

"And did you find him?" Seraphina asked, stroking his arm. Noah nodded.

"Yes, but he died a few minutes later. His eyes were filled with such sorrow, Seraphina. Such pain! How I grieve for what might've been."

"Perhaps his sorrow led him to repentance."

Her remark gave Noah pause for thought.

"I hope so," he sighed. Seraphina did not answer. Nothing she said could make Noah's grief easier. Snuffing out the lamp, she held him tightly.

CHAPTER 21
TABITHA

... the LORD is a faithful God. Blessed are those who
wait for Him to help them.
Isaiah 30:18b

Noah stood in the belly of the Ark and looked up at the rafters. It was hard to believe every nook and cranny would one day be filled with creatures. How on earth was he going to feed them all? Although it had taken almost a century to build the great ship, neither he nor anyone else had had the foresight to fill the storage vats. While Seraphina's garden might provide amply for their own needs, it would take years to grow enough fodder for their cargo of livestock!

He looked miserably at the narrow windows situated just beneath the Ark's roof. The sunlight flooded through them briefly at dawn and sunset, but the boat's interior remained in shadow for the rest of the day. The prospect of surviving the Flood in an almost constant state of gloom was even more depressing than having to subject his family to yet another trial. He sighed. They had been so excited this morning, when he had painted her name on the bows. After much deliberation, they had decided to simply call her *The Ark* and the white letters stood out boldly against the darkened wood.

Noah's thoughts were rudely interrupted when the timbers beneath his feet began to throb. The Presence that suddenly filled the vessel shone like the sun and he threw up an arm to shield his eyes. Methuselah had often tried to describe how the Most High had appeared to him in the grotto, but had been lost for words. Noah could now understand why. Wonderstruck, he fell trembling to his knees.

You have done well, Son of Lamech.

Elohim's[7] voice rumbled like a mighty waterfall, and Noah longed for the Lord to speak again. But the silence remained unbroken. It was with a tingle of fear that he realized the Sovereign Lord awaited his response.

"I've not done as well as I should have," he whispered.

He felt the Lord's Hand upon his shoulder, like warm sweet oil, and wept.

You have done well, Elohim[7] repeated softly. *The Ark is complete and the season for prophesying has begun. My call to repentance will burn in you until you cry in agony of soul. Then I will give you strength to speak with an authority that will draw people from far and near, so that all who have not heard may hear.*

And while you prophesy, your family is to plant and reap. I will multiply your crops a hundredfold and your vats will overflow on the day Japheth is wed. You will invite the hungry to eat of your surplus, but terror will grip them and they will not.

And thus will begin my season of vengeance. No longer will I allow the wicked to corrupt what is good. Yet, if as few as fifty repent, I promise to stay my hand from destroying the Earth and all who live upon her. So speak, my son, with all the love you have for me.

The exhortation filled Noah with sorrow. Falling so far short of God's glory himself, he wondered if there were that many righteous people left.

"How, then, is it possible for *any* to be saved?" he cried. But there was no answer from within the fading light.

Although Noah had shared the prophecy with Seraphina, she was unprepared for the effect it had on him. Her husband's relentless preaching left him with little time to eat or sleep, and he was soon an unkempt caricature of the man she had married.

"This can't go on, Noah!" she exclaimed irritably, as she helped him back to bed in the early hours of one morning. They had been asleep for just a short while when his cry had startled her awake. She knew from his terror-stricken eyes that the nightmares had returned. It had been years since Noah had had one. Years, too, since he had been under such strain.

"This can't go on," she repeated, tucking the blankets around him. "I understand your urgency, but you've become so busy preaching that you don't have time for God. You need to do some serious praying before you burn out altogether. Now, stay here while I go and heat some milk and honey."

Noah nodded wearily.

"Do you know they call me God's Madman out there?" he murmured. Seraphina's eyes welled with tears. She had heard the derogatory nickname often, but only when Noah was out of earshot, and wondered how he had got wind of it.

"I've known for a long time," he said, interpreting her thoughts. "I used to smile because no one had the courage to call me that to my face. Now they blatantly shout it out. The thing is, Seraphina, I'm beginning to believe it's true. I walk up and down, day after day, pleading in vain for repentance, and I do feel like I'm going mad! I know it can't go on, dear heart, but how can I stop it?"

Seraphina's temper flared.

"I've already told you," she answered impatiently. "Pray! Cry out to Elohim[7]! He called you to this in the first place. He will make His ways plain if you but ask." She immediately regretted her hot, accusing words. Leaning forward, she brushed her fingers across her husband's unhappy brow and kissed him lightly.

"There really is no other way but prayer," she insisted as she left the room to warm some milk and honey. Alone and aching, Noah hugged himself and began to weep.

"No more!" he cried between sobs. "Please, no more!"

Emotionally and physically exhausted, he slumped back against the pillows and shut his eyes. Sleep came quickly, but it was a week before he rose from his bed, fully recovered and hungry as a gannet. He soon regained the weight he had lost and prophesied with a fire that burnt through the fabric of his listeners' lives. Yet few accepted God's message as fervently as they came to hear it.

Tabitha was one of thousands who made the long journey to hear Noah preach. She had only been a child and desperately ill when Joanna had first told her about the great man. Never had she heard a story so wondrous, or so full of hope! Her pulse quickened at the thought of listening to him for herself. Would his message change her heart in the same way it had changed Joanna's? The prospect made her smile. She had been branded a leper from birth, and would have perished had the kind widow not given her refuge. The feel of the cool water on her fevered brow was as memorable as ever – as was the gasp of surprise when the filth was washed off to reveal the unblemished skin beneath.

"Why, you're not leprous!" Joanna had exclaimed indignantly. "Just a little different, that's all."

It had been several days before Tabitha was sufficiently recovered to understand what her benefactor meant. Her eyes had filled with tears as she had gazed into the bronze mirror and seen her body for the first time. Her skin and hair were uncommonly pale, setting her apart in a way she did not find particularly pleasing, but she was *not* a leper. The realization had been a turning point in her life. She had vowed to never again hide behind sackcloth and ashes, or allow herself to be forced into poverty! Joanna had promptly applauded her decision and offered her employment.

Tabitha had taken to the art of silk making like a bird to the sky and had soon surpassed her teacher's skill. Her superior cloth had rapidly turned the modest home industry into a thriving business.

"How fortunate I took you in, Tabby," Joanna had said fondly. "The master would be livid if he knew how well we're doing."

It was the first time the widow had mentioned her loveless marriage. Her husband had been killed in a brawl some years before, leaving his wife and three daughters destitute. A high-placed friend had kept the debt collectors from their door, but it had taken years to repay the man's kindness.

Sadly, Joanna had died ten summers ago, but the crippling disease that had rendered the robust woman to skin and bones had been unable to touch her spirit. Tabitha remembered their last conversation well.

"Death isn't the end," Joanna had said in earnest. "It's coming face to face with God, like Adam and Eve did before they sinned. I yearn to be with my Lord, Tabby, so don't grieve when I die. There's too much to live for. That's why you need to go and listen to the Prophet. His words will change your life, as they did mine."

Tabitha had been eager to make the trip ever since, but had been forced to wait until her adopted nieces were able to run the business without her. Now it seemed like every person she met was on their way to hear the Prophet. What a pity most were motivated by mere curiosity.

As she listened to the brawny, white-haired man, Joanna's words impacted her anew. Believing in Elohim[7] had been the widow's key to living a fulfilled life. But her belief had been more than just a nice idea. It had been a total submission of her will to His plans and purposes. A great longing overwhelmed her and she fell to her knees. If only she had Joanna's faith!

"Please forgive me, Lord, for ignoring You for so long," she whispered. A warm peace flooded her breast. A peace like no other. Her eyes welled with tears and she bowed her head in worship. God was here, in this place. With her!

"Thank You! Thank You!" she breathed. The brush of invisible wings against her face sent a tingle up her spine. Laughing, she leapt to her feet, then gasped. Standing beside the Prophet was a man so like her in appearance that she thought she was looking in a mirror. Her heart stirred in a strange new way. Had God brought her here for a reason other than her own?

She closed her eyes and took a deep breath. Nothing Joanna had taught her had prepared her for this! Setting her lips in a determined line, she began pushing her way towards the front of the crowd. People grumbled, but quickly stepped aside when they saw her unmistakable likeness to Noah's pale-skinned son.

Japheth forgot about giving Noah his lunch when he saw the fair-haired woman. Dropping the bread and cheese, he ran down the gangplank, his hands outstretched. Tabitha smiled uncertainly, then offered her own. Japheth squeezed them warmly.

"I've been waiting for you all my life!" he exclaimed.

"And I you," she whispered.

The ribaldry of the amused onlookers made Japheth blush, and he looked up to see his father twinkling with mirth.

"You'd better get used to it, lad," Noah teased, "especially now that your wedding is imminent."

Tabitha heard Noah's approval in the quip and bowed graciously. She then turned back to Japheth.

"Please, take me to my new home," she said. Grinning broadly, Japheth offered her his arm and led her away from the crowd.

Noah shook his head in wonder as he watched his son escort the blue-eyed woman to the house. Japheth's betrothal might have been slow in coming, but the girl God had chosen was perfect.

Shem and Ham were both fascinated and shamed by the tall blonde woman. They had always thought their brother's pasty skin ugly, but in Tabitha it was strikingly beautiful. Seraphina saw they were perplexed but said nothing. It was good to see Japheth so happy. Smiling, she slipped from the room to prepare dinner.

It was not long before Noah stuck his head around the kitchen door with an offer of help.

"What a day it's been!" Seraphina sniffed as she sliced onions. She worked in silence for a few minutes, then leaned towards her husband.

"Have you ever wondered why Japheth and Ham look so different from us?" she asked. Noah shrugged.

"Not all children resemble their parents," he answered. "Take me, for instance. I don't look anything like Lamech."

"True, but you do take after Methuselah."

"What are you saying, Seraphina?"

"I'm saying our two younger sons don't seem to resemble any of our ancestors – or anyone else's for that matter."

"Then explain why Japheth and Tabitha look sufficiently alike to be taken for brother and sister. As for Dinah, her skin is almost as dark as Ham's."

"How can I explain something I don't understand?" Seraphina grumbled. "All I know is that our sons are as different from each other as blood is to water. Indeed, the more I think about it, the more I'm convinced Elohim[7] wants to use their offspring to father three diverse races of people[36]."

"But why would He do such a thing, Seraphina? What purpose would it serve?"

"How would I know?" she muttered as she returned to her chopping board. Noah's face clouded with worry. There was already so much violence and discord in the world. Racial diversity would only make matters worse. Sighing, he threw the onions into the pot. The thought of his grandchildren warring against each other was unsettling.

Although Lamech could not see the betrothed couple, he could hear their chatter and silently thanked God for attending to his prayer. Tabitha lit up Japheth's soul like no other and would be a wife worthy of his love. Just as Orpah had been worthy of his. He smiled. There was only one thing left to do before he departed to be with her. Hopefully, Methuselah would be strong enough to participate in the ritual. The Patriarch[23] could scarcely speak, let alone raise his hand. Lamech's eyes prickled with tears. The last few years of renewed fellowship with his father had been precious. Clearing his throat, he leaned across the bed and beckoned Japheth.

"Please call the family, son. I want to see them."

Japheth immediately left the room with Tabitha to do his grandfather's bidding. As Lamech waited, he wondered how he could say what was on his heart. He had never been a good orator and had prayed throughout the night for God to enable his tongue. Hearing the noisy voices outside his room, he silently did so again.

"You called for us?" Seraphina asked, pushing open the door and helping Methuselah into a chair. Lamech heard the others close behind her and inclined his head in greeting.

"Thank you for coming at this time of day, when you've so much to do," he said warmly. "I would have waited until later but fear I've little time left."

"Don't say that, Father!" Noah cried.

"Hush, Noah," Lamech said softly. "Much as I love you, my body is tired and I'm glad to be going. It is time, now, to bestow my final blessing before I'm too weak to do so. Have your sons kneel at my feet. Then come and sit beside me. You, too, Father. I want you to lay your hands on mine and give me direction should my tongue fail."

The thought of Lamech dying was distressing and it was several seconds before Noah could respond. Heedless of their father's hesitation, the brothers knelt and embraced their grandfather.

"You're good lads," the old man said with tears in his eyes. "Elohim[7] gave you to us. We in turn dedicated you to Him. Now it is time to pronounce a blessing over you that will pass down through your generations. So listen carefully and take heed to my words." He peered blindly at the three young men, then closed his eyes and began to prophesy.

"Shem, Japheth and Ham, God has shown me that you will survive the Flood to become founders of the generations to come. A multitude of nations and tongues will come from your loins and fill the whole earth."

Pausing, he invited Methuselah and Noah to place their hands with his on Japheth's head, then continued.

"Japheth, you will leave your brothers and settle in the lands of the North, where your desire to learn and to serve will be gratified. Beware of being led astray by pride. It is the Most High who blesses the work of your hands and clothes you with salvation. Seek to honour and glorify Him, and He will make you prosper."

Lamech smiled and stroked Japheth's face with his finger, then shifted to Noah's youngest.

"Ham, your restless spirit will make you spread like the limbs of a tree. You will extend to the unknown lands of the South, where you will wander until you find a place to settle. Beware of falling prey to greed, idolatry and slavery. Guard your heart, for out of it springs the well of life. Stretch your hands to the Most High for mercy. Honour Him and He will direct your paths."

Lamech tenderly embraced Ham, then leant forward to plant the kiss of the first-born on Shem's forehead.

"Shem, the Most High sees your faithfulness and knows your heart. He will give you the lands of the South-East, where you will establish an everlasting kingdom. It is through your seed that the Saviour of all the nations will come. Pray you know Him in that day. Delight in Him and He will abundantly supply your needs, and through you the needs of multitudes. He will also entrust you with His Words and Statutes. Be faithful to obey them. Guard against the pride that so easily destroys. Seek God's mercy that you may not be ashamed on the day of His reckoning."

Lamech concluded his prophecy with a shuddering sigh, then opened his arms for the final benediction.

"Lord," he said in a loud voice, "You have called these men to become the fathers of kingdoms and nations. May You bless them bountifully and guide them in Your ways. Shine the light of Your countenance on them. Give them Your peace. Hear our prayer, O Elohim[7], for the sake of Your great Name. Amen."

Exhausted, Lamech flopped back against his pillows. What he had begun was now finished and so was he. Turning his head towards Methuselah, he winked. The Patriarch[23] chuckled and shakily ran his hand across his son's hair. The two men had joked for some time over who would be first to obtain life's final crown. Methuselah now knew it was not he. A lump formed in his throat and he impulsively wrapped his bony arms around Lamech.

"Until we meet again, my son," he whispered.

"Until then," Lamech agreed wearily.

Noah's eyes filled with tears as he helped his grandfather to his feet. Lamech's blessing confirmed what Seraphina had already suspected. Their sons were destined for great and terrible things.

Seraphina was alarmed to find Lamech barely conscious the following morning. She immediately called for Noah but there was little either of them could do. The old man died two days later.

Noah's heart ached as he looked down at the mound of newly dug earth.

"I'll miss him, too," Seraphina murmured, slipping her hand into his. "Thank God he died believing in Elohim[7] for the salvation of his soul." Noah considered how much Lamech had changed over the years and nodded.

"That in itself is a relief," he agreed.

He watched Seraphina place some anemones on the grave. The bright flowers were among the few things Lamech had been able to see in his near-blind state. Hopefully, the women would continue to fill the house with the blooms in memory of him.

Seraphina wiped her eyes and rose to her feet. Several graves now occupied the small burial ground. The thought of who else would be interred there before the coming of the Flood made her sad. Tenacious as Methuselah's grip on life was, he could not endure for much longer. Sensing her thoughts, Noah draped his arm around her shoulders and gave her a squeeze.

"Death is not the end for those who love the Most High, dear heart. It's the beginning of living in His radiant Presence." Seraphina looked up into her husband's craggy face and returned his embrace.

"Thanks for reminding me," she murmured. "It's still hard, though, isn't it?"

"True, but nothing is impossible to bear when we believe in God wholeheartedly. Our faith in Him is our victory over the devil."

Seraphina nodded. The Sovereign Lord had enabled her to cope with things she had not thought possible. She would trust Him to carry her through to the end.

Much as Tabitha hated to leave her betrothed, she had to return to Beth Shamir. The tax collectors were due to assess her profits for the year, and her nieces did not know how to deal with the crooked officials.

"I'll be lost without you," Japheth objected.

"You know I have an obligation to Joanna," she answered, running her finger down his bearded cheek. "I promise to return once I've trained the girls to take over from me."

"But a year, Tabby! Why so long?"

"It may take even longer than that, but I swear it will not exceed two. I long to marry you, Japheth, but I must first attend to this responsibility. We may never have met had it not been for Joanna. It's important I return her kindness by setting her grand-daughters on their feet."

"What if they prove incapable?" he asked. Tabitha shrugged.

"I can only teach them everything I know and hope for the best," she said. "Now, let me go and do what I must. The sooner I start, the sooner I'll be able to return." Japheth reluctantly released her to say goodbye to the rest of the family. She then returned to his arms and kissed him fervently.

"I promise to come back as soon as I can," she said in a choked voice.

"I know you will, Tabby," he whispered, gently returning her kiss.

His throat burned as he watched her walk away, her body taut with determination. A thought suddenly occurred to him.

"Be sure to bring back some of your finest silk for your bridal robe," he called after her. She turned and looked at him with eyes shimmering with tears.

"Only the best will you have," she answered brokenly. "I'll weave it myself."

Japheth watched until she was no more than a speck in the distance, his heart heavy with loneliness.

"I know how you feel," Noah said as he placed a comforting arm around the young man's shoulders. "But there's a greater plan at work than what you can see."

"How so?" Japheth asked dully.

"Do you remember me telling you about the Prophecy Elohim[7] gave me when we finished building the Ark? Well, not only did the Lord say I would enter into a new season of preaching, He also told me the Ark's vats would overflow on the day you wed your bride."

Japheth stared at his father in disbelief.

"But our vats aren't even close to being full!" he cried. Noah hunched his shoulders in apology.

"No, they aren't and probably won't be for many harvests to come," he admitted. "I fear your marriage to Tabitha may have to be postponed for a lot longer than she predicts."

"No!" Japheth shouted. He took a deep breath to calm himself, then continued in a low, strained voice. "All these years I've waited. Now I'm told I have to wait some more! How much longer, Father? What if Tabby grows impatient and leaves me for another?"

Noah frowned sternly.

"This is not about you and Tabitha," he said. "It's about God's mercy. You can resist all you like, Japheth, but Elohim[7] will only allow our vats to overflow once every person on Earth has had opportunity to repent. He has already begun to fulfil His promise to multiply our crops. Perhaps there's more to come."

Noah's words quickly cooled Japheth's temper.

"You're right, Father. I am being selfish," he apologized ruefully. "But if Almighty God wants me to wait longer than I've bargained for, He must give me grace to be patient."

"Amen to that. But, long time or short, Elohim[7] *will* undertake for you and Tabitha," Noah said, giving Japheth a hug before returning to the house. It was some time before the young man followed, a look of resignation in his blue eyes.

CHAPTER 22
JOY COMES WITH THE MORNING

Weeping may go on all night, but joy comes with the
morning.
Psalm 30:5b

Dinah found Ben Hazar in a state of collapse on the storeroom floor two days after Tabitha had left. Falling to her knees, she felt for a pulse, then quickly covered the sick man with some empty sacks. While far from adequate, the hessian would do until she returned with blankets and warm stones.

Hadassah was working in the kitchen when she heard Dinah's urgent call.

"What's wrong?" she cried, casting aside her apron.

"Ben Hazar's collapsed in the storeroom," Dinah answered breathlessly. "Go to him, quickly. I'll join you as soon as I can." Hadassah hastily did as she was bid. She had known for some time that her uncle was ailing, but he had made light of her concern.

"Bad living has to catch up with a man sometime, daughter," he had said. "No one can carry on as I've done and expect to still be vigorous at the end of it all. I've had my time. Now I'm being forced to slow down, that's all."

But, as she rubbed her uncle's icy hands between her own, Hadassah knew he was very ill. Weeping, she slipped under the sacks and wrapped her arms around him.

"Dear Elohim[7]," she prayed, "please give me one more chance to tell Uncle Ben how much I love him."

Dinah returned a few minutes later with warm stones and blankets. Noah followed, holding a glowing brazier at arm's length.

"This has always been a cold room," he said, placing the brazier near the makeshift bed. Hadassah threw back the sacks and packed the stones around her uncle's cold body. She then covered him with the blankets and forlornly sat back on her heels. Noah placed a comforting hand on her shoulder and held out a corked bottle.

"Methuselah gave me some red lavender[24], to stimulate Ben's heart," he told her.

"What if it's *not* his heart?" Hadassah objected.

155

"Even so, the potion should revive him temporarily. We can then decide what to do next."

"I suppose you're right," she agreed reluctantly.

Kneeling, Noah carefully measured out a dose and spooned it down Ben Hazar's throat.

Hazar sighed as he savoured the sweet fragrance of Heaven. The millions of flowers swaying to the songs of angels filled him with longing. But his time had not yet come. Closing his eyes, he focused on those left behind. A sudden burning in his chest startled him awake. He looked up to see those he loved bent over him.

"It's alright, old friend," Noah said, slipping a pillow under Hazar's head. "You took a bad turn, that's all."

Hazar's heart was hammering madly and he took a deep breath to steady it.

"This isn't a bad turn, Noah," he whispered. "I'm dying."

"Don't say that, Uncle!" Hadassah cried. "There must be something we can do!" Hazar felt the warm tears on his face and reached up to stroke her hair.

"I'm so sorry," he said tenderly. "Sorry to have not been honest with you before. I'm ill, Hadassah. Ill with a disease that causes no pain or discomfort. Yet it weakens the body until there's no strength left for living. It won't be long, now, before I fall asleep and wake up in Heaven. So be happy for me, daughter! Don't break my heart with your tears."

"But why does it have to be like this?" she asked, her large eyes stricken with grief. "Why can't things go on as before?" Hazar tried to smile through his own tears.

"Dear Hadassah! You know it's impossible for things to remain the same. You will soon be called to enter the Ark and I'll not be able to follow. The Lord has not ordained it. So my leaving like this is actually easier for us both, in many ways."

"But what will I do without you, Uncle? I love you so much."

Ben reached for her hand and pressed it to his lips.

"I love you, too. But if you knew how wonderful Heaven is, you'd be happy for me."

Although Hazar's words were not intended for her, Dinah was both thrilled and disquieted by his reference to the afterlife. She had always had a deep fear of death. Pushing her thoughts aside, she raised her eyes to Noah's.

"I think we should get Ben up to the house, where it's warmer," she suggested. To her dismay, Hazar immediately resisted the idea.

"No, not yet!" he cried, agitated. "There's something I must say and I have little time left. Don't waste it on things that will make no difference in the end."

"There's no need to get upset, Ben," Noah soothed. "We'll first hear you out, if that's what you want."

"It is," Hazar answered weakly. He lay back in an effort to rally his strength, then continued in a voice hoarse with fatigue. "Noah, you must do something about your water reserves if you want to survive the Flood," he said. Noah raised his eyebrows in surprise.

"We've already filled the Ark's cisterns with enough water to last two months," he responded. "I know we'll need a lot more than that, but we can replenish our supply from the floodwaters."

Hazar shook his head.

"Don't you see?" he rasped. "The ratio of pollutants in the dropping water levels will increase to the point where it will become undrinkable."

"But we've never had a problem with evaporation making fresh water undrinkable before."

"We've never experienced a flood of such magnitude either! Imagine the thousands of people and animals crushed by the torrents. The poisons emitted by their rotting flesh and night soil[21]!" The thought made Noah's stomach heave.

"You've made a valid point, Ben," he admitted wryly, "but how do we address the problem?"

"Distil the water," Hazar said. Noah blinked at the suggestion.

"Good idea, but we've no room for a still and the fuel to run it."

"I'm not talking about a still," Hazar started to explain, when he was overtaken by a coughing fit that left him fighting for air.

"Father! Do something!" Hadassah cried. Nodding, Noah administered a second dose of red lavender[24], but it was several minutes before Hazar could continue.

"I waste too much time on details," he wheezed. "Now listen carefully, Noah, before it's too late." Noah nodded and gently squeezed the old man's hand.

"I'm listening," he answered quietly.

"The drainage channels just beneath the top wale of the prow – they're part of a water-purifying system, to which the hothouse is the key."

Noah looked at him blankly. The hothouse was a structure made of gossamer[9] coated with clear resin. Ben had come up with the idea of growing vegetables inside the semi-transparent shed to prevent water loss by evaporation.

"How can the hothouse replenish our water supplies on the Ark?" he asked quizzically.

"Easy," Hazar answered with a feeble wave of his hand. "Affix the hothouse's gossamer[9] to an A-frame on the Ark's open prow. Evaporation will cause water trapped there to condense and run off into the drainage channels, straight into the Ark's cisterns."

Noah frowned. Hazar's idea was sound in theory, but the prow – which was sealed off from the rest of the Ark – would need constant topping up for the plan to work.

"The window, Noah," Hazar said hoarsely. "The channels just beneath the window!" Noah stared at the sick man, then threw back his head and roared with laughter. Of course! The channels just beneath the Ark's fore window emptied onto the prow deck. A few buckets of floodwater into those every day, and they had an effective method of replenishing their water supplies.

"Ingenious!" he exclaimed.

"The cleverest ideas are always the simplest," Hazar croaked.

"You've really thought this out, haven't you?" Noah mused. Hazar sagged against the pillow, his face grey with exhaustion.

"You credit me with too much, Noah. God gave you the specifications for the drainage system. He simply showed me how to use them, that's all." The barely audible whisper brought a lump to Noah's throat, and he beckoned Hadassah to her uncle's side.

"Thank you so much for everything!" she cried, the tears streaming down her face.

"I told you not to weep," Hazar admonished weakly. "A stubborn woman is what you are." Then, gathering the last of his strength, he placed his hand on her head and spoke in a loud voice.

"The Lord bless and keep you, my daughter. May He cause you to become a woman of women and a mother of mothers, the bearer of many sons and daughters of noble character. May your husband praise you in the gate and call you blessed. May your children rise up and honour you. May your descendants see in you a model of grace and beauty. May all these things be yours from the Lord."

Hazar lowered his arm and smiled at Hadassah with eyes that had already begun to glaze over. Heartbroken, she pressed his hand to her lips and mourned.

Hadassah reconciled herself to Ben Hazar's death during the early hours of morning, and attended his funeral with dignity and peace. It would not be long before she would be glad he had gone to be with the Lord – as she would, too, one day. The thought of their reunion made her weep anew.

Noah remained long after the others had left the graveside, staring at the earth-covered remains of a man he had come to love and respect. He would miss his friend's good sense and sharp wit, his drive and initiative. If only his sons were so motivated! Little did he realize how much they were awed by his own driving passion. Men of Ben Hazar's calibre were rare.

Sighing, he remembered with sorrow and gratitude those who had touched his life. Lamech, so firm in his faith once he had returned to it, and Enos – without whom they would have perished. Doughty old Beulah and poor embittered Obed, whose unbelief had driven him insane. And John, who he believed had been caught up to Heaven in a glory reminiscent of what he had only experienced in dreams and visions. He wondered if Enos had seen it happen.

Noah's train of thought led him to Methuselah. It would not be long before his grandfather also left them. The Patriarch's[23] bedridden state had begun taking its toll on his spirit – especially since the last of the animals he loved so well had succumbed to death. Sighing, he shut the graveyard gate. The only member of his team unaccounted for was Jasper. He wondered if the old man was still alive, and whether or not he had found his sister.

With the exception of Tabitha, and Methuselah whose death was imminent, only those destined for the Ark remained on site. Noah yearned for the period of waiting to end, but could not foresee that happening for months to come. At least they had the building of Hazar's water-purifying system to occupy them for a time. He would have to be careful when drawing up its dimensions. With so little gossamer[9] on hand, a single mistake would cost them dear.

Much as Seraphina objected to the disassembling of her hothouse, she had no choice but to let it go. Fortunately, all but two of her barrels were now full. With one yield on the drying tables and another hanging heavy on the vines, it wouldn't be long before they, too, were filled and sealed. If only they had also had a hothouse to boost the wheat, barley and millet crops! While their recent harvests had been bountiful, it would be months before the Ark's vats were full. *How much longer, Lord?* she silently pleaded. Her main concern, of course, was Japheth. He was becoming more and more of a recluse, waiting for his bride.

Noah was just as aware of his son's loneliness and went out of his way to keep him occupied. The two men were installing the water-purifying system when they noticed a disturbance in the crowd below. Muttering to himself, Noah downed his tools.

"I swear these people are getting worse by the day!" he grumbled as he climbed down from the scaffold. He raised his hands for silence, then stared in astonishment at the familiar figure running towards him. Laughing, he embraced her.

"Is it really you?" he asked with an ear-to-ear grin. Tabitha's face glowed with excitement.

"Yes, it is I," she said, hugging him tightly.

Noah wondered why she had returned so early, but refrained from probing. There would be time enough to ask questions later. Turning, he bellowed for his son to join him. Japheth was unaware of Tabitha's return and irritably poked his head over the wale of the prow, then blinked in surprise. Clambering to the ground, he threw his arms around his betrothed and tasted the salt of her happy tears.

"Dear Japheth!" she cried. "I came as soon as I could. And I've brought that silk bridal robe you ordered. Please let us marry soon. We've waited far too long."

Although Japheth had envisioned this day often, Tabitha's words were sobering. He shook his head and drew her aside.

"We can't – not yet," he said.

"Why ever not?" she asked. Sighing heavily, Japheth proceeded to tell her what his father had told him.

"So we can't marry until the vats on the Ark are full," he concluded sadly. "To do so would be rebelling against God."

Tabitha's eyes welled with tears.

"Oh dear Elohim[7]," she whispered as she gently ran her finger over Japheth's lips. "How good and merciful You are."

Her words of praise made Japheth angry.

"Merciful? I think not, Tabby!" he exclaimed.

"Oh, but He is, Japheth!" she said, grasping his hands and squeezing hard. "Come, there's something you must see. Then you will know just how great the Most High is." Intrigued, Japheth followed her through the crowd to the breach in the city wall and stared in amazement at the train of laden drays.

"All the wheat, barley and millet you need," Tabitha said proudly. "There're also two barrels of oats and six drays of straw."

Japheth gaped at her, his eyes full of questions.

"My stepsisters refused to receive my share of the business as a gift," she hastened to explain. "Their husbands are among the few farmers left, so they compensated me with what you see here."

"This is wonderful!" Japheth said in awe. She smiled.

"I may not have planted or gathered like you have, Japheth, but God has provided me with a great harvest. Hopefully, there's enough here to fill the Ark's vats. I don't know if I can wait longer for you than I already have."

"I suppose we'd better unload your wares, then," Japheth grinned. "How we're going to fit so many drays into our yard I've no idea!"

"Neither do I," she laughed. "But I'm sure Noah will sort something out."

"He always does, so what're we waiting for?" The couple eagerly linked arms and hastened back through the crowd.

Noah was both delighted and worried when he saw Tabitha's gift. It had been a long time since anyone in Je'el had seen such bounty. Would the city allow him to keep it? To his surprise, the resistance he expected was not forthcoming and the offloading proceeded smoothly, with each dray being driven in turn up the gangplank into the Ark. Once inside, the horses had plenty of room to manoeuvre and tip the contents of their drays into the vats. Noah knew it would take hours to transfer the precious cargo, and insisted they work through the night. Dawn was just beginning to break when the last vat overflowed.

"You've done it!" Japheth cried, swinging Tabitha round and round until she was dizzy.

"Don't be silly," she laughed. "We've done it together, with Elohim's[7] help." His eyes softened and he grasped her hands.

"Yes, we have, haven't we?" he agreed. "And the Lord promised we would marry on the day the vats overflowed. That's today, Tabby! Today!"

"Are you crazy?" Seraphina exclaimed. "Me prepare a wedding feast in a single day? Never!"

Noah stared at his wife, then broke into helpless laughter.

"You've no choice!" he spluttered. "Unless, of course, you're willing to argue with Elohim[7]?"

"And here I was, looking so forward to resting after such a long night!" she cried, throwing up her hands in frustration. Noah laughed again.

"Seraphina! You were just as eager as I to get the offloading done in one go. You wouldn't have given us a chance at sleep had we called for a break."

"You know me too well," she answered wryly. "Well, what're we waiting for, daughters? We've a celebration to prepare for."

Smiling wearily, Tabitha began to follow but Seraphina gently restrained her.

"Not you, Tabby," she said. "You've done more than your fair share and need to rest if you're to be bright-eyed for your groom. I'll bring you some breakfast in a short while. Then you must sleep until I call you. We'll not be celebrating before the sun sets, anyway. I want to take as much time over this wedding as I can."

PART 3

THE FLOOD
2164–2160 BC

*And God did not spare the ancient world – except for
Noah and his family of seven. Noah warned the world of
God's righteous judgment. Then God destroyed the whole
world of ungodly people with a vast flood.*
2 Peter 2:5

CHAPTER 23
FINAL WARNING

I will send great troubles against them... For when I
called, they did not answer. When I spoke, they did not
listen. They deliberately sinned – before my very eyes –
and chose to do what they know I despise.
Isaiah 66:4

The setting sun made Tabitha's gold-threaded gown shimmer brightly. Yet it could not match the glow on her face as she and Japheth exchanged their vows. So intent were they upon each other that they did not see the glorious white Bird hovering above them. Neither did they hear the low rumble in the darkening *shamayim*[27].

The phenomenon did not go unnoticed by Noah, however. Shivering in the early evening breeze, he turned and stared at the increasing flow of people into his yard. Most were already in an advanced state of drunken debauchery, and their lewdness was heightened even further by the wedding. Unable to ignore such lack of restraint, Noah ushered his family inside.

"Forget about your prophecies of doom, madman!" some in the crowd shouted as he firmly shut his door. "Come, enjoy the wenches! You know you'd like to!" Laughing uproariously at their profanity, the mobsters began to revel in earnest. The orgy soon turned into a vicious brawl.

"Enough!" Noah roared as he bounded out of the house, his chest heaving with anger. Cowed into silence by the big man, the crowd backed away.

"Enough!" Noah repeated more quietly. "Have you gone mad, beating each other to a pulp? And for what? Fools! Does your wickedness satisfy you? Does it bring honour or dignity? Does it glorify the Most High? No, it does not! Turn from your sin now, or be held accountable for it by God." The challenge elicited several outcries that made Noah's throat ache with sorrow.

"It is enough!" he cried again. "For years I have begged you to turn from your wickedness. Yet you do nothing but scorn me, little realizing you speak against the

Almighty Himself! No longer will I plead with you. God has set before you life and death. Return to Him, or be destroyed in the Flood of His wrath!"

"What Flood, old man!" a bold youth challenged. Spurred on by the boy's audacity, the crowd began to harass Noah, pushing him and pulling at his beard, demanding he prophesy. A loud crack suddenly rent the heavens. The mob froze in terror, then began to frantically disperse to their seedy haunts to hide from God. Noah grieved for them as one would grieve an untimely death, and it was several minutes before he returned to the subdued bridal feast.

For three years, famine and starvation ran rampant through the land. Yet the hungry refused to help themselves to the surplus grain rotting on the wharf. The fire and rumblings in the lowering sky were too reminiscent of the burning torch so many years before! Despite their fear of God, however, people by and large became even more depraved – much to Noah's despair.

He was filled with even greater sorrow when Seraphina told him Methuselah had died in his sleep. The Patriarch[23] had asked for his funeral to be full of joy and laughter, but the bereaved family could not help weeping as they laid his body to rest. The feisty old man would be sorely missed.

As Noah closed the graveyard gate for the last time, he knew the Patriarch's[23] death was a sure sign that the day of God's vengeance was imminent. Did not the very name Methuselah mean 'when he is dead it shall be sent'[16]? A shiver ran up Noah's spine. The need to call the lost to repentance was more urgent than ever!

It was with deep sadness that Noah joined his family for dinner. The look in his eyes made Seraphina's heart constrict.

"Has it started?" she asked tremulously. Noah shook his head.

"No, but the sky's darker than ever. As are the hearts of the crowd! I wonder if they would mock God so carelessly if they knew how little time they have left."

"Then why're we sitting here idle?" Ham demanded of his father. "Shouldn't we be rounding up the animals or something?"

"Good point, son, but I've no idea where to start."

"We should've figured this out long ago," Hadassah said.

"I tried – several times in fact – but there was always something else Elohim[7] wanted me to do first," Noah answered. "I finally assumed He would sort it out. Perhaps I've been presumptuous."

"I doubt it," Seraphina said firmly. "The Lord has always been specific in the way He's led us. Gathering and boarding the animals will be no different."

"Mother's right," Tabitha agreed. "We need to ask God for direction."

"Well spoken, daughter," Noah commended her. "Let's pray now, together." Linking hands, the small group began to quietly seek the Lord's counsel. Within seconds, each sensed His unsurpassable peace. He wanted them to still their hearts and wait.

Unable to sleep, Noah quietly left the warmth of Seraphina's arms and went outside. A flash of light cleaved the heavens and he stepped back, startled by what he had seen. He peered into the murky darkness, but could not discern object from shadow. Curious, he fetched a lamp and was overjoyed to discover his eyes had not deceived him. It had been a while since animals had dared to venture into Je'el. Yet the tawny owl and two sheepdogs sat side by side, calmly awaiting his return. Noah stooped to stroke the canines and grinned when they licked his hands. They reminded him of Methuselah's wolfhound, long since dead. These creatures were more than just pets, however. Of that he was certain.

As though confirming his thoughts, the dogs suddenly sped into the night with the owl. Intrigued, Noah sat and waited. He was astonished when the trio returned a little later, with a variety of creatures in tow.

The gathering of the animals over the next seven days was watched by an increasingly perplexed crowd. Yet even now, with the end so near, they were as hard-hearted towards God as ever.

Seraphina was about to serve that week's Sabbath[25] meal, when she saw the look in her husband's eyes.

"Is it time?" she asked, her voice barely audible above the howl of the wind. He nodded.

"I fear we'll be having dinner onboard the Ark tonight," he replied. Hadassah looked out at the yard with tears in her eyes.

"I know Elohim[7] has been merciful to those who trust Him," she said wistfully. "But what about the thousands of innocent animals who're still out there?"

"We can do nothing but believe God will undertake for them," Noah answered sadly.

"Be that as it may, my immediate concern is for these creatures on our doorstep," Seraphina grumbled. "We've still to get them onboard and into their pens."

"Stop worrying!" Noah exclaimed impatiently. "God has proved time and again that He is more than able. Now, let us commit our lives to Him for the voyage ahead."

Joining hands, the small group solemnly bowed their heads.

"Dear Lord," Noah prayed, "You've led us thus far. We now ask You to take us the rest of the way. Protect us. Guide us. Help us accomplish all You have called us to do. We ask this for Your great Name's sake. Amen."

Opening his arms, he wept with his family as memory after memory flashed through his mind. They were about to lose so much – and all because God's call had been rejected! His spirit buckled at the thought of those who would perish in the Flood, but he knew his sorrow was nothing in comparison to the Lord's.

"Come," he said, gently pulling away. "We must be onboard by nightfall. Gather your belongings, then meet me back here."

He ran his hand over the colourful furnishings of Seraphina's kitchen while he waited. Would their home in the post-Flood world be just as pleasant? Or would the Earth be plunged into a chaos from which it would never recover? He was so lost in thought that it was several seconds before he was aware of Seraphina's small hand in his. Suddenly, the future did not seem so bleak.

"We're ready," she said, looking up at him with those lovely green eyes of hers. Nodding, he led his family out of the house for the last time. They paused at the grave-yard to make their silent farewells, then proceeded to the workshop yard, where the Ark rose tall and dark from her cradle. As the small group ascended the gangplank, the animals began following two by two.

"I told you so," Noah grinned, as the menagerie filed past them into the ship.

"Don't be so cocky!" Seraphina retorted.

After ensuring the creatures were safely in their pens, Noah gathered his family about him.

"There's one thing left to do, and I'd like us to be together for it," he said soberly. Leading them back to the Ark's giant door, he looked long and hard at the morose spectators.

"It's not yet too late!" he cried above the screeching wind. "There's still time to repent and stay God's Hand of judgment." A silence pregnant with hope fell upon the land, but the crowd remained grim and unyielding.

"Please!" Noah cried again. But his anguished plea was met with a grumble of anger. He held out his hands in one last, silent gesture – but to no avail. Grief-stricken, he re-entered the Ark with his wife and children.

Fear clutched at Seraphina's stomach when the enormous door was slammed shut and barred from the outside.

"Hush, dear heart," Noah whispered when she began to sob. "Only God could close the Ark's door with such speed and force. No other is strong enough."

"Why didn't you tell me before?" she whimpered. Noah shrugged uncomfortably.

"To be honest, I hadn't considered it until now," he said.

"I wonder if the people saw Him do it?" she murmured. Noah did not answer. He did not know.

Outside, the white Dove perched on the bar of the sealed door and watched the dispersing crowd with a longing that spanned both time and space.

Noah had never experienced such an intense time of waiting. Man and beast huddled together in the gloom and listened in wide-eyed silence as the storm mounted in fury. By dawn, the wind was a force to be reckoned with. The earth beneath the Ark began to violently quake, causing Seraphina to fall to her knees.

"Are you alright?" Noah shouted above the ear-splitting noise, as he helped her to her feet.

"A bit bruised is all," she shouted back. "What's going on out there, Noah?"

"I'm not sure, but the Ark's handling it well so far," he answered. "I don't know what will happen if it gets worse, though. Do you want to come with me and have a look?"

"Dare we?" she asked, cringing as a flash of light lit up the inside of the boat.

"How else are we to record it for the generations to come?"

Seraphina gingerly followed her husband up the ladder to the Ark's top deck. The sight that met her eyes made her recoil. The earth had split open like an overripe fig and was spewing her underground fountains hundreds of cubits[5] into the vapour-laden sky. Roiling against the onslaught, the heavens also began disgorging their load. The pelting sheet of water and ice soon turned fissures into fast-flowing streams that fed the Tigris, causing the river to overflow and wreak a destruction of its own.

Yet worse by far were the screams of those left behind. Faces stark with fear, they ran from their homes pleading to be saved. But it was too late! A vast chasm had opened between them and the Ark. Those attempting to breach it quickly fell to their death. Unable to watch any longer, Seraphina turned and clung to Noah.

"It's such a waste!" she wept. Noah rested his head on top of hers and gently rubbed her back.

"We must believe we did all we could, dear heart, or go mad with grief," he said.

Seraphina knew her husband was right. Even so, she wondered if she would ever recover from her sorrow.

It was not long before the torrents floated the Ark off her cradle and drove her relentlessly before the wind. Noah listened fearfully to the creaking and groaning of the timbers. If ever the caulking would fail, it was now. But, except for some seepage through the high shuttered windows, the vessel remained watertight. When the worst of the buffeting was over, Noah climbed up to the top deck and wept at the devastation he saw.

"If only!" he sobbed. "If only …"

But his cry fell on ears that could no longer hear God's call to repentance.

CHAPTER 24

TRAVAIL

In my distress I prayed to the LORD, and the LORD
answered me and rescued me.
Psalm 118:5

Although the Ark sailed the floodwaters on an even keel, the ordeal was far from over. Day after day the water continued to fall, its relentless tattoo testing the endurance of the survivors to breaking point. Living in such a state of monotonous, damp gloom frequently gave rise to heated arguments. Ham in particular was quick to voice his frustration, and Noah often wished this son of his was more like the animals, who lived together in quiet harmony.

"You wouldn't be onboard if it wasn't for the Lord's loving kindness towards us," Noah chided one day. "I swear you're as bad as the unbelievers in your thinking!"

He would have regretted his hot words had Ham not shown such indifference. Noah had for some time suspected his son of growing cold towards God. It was disappointing to have his suspicion confirmed.

Unlike Ham, the others were grateful for the many hours it took to complete their daily chores. The mucking out of stalls, laying clean straw, topping up water troughs and refilling feed bins helped them cope with the tedium of their floodwater lives.

When work for the day was done, Noah would take time to record their voyage, and all that had preceded it. Little by little, the Scroll of Remembrance grew. Hopefully, he would complete the amazing record before they made landfall.

It was just before dawn of the forty-first morning that Noah awoke to silence[37]. He lay uncertain, staring at the bands of light that laced the floor, then sat up in amazement. The water had stopped falling! Breathing a prayer of thanks, he leapt out of bed and clambered up the ladder, hoping to see signs of new life. But not even a mountaintop stood against the crimson horizon. The thought of living on the Ark a moment longer made him yearn for the wooded valley and limewashed house that had been his home. But that comfort was his no more. The months ahead would be his greatest trial yet. A trial only Elohim[7] could enable him to endure.

Looking down, he noticed the others beginning to stir.

"Come and see!" he called. "The water's stopped falling."

"Dear God! The sun's shining!" Seraphina cried, shielding her eyes against the glare. "At last we can get our clothes dry!"

Her remark made Noah laugh. For days the women had been complaining about the soggy clothing. Hanging the wash like festive flags down the side of the Ark would be an apt way to celebrate their survival.

The warm sunshine did much to boost morale, as did Tabitha's announcement that she was with child. Noah was overjoyed and relieved when he heard her news, for it gave him a time frame. With no room on the Ark for anyone else, he assumed all offspring would be born after their journey's end – which he now estimated would be within the next seven to eight months.

Seraphina believed Tabitha's pregnancy would be the first of many. Her heart sang at the prospect of dangling a baby on her knee again.

"There was a time when I thought I'd battle to have children. Now I'm a grand-mother-to-be!" she laughed merrily.

Dinah, who had longed for years to bear Ham's child, did not welcome Tabitha's news. When weeks followed without any change in her cycle, her jealousy mounted into a deep-rooted bitterness she desperately tried to hide. But Hadassah knew her sister-in-law too well to be fooled.

"For mercy's sake, tell me what's wrong!" she implored one day, after a particu-larly cold rebuttal. Tears sprang to Dinah's eyes and she angrily brushed them away in an effort to hide her pain. But her heart was too sore, too desperate for sympathy. No longer able to resist, she looked at Hadassah defiantly.

"You want me to talk, then I'll talk," she said sharply. "Why is it that I'm the first of us to marry, yet my womb remains empty and nobody cares? I earnestly pray for a child, and what do I get? Nothing! I'm barren, Hadassah! Barren! Ham would have been better off marrying someone younger."

"You know that's not true," Hadassah chided gently. "As for being barren, I haven't fallen pregnant either. But that doesn't mean we won't."

Dinah shook her head vehemently.

"*You* might find that easy to believe, but I don't," she said.

"I understand what you're feeling, Dinah. But, in this instance, God's promise speaks for itself. He has called our husbands to be the fathers of the post-Flood world. How can that happen except through us bearing their children?"

"Then why don't I fall pregnant?" Dinah wailed.

Hadassah looked at Dinah so tenderly that she began to weep.

"I think He's withholding the child of your dreams until you allow Him to heal your soul," she said. Dinah bristled. To be reminded of her dark secret was intolerable.

"Don't talk rubbish, Hadassah! Many children have been conceived by hurting women."

"True, but Elohim[7] sent the Flood to destroy the old wicked order, that we might found a new righteous one. Perhaps the bitterness you should've left behind is depriving you of the blessings God has in store for you now. He doesn't want your children affected by the sins of the past. You must deal with them if you're to go forward."

"But I can't forget my past," Dinah protested. "Nobody can."

"Agreed, but you *can* lay it to rest by forgiving those who've abused you. The Lord does not harbour resentment, Dinah. Neither must you."

"I know that," Dinah answered in a small voice.

"Then let your past go and get on with living!"

"I can't – not until I've told Ham."

Hadassah sighed and shook her head.

"It's too late for that now," she said.

"Perhaps, but I've got to try," Dinah insisted.

Perplexed as Ham was over his wife's barrenness, he was unprepared for her confession. He could not face it – not after all these years!

Despite being little more than a boy when he had married Dinah, he had known enough to suspect she was no longer a virgin. Her innocent shyness on their nuptial night had, therefore, been a surprise. It had only been afterwards, when she had lain beside him weeping, that he had discovered he was right after all. Although disappointed, he had realized that Dinah's tears and inexperience could mean only one thing.

He had lain awake for hours, holding her and wishing he could take away her hurt. Wishing she would confide in him. But she never had. He had decided to not pursue the matter and soon forgot about it altogether. It came as a surprise to discover Dinah had not.

"Dinah, please! I don't want to know," he said, raising his hands in protest.

"But you don't understand," she persisted.

"I understand more than you think!" he said through clenched teeth. "The thought of some brute taking you by force tears me apart inside."

Dinah stared at him in shock.

"You know?" she whispered. Ham took hold of her icy hands and kissed them.

"I may be selfish," he said thickly, "but I'm not blind or stupid. Of course I noticed you weren't a virgin when we consummated our marriage. But you were so frightened, so innocent, I guessed you'd been raped when you were a child. That made me furious, and I would have gladly murdered your assailant had I known who he was. But you weren't telling and I didn't know how to ask without making you feel even more ashamed. So I did the only thing I could, Dinah. I vowed to love and look after you always."

"But how could you, knowing I came to you like soiled goods?" she asked hoarsely. Ham gently pulled her into his arms.

"No one ever becomes soiled unless their will is involved," he said. "Yours wasn't, Dinah. I love you and always will. And I know you'll stay faithful to me. That's all that matters."

"But don't you see? That's not all that matters, not to me!" she cried. Ham groaned.

"For goodness' sake, Dinah!" he exclaimed. "I love you just as you are. No strings attached. Surely that's sufficient?"

"If only it were, Ham. Hadassah believes the bitterness of my past is what makes me barren. She says I need to forgive and let go. That's all very well if you love God as she does. But I don't. And even if I did, would He forgive me for trying to deceive you?"

"You know what Mother would say to that."

"She always has much to say, especially when it comes to God," Dinah grumbled. "What pet phrase are you thinking of in particular?"

"How about nothing being impossible to God? Or, He casts our sins into the Sea of Forgetfulness? Her favourite, of course, is how much bigger than our problems Elohim[7] is. They're all good words, Dinah, but with little impact if you don't believe them."

"That's all very well for you to say, but you don't believe them either!" she said pointedly. Ham flushed.

"It's not me we're talking about," he retorted. "I know you want a child, but maybe Hadassah is right. You need to let go of your hurt and get some joy into your life. Do that and you'll probably bear more babies than Hadassah and Tabby put together."

"You think so?"

"Yes," he answered, kissing her. "Yes, I really do."

Despite the earnestness of Dinah's prayers, the memories of her past continued to tax her temper and strength. Seraphina noticed her daughter-in-law's abnormal weight loss and wondered what ailed her. Sadly, Dinah confided little. She could only hope the girl would become more trusting over time. Meanwhile, there was much to worry them all.

They had realized they would have to ration provisions. What they had not foreseen was the possibility of supplies running out long before the floodwaters receded. Noah estimated the vats would be empty within a fortnight and apportioned to Tabitha enough food for the duration of her pregnancy. What remained was then divided into meagre lots, upon which he and the others fed every second day. It was not long before there was nothing left. Desperate, the animals took to feeding on the straw that served as their bedding. But their respite was short-lived. The Ark was soon filled with the sounds of hungry, complaining stomachs, as the ravages of starvation began to take hold.

With little energy left for anything other than filling water troughs, family tensions grew. While no one blamed Noah for their predicament, he could not help but feel responsible. Elohim[7] had told him to bring enough food and he had grossly under-estimated. If only he had made his vats bigger, packed the provisions more tightly! Depressed by the thought of the enormous vessel becoming a floating tomb, he spent days in silent prayer, pleading for strength to endure.

Ham mistook his father's silence for apathy and became increasingly agitated. On the morning of the thirtieth day with nothing to eat, he could maintain his self-control no longer. Storming from the alcove he shared with Dinah, he grabbed Noah by the shoulders and shook him.

"I can't take this anymore!" he shouted.

Alarmed, Noah looked up into eyes stark with fear.

"What can't you take, son?"

Ham's face registered shock. How could his father be so callous, so uncaring?

"Don't pretend you don't know!" the young man cried angrily. "What are we waiting for, Father? To die? It would have been better had we perished with the rest! At least death would have been quick, if not painless. Instead, we're adrift in this boat, withering away to nothing! If God is so great, why doesn't He feed us?"

Exhausted by his tirade, Ham sank to the floor and wept. Noah gently ran his hand across his son's heaving shoulders, then ascended the ladder to stare out at the ocean. The bitter sea was now the only thing keeping them alive, yet the inspiration for the water-purifying system was only one of God's many miracles. Would the Most High add to His wonders by providing the food they needed now? Noah fell to his knees. Never had he felt so inadequate, so dependent on the Lord for mercy.

"Will You do it, Elohim[7]?" he cried.

For hours he sought the Most High with tears. He finally rose from his travail with the understanding that life was more than mere survival. Life depended on Almighty God being with them in all circumstances.

He was startled by a flutter of wings and looked up to see a white Dove hovering above him. The Bird's eyes held him fast, looking deep into his soul. In that moment, Noah realized the Creature and the Sovereign Lord were one and the same.

"My God!" he cried, falling to his knees and shivering when the Lord touched his face. Then the Bird was gone, leaving behind a golden glow. Overjoyed, Noah extended his hand towards the warm, fading light. Never had he felt so encouraged, so full!

Noah's new-found exuberance was thought to be hysteria by everyone but Seraphina. She was convinced her husband had experienced something wonderful during his time of travail and refused to discuss the matter further. Quietly excusing herself, she climbed the ladder to haul in a line of washing. The sight that met her eyes made her gasp. Chore forgotten, she cupped her hands to her mouth to call the others.

"Look!" she cried, as her family clambered up beside her.

Although God had assured Noah He would provide the food they needed, the sight of the ocean purple with seaweed was nonetheless overwhelming.

"Yes!" Noah shouted excitedly. "Yes!"

Soon everyone was laughing and crying with relief. Roused by the noise, the animals also began to sound forth with cries of hope that set the Ark rocking.

CHAPTER 25
DELIVERED

*Look at the birds. They don't need to plant or harvest or
put food in barns because your heavenly Father feeds
them. And you are far more valuable to Him than they
are.*
Matthew 6:26

N oah watched in dismay as the buckets were repeatedly lowered and hauled
up full of nothing but water. The seaweed – thick as a man's arm and many
times as long – was too large for the narrow containers. Frustrated by their
fruitless efforts, the survivors sank into an even deeper despair than before.

"Damn you and your God!" Ham muttered as he pushed against the Ark's sealed
door. "You didn't even think to bring a grappling iron, or an axe to smash open a
hole for us to crawl out of." Noah stared into the hot, frightened eyes and suddenly
understood why God had told him to leave his heavier tools behind.

"I am neither stupid nor forgetful, Ham," he chided. "Our safety depends on us
staying inside the Ark. And stay we will until Elohim[7] tells us to leave. In the meantime,
we must trust Him to sustain us."

"*You* may have faith in Him, but I don't!" the young man shouted. "How can I
believe in someone who allows such hardship?"

Noah shook his head in frustration.

"Your unbelief is what makes Elohim[7] small in your eyes, Ham. Yet His power has
no limits. He is able to save us to the uttermost."

"I still don't understand how I can believe in someone I cannot see, smell or touch,"
Ham objected.

"The Lord Himself will help you believe, just as He helped me," Noah said as he
saw the white Dove alight on Ham's shoulder. Ham frowned. He was unaware of the
Lord's presence, and wondered why his father looked at him with such an expression
of awe.

Noah saw the Dove touch each member of his family that day, but remained silent. The Lord would reveal Himself when they were ready.

Seraphina was first to notice the indescribable peace. She had become increasingly anxious over their impossible situation. Grieved, too, that her faith had been so easily shaken. But her fears had steadily faded throughout the day. By dusk, she was confident they would eat that night and eagerly set the table. Noah grinned when he saw the empty bowls. His wife never did anything bizarre except by faith. Had she received a specific word from the Lord?

"Are you crazy, Mother?" Ham demanded when she summoned him for dinner.

"Why so shocked?" Seraphina quietly answered as she took her place beside him. "Elohim[7] has proved time and again that nothing is too hard for Him to do. He promised to bring us through the Flood. We therefore know He will feed us."

She then turned confidently to Noah.

"Will you ask God's blessing over what we're about to eat?" she asked. Noah eagerly grasped her hand.

"I've never given thanks for a meal not yet in the dish," he said, "but I think it's an excellent idea. We often take things for granted until we're in a hard place. Elohim[7] is our provider. He knows what we need. Let's ask Him to supply it."

Nodding, the family bowed their heads.

"Dear Lord," Noah prayed. "You are Father of all. Everything comes from You and of Your own we give You. You alone are worthy of our trust and praise. We look to You to meet our needs and thank You for Your provision. Fill us now, most merciful Elohim[7]. We ask this for the sake of Your honour and glory. Amen."

A warm silence descended on the group as the wonder of God's love began filling their hearts. Empty dinner bowls forgotten, they lifted their voices in praise to the One who held their lives in His hands. It was only when they fell onto their beds hours later that they realized their hunger had been miraculously satisfied.

Although weary, Hadassah was reluctant to retire for the night. She was convinced the Lord would do something wonderful before sunrise and wanted to see it.

"Please, Shem, we'll miss out if we don't stay awake!" she pleaded, but to no avail. Her husband was asleep before his head touched the pillow. Hoping one of the others would agree to keep vigil with her, she emerged from her alcove and was delighted to find her sister-in-law still up.

"Shouldn't you be in bed?" Dinah asked as Hadassah eagerly snuggled down next to her.

"I'm too excited," Hadassah answered. "Wasn't tonight amazing?"

"That it was."

Hearing the catch in Dinah's voice, Hadassah moved the lamp closer.

"What's wrong?" she asked, looking at Dinah intently.

"Nothing's wrong," Dinah said, wiping her eyes. "Quite the opposite, in fact. What happened tonight, Hadassah? I feel so clean! Like I've been washed from the inside out. I never knew God could be like that."

The look of worship on Dinah's face was overwhelming and Hadassah began to weep.

"Oh dear! We don't want another Flood, do we?" Dinah laughed sweetly. Hadassah shook her head and dried her eyes.

"I'm just so glad for you," she whispered.

"No more than I," Dinah stated simply. She then reached for Hadassah's hand and held it tight.

"I have this wonderful sense of belonging to the Lord," she said earnestly, "like I've really been found by Him. But I also feel a little lost, too. I know He's forgiven me, yet there's so much I have to learn about Him, it's frightening."

"It's natural to feel that way, Dinah. We're all overcome by God's love and mercy in the beginning. That's why it's important to have fellowship with people of like faith. Even then, it's the Lord who teaches us most and strengthens our belief. Keep your heart close to His, Dinah, and you can't go wrong."

"And how do I do that?"

"By praying and doing what you know will please Elohim[7]. He will show you what's right and what's wrong, and how to resist temptation. He will always lead you to those places and situations that are best for you – even when they don't appear to be."

Dinah hugged her knees close to her chest.

"I'm glad we had this talk," she said warmly.

"You know I'm here for you."

"And always have been. Thank you, Hadassah."

Dinah paused, her thoughts far away.

"I wonder if I'll fall pregnant, now the guilt is gone," she pondered.

"I'm sure you will. But would it matter if you didn't?"

"Strangely enough, no. Isn't that odd?"

"Not really. Your burden is finally where it should be – on Elohim's[7] shoulders."

"Thank goodness for that!" Dinah answered sleepily. "I don't know about you, but I'm ready for bed now."

"Please don't go," Hadassah begged. "I'm sure God's going to do something special tonight."

"Such as?"

"I don't know, but it has to be something great. He never does anything by halves."

"No, He doesn't, does He? Very well, I'll stay up for as long as I'm able."

"Perhaps praying will help us stay awake," Hadassah suggested. Dinah nodded.

"I'd better do it with my eyes open, though," she yawned. "They'll probably stay closed for days once shut!"

The two women began to pray in earnest. Dinah wept anew when she heard Hadassah's thanksgiving for her new-found faith.

Hadassah awoke with a start to an ear-splitting cacophony. Her neck was painfully stiff from having rested against Dinah's shoulder for most of the night, and the thought of tending to the unhappy creatures was unappealing. She rose groggily and sought to identify the cries, only to discover they did not originate from inside the Ark. Tingling with excitement, she stooped to rouse her sister-in-law.

"Dinah!" she called urgently. "Dinah! Wake up!"

"What?" Dinah mumbled, rubbing her eyes.

"Don't say anything – just listen!"

Dinah inclined her head, then looked questioningly at Hadassah.

"I think we're in for something marvellous," Hadassah grinned. "Come. Let's go and have a look."

The two women eagerly climbed up to the top deck and looked out on a spectacle that made them gasp. Glinting like polished silver in the early morning sun were hundreds of leaping dolphins, their high-pitched chatter cutting merrily through the silence. Hadassah laughed. She had always loved the vivacious sea creatures and was grateful they had survived the Flood. Hopefully she, too, would once again be just as free.

She watched in fascination as a big fellow rose from the ocean and swam towards them on his tail, a piece of seaweed dangling from his jaws. She had often seen dolphins play with one another in like fashion, but was suddenly aware this was no game. She turned to warn Dinah, but it was too late. The tossed seaweed hit her sister-in-law smartly in the face and landed, dripping, at her feet. The two women looked in amazement at the offering, then jumped back as another piece was thrown through the window to land beside it.

"Who'd have believed Elohim[7] would send dolphins to feed us?" Hadassah cried as they watched the pile of seaweed rapidly grow and spill over to the living quarters below. Dinah smiled broadly. Never had she felt so excited or so sure of God's love!

CHAPTER 26
COMPLETION

I have fought a good fight, I have finished the race, and I
have remained faithful.
2 Timothy 4:7

Although Ham was just as amazed as everyone else by the Lord's provision, he knew his enthusiasm could not survive his unbelief. If only he had the same hunger for God his parents had! His indifference was no longer an option, however. The wonderful change in Dinah demanded he make an effort – for her sake. He sighed. Had the transformation in his wife happened sooner, she would not have fallen prey to the dark moods that had almost destroyed their marriage. Listening to her laugh while she hung seaweed out to dry made him glad he had persevered with the relationship. Dinah was no longer an acerbic woman with a hurting heart. She was an animated miracle who infected them all with joy.

Dinah knew Ham was proud of her in a new, more meaningful way. Circumstances had kept them together against all odds, and she praised God for it. They were happier now than they had ever been. The only thing lacking was Ham's spiritual breakthrough. Hopefully, that would happen before their little ones arrived.

She stopped what she was doing to run a hand across her stomach and grinned. It still seemed too good to be true!

Seraphina was sure Dinah was pregnant and longed for the girl to share her news. Not that she had any right to be impatient. Her daughter-in-law was probably guarding her secret for no other reason than to be certain. Even so, it would be prudent to keep an eye on her. The effects of the girl's former state of mind could still be seen in her overly thin face.

Her thoughts were interrupted when Dinah placed a huge griddlecake on the table. Shem eagerly helped himself to a piece.

"This is delicious!" he said. "Where did you get the flour from?"

"Tabby gave me some of her rations," Dinah answered with a wide smile. "It's a pity we haven't any milk to wash it down with. I don't suppose the animals will begin lactating until after they calve."

"I wonder how many are pregnant," Noah mused.

"Definitely all the larger species," Dinah said with a twinkle, "and some not so large. Like myself, for instance."

Her casual remark took everyone by surprise and it was several seconds before Seraphina excitedly clapped her hands.

"You certainly know how to pick your moment, daughter!" she laughed in delight. Dinah grinned.

"I've been far too serious all my life, Mother. It's time to stop, don't you think?"

"Are you saying we're expecting a baby?" Ham blurted.

"Yes, Ham! That's exactly what I'm saying!" Dinah exclaimed joyously. Lost for words, Ham tightly embraced his wife. Only now did he realize just how much he shared her desire for children.

A grinding shudder suddenly shook the Ark and the enormous boat listed, tipping the griddlecake onto the floor. Laughter forgotten, the group stared at each other, wide-eyed. For weeks they had awaited this moment.

"We men need to check for flooding," Noah told Seraphina. "You women go to the top deck and see what we've run aground on." Nodding, Seraphina climbed the ladder, closely followed by Hadassah and Tabby. Dinah, however, hung back. The day had been extraordinary and she was reticent to break the spell. No longer did she doubt Elohim's[7] call on her life. She *would* be a mother of nations and her destiny would start being fulfilled somewhere near this place. A thrill of excitement ran through her. For the first time in her life, she was ready to grab the future with both hands.

The men were relieved to find the hull still intact and eagerly joined the women on the top deck. To their disappointment, they saw nothing but mil[17] upon mil[17] of glassy sea.

"At least we're a lot closer to getting off this boat than we were yesterday," Noah said.

"But we've already been cooped up 198 days," Ham grumbled, "and still no land in sight!"

"Why so glum?" Tabitha chided gently. "We'll be home and dry by the time my baby's born. That's not too far off now."

"It's at least another five months," Japheth reminded her.

"A mere drop in this ocean when compared to the lifetime ahead of us," she insisted.

"Tabitha's right," Seraphina agreed. "Our time of waiting is small in the whole scheme of things. We should be grateful God has brought us to the doorstep of our new home, and not left us floating in the middle of a vast sea."

"I suppose you're right," Ham muttered.

"Right? Of course I'm right!" she said, tossing her head. Laughing at his mother's cheeky confidence, Ham descended the ladder to where Dinah was waiting. To his surprise, she was content to remain onboard a little longer. Not that he could blame her. It was here she had found peace with God. What he did not know was how eagerly his wife wanted him to share her faith. Leaving the Ark prematurely might well interrupt the work Elohim[7] had already begun in his life.

It was two and a half months before Noah could see a little of what the Ark had run aground on. Cupping his hands around his eyes, he scanned the ocean for other land-masses, but still could see nothing. The boat had obviously settled on the highest peak within his scope of vision. At least they were in water deep enough for the dolphins to continue feeding them. This could not last for much longer, however.

Curious as to what lay beyond the horizon; Noah finally decided to use a raven to scout the area[38]. The greedy bird would be sure to return if there was no food to be found. To his dismay, the creature clung to its freedom. It was clearly feeding on something. The question was what?

"You know ravens are born scavengers," Seraphina said one day, as she served Noah his lunch. "He's been living on seaweed long enough to recognize it, and probably gets his share from the dolphins before they bring it to us. Besides, you can't blame him for getting out of here once and for all. I think I'd do so, too, if I could."

"Then it's just as well you can't!" Noah grinned. "Elohim[7] has decreed one way off this boat, Seraphina, and that's through the door. Jests aside, what if that bird *is* feeding on something other than seaweed? I would send another bird to find out, but you saw what happened with the raven."

"It's your own fault, Noah. You used the wrong bird. Have you forgotten Enos's faithful pigeon? She always returned, even when the odds were against it."

"I remember Sheba well. It's a pity our pigeons aren't trained to home in."

"Then what about using a dove instead?" she suggested. "The pearly grey is so sweet and friendly. She's also a creature of habit and should return if she finds nowhere to settle or feed."

"Good point," Noah said. "Fetch her, then. I'm longing to know what else is out there."

The dove came to Seraphina so eagerly that she wondered if it had been told what to do.

"I think she knows," she said, placing the bird into Noah's hands.

"Perhaps she does," Noah answered, stroking the soft, downy chest. Unafraid, the dove stared at him for several seconds, then flew out the window[39].

Awaiting the bird's return seemed to drag on forever. Noah began to wonder if he had again made an error when he heard the unmistakable flutter of wings. He was glad the dove had not let him down, but also somewhat sorry. She would not have come back so soon had there been a place for her to roost.

A week later, Noah sought out the small grey bird again.

"Bring back whatever you find," he murmured as he released her.

Unable to concentrate on anything else, Noah spent the entire day crouched at the window, staring at the empty horizon. He finally saw the dove just before sundown, a tiny speck against the scarlet sky. Tears filled his eyes when she flew into his eager hands, a sprig of olive in her beak[40]. At last! She had found what he had been hoping for!

Noah waited another week before sending the dove out again. When she did not return[41], he knew the time for disembarking was near. Not only had the floodwaters receded almost completely, there was also new growth on the emerging land masses.

Yet days dragged on into weeks, and still the massive door remained sealed, causing Noah to fret. It had been a long time since the dolphins had been able to bring them seaweed. What little they had laid by was now depleted.

Ham, too, was anxious. What if Dinah miscarried because of malnourishment? His fear made him feel guilty. How could he possibly doubt Elohim[7] now?

Dinah knew the extent of her husband's worry, but nothing she said could reassure him. That morning's breakfast had emptied the larder and their water supply was critically low. Only God could sustain them now. She wondered how her sister-in-law was feeling. Tabby's baby was due any day and would need nourishment to survive. Sensing Dinah's thoughts, Tabitha patted her hand.

"It's going to be alright," she said firmly. "Especially now we have nothing left but faith. Remember how often the Lord has saved us just when we reached rock bottom. He'll do it again. Just wait and see."

"As if we haven't done enough waiting!" Noah said dourly. "But you're right, daughter. God *has* allowed us to come to the end of ourselves time and again, and only then supplied our needs."

"But the Most High doesn't always follow this pattern," Hadassah argued. "If He did, our lives would be in constant turmoil. I believe He's tested our faith over the past few months to show His goodness and power. It's so easy to forget about Him when life's running smoothly. We need something to help us remember, especially in the days to come."

"You've made a valid point, Hadassah," Noah said quietly.

"And you must record it as such," Seraphina urged. "Our descendants need to know how richly Elohim[7] rewards those who trust Him. And to think, this is just the beginning of everything He's planned for us."

Noah began to answer, but was silenced by the sound of wood against wood. Swinging round, the group shielded their eyes as the door of the Ark opened, admitting a flood of warm sunshine and the light of God's Shekinah[29] Glory. Awestruck, they fell on their faces.

It is time. Time to come out of the Ark, Elohim[7] said, gently touching each one. *Time to multiply and fill the Earth with your fruit.*

Noah rose shakily to his feet and descended the gangplank in a daze. The others slowly followed, staring in wonder at a world of vibrant colour. Tabitha suddenly sank to her knees in pain, her unborn child pushing hard against her.

"Now?" Seraphina asked.

"Yes, now!" Tabby cried, clutching her stomach. "Mercy in Heaven, Mother! It hurts!"

"I know it does," Seraphina sympathized. "Come now. You'll be having your baby right here if we don't get you back to bed."

The young woman turned to obey and nearly tripped over the ewe in her haste. The animal bleated piteously, its plump body heaving in labour. Tabitha was filled with such a sense of wonder that she forgot about her own pain. She had never seen a birthing and was enthralled when the mother nudged her lamb, urging him to suckle. A determination for her child to also begin life in the clean, open air filled her and she refused to return to the Ark.

Japheth was dismayed by her decision, but there was nothing he could do. The child had already begun to crown! He looked on helplessly as his mother squatted with Tabitha at the foot of the gangplank and helped deliver his son. The squalling newborn was quickly silenced when Seraphina placed him against Tabitha's breast. A lump the size of a fist filled Japheth's throat and it was several seconds before he could speak.

"I'd like to call him Gomer," he finally whispered as he gently stroked the feeding babe's head. Tears sprang to Tabby's eyes and she laughed for joy. The name meant 'completion' and was her husband's way of telling her she had fulfilled all his dreams.

CHAPTER 27
THE COVENANT

"For I know the plans I have for you," says the LORD.
"They are plans for good and not for disaster, to give you
a future and a hope."
Jeremiah 29:11

The day was spent in offloading their cargo, and the Ark was empty of all but their personal belongings by sunset. Scratching his head, Noah looked around him. He had hoped to set up camp in the sheltered gully below, but doubted they could safely make the descent in the fast-fading light.

"The mountain is covered in too much debris to risk the climb tonight," he told the others. "We'll have to bed down in the Ark."

Hadassah shook her head adamantly.

"*You* may sleep there if you wish, Father, but not I," she said.

"I agree with Hadassah," Tabitha interjected. "Gomer was born here, in the fresh air, and this is where he will stay. Besides, the Ark is no longer our place. We stepped into the fulfilment of God's promises when we disembarked. To take refuge in the boat every time a difficulty arises would be wrong."

"Be reasonable, Tabby!" Japheth implored her. "Our baby needs warmth and shelter if he's to survive."

"We'll be warm enough under those woollen blankets we brought," Tabitha insisted. Japheth groaned in frustration.

"They'll not be much protection against the icy night air!" he exclaimed.

"Japheth's right," Shem said. "The weather's cooler than it was before the Flood and the mountain will be bitterly cold."

Despite Shem's observation, Hadassah and Tabitha stood their ground. Seraphina listened with growing conviction to their argument.

"Don't tell me you agree with them?" Noah asked quietly.

185

"I hate to admit it, Noah," she answered, "but our daughters are correct. The Ark will always be a strong reminder of what God has done for us, but it is no longer our haven. I don't suppose we can camp on the rock face, can we?"

Noah shook his head. There was not even a tree stump to which they could secure the tent stays – without which the canvas shelters would be blown over by the gusty wind.

"There must be a solution," Seraphina continued. "What's left onboard, Noah?"

"Three chests of clothes, the lamps, a brazier, the buckets and the tents. There're also those two bolts of heavy fabric."

Seraphina nodded thoughtfully. The awful material had been a wedding present she had all but forgotten about until the eve of the Flood. The urge to stow it onboard had been irresistible and she was now glad she had obeyed her impulse.

"There's actually no need to stay onboard the Ark tonight," she said, looking intently at the broad gangplank.

"How so?" Noah asked.

"It's obvious. Drape the gangplank with the fabric and we have a makeshift tent that will adequately shelter us all from the chill."

Noah grinned broadly. The gangplank was half as wide as it was long and would be ideal.

"An excellent idea if we've enough cloth," he agreed.

"There's sufficient to drape it twice over."

"Then it's a genius you are!" he exclaimed.

Hadassah, however, was incredulous at the idea.

"You can't be serious?" she said.

"It's the best plan anyone has come up with so far," Dinah pointed out.

"But we'd still be using the Ark as a refuge then!"

Noah scowled. It was not like Hadassah to be obstinate.

"Have you forgotten that Japheth's son was born on the Ark's gangplank?" he reminded her sternly. "I hardly think the Lord will object to us being sheltered under it now!"

"Noah's right, Hadassah," Seraphina said, putting her arm around the girl's shoulders. "This gangplank between the old and the new is symbolic of something we do not yet understand – something significant. Not only was little Gomer delivered at its foot, the lamb was born right in its middle. Besides, you'd be foolish to resist what God ordained from the beginning."

"I'm not sure what you mean," Hadassah frowned.

"Then let me tell you. Let me tell you all." Seraphina then proceeded to explain why she had stowed the cloth onboard in the first place. "Considering how much I dislike the fabric, the idea of bringing it along seemed ridiculous. But I couldn't resist the urge to pack it. I'm now grateful I did. Elohim[7] knew just what we would need this day." Smiling, she again embraced her daughter-in-law. "So tell me, if we're not to sleep onboard the Ark tonight, what better place *is* there but under the gangplank?"

Hadassah's eyes prickled.

"Oh, Mother! I wouldn't have been so stubborn had I known," she apologized. Seraphina shrugged.

"None of us are perfect," she said.

"No, we're not, are we?" Hadassah admitted. Tears forgotten, she looked at her father-in-law with a sunny smile.

"Well, what're you waiting for?" she said. "It really *is* beginning to get cold out here."

Cosy as their first night off the Ark proved to be, Noah lay awake for hours, in turmoil over what God had told him to do. The firstborn of the flock had been considered holy since the son of Adam had sacrificed his lamb[42]. Yet the significance of Abel's offering, and the value God placed on it, remained a mystery. The ancient Commandments forbade the shedding of blood. Why then would Elohim[7] favour such a sacrifice?

Although God held Abel and his offering in such high regard, no other had ever ventured to follow in their forebear's footsteps. Neither had the Most High required it. Noah had therefore been appalled when he had been commissioned that morning not only to build an altar[43] on which to offer his firstborn lamb, but to also eat of it afterwards. The consuming of flesh was thought to be the vilest of devilries!

Despite his revulsion, Noah had no choice but to obey. God said the lamb symbolized the sacrifice He would one day make of Himself, to save Man from sin, and must be offered. But how was it possible for the Most High to die like an ordinary creature? And why was it necessary for them to eat of the lamb in order to appropriate the Lord's forgiveness?

Exhausted, Noah buried his head in his pillows. Everything concerning the burnt offering was hard to stomach! How could he tell the others what Elohim[7] had commanded when he did not understand it himself? He only had a week in which to prepare the altar and prayed he would have strength to do the awful thing. Sighing, he closed his eyes and drifted into a troubled sleep.

Seraphina was perturbed by Noah's uncharacteristic silence.

"What's wrong?" she asked, clearing away his untouched breakfast of figs and milk. But her husband was so lost in thought that it was seconds before he realized she had spoken.

"Sorry. What did you say?" he apologized.

"I asked if there's anything wrong. You've been so quiet lately."

"You're right, I have been distracted," he nodded slowly.

"Do you want to tell me about it?"

Noah shrugged uncomfortably. He did not know where to begin. Seeing the struggle on her husband's face, Seraphina suddenly recognized what she had failed to see before.

"God's spoken to you again, hasn't He?" she said excitedly.

"Yes, He has," Noah answered soberly. "I wish I could tell you all He's shown me, but I can't – not yet. It's too hard."

He laid his hand against Seraphina's cheek, then walked away, leaving her feeling hurt and sidelined. Never before had he withheld from her the words God had spoken.

It was Tabitha who noticed Noah's obsession with the lamb.

"He's made a pet of the creature," she said as the four women laboured over the weekly wash. "Indeed, he spends as much time with the lamb as he does with his grandson – something I would find disturbing if I didn't know him better."

"Well, I would be bitterly jealous if it was *my* son he was neglecting," Dinah grumbled as she stretched her aching back. She felt like she had been pregnant forever and longed for the day her baby would be born.

"But why would Noah be so attentive to a lamb?" Seraphina asked crossly. "The only animals he's passionate about are horses."

"The story of Abel does show us that lambs are special to God," Tabitha reminded her mother-in-law.

"So it does, but what has *that* got to do with anything?"

"Well, Father's been gathering huge stones all day. I'm wondering if ..." Tabitha hesitated, unsure of how to share her thoughts. But the unfinished sentence spoke for itself.

"That's it!" Seraphina exclaimed with certainty.

"Surely not!" Hadassah protested in horror.

"I fear so, daughter. And, whether we like it or not, we must support Noah. This is not something to be borne alone."

The incomplete altar stood like a beacon at the top of the mountain, but Noah was nowhere to be seen.

"He's probably gone looking for more stones to finish the altar," Ham said. "There're none here."

Seraphina nodded unhappily. Apart from loose rubble, the rock face offered nothing in the way of building blocks. She wondered how far afield Noah would have gone to find them.

"If only I knew where he was," she muttered.

"There's no chance of him getting lost, Mother," Dinah said matter-of-factly. "Not with the Ark sitting like a sore thumb on top of the mountain."

"You misunderstand, daughter," Seraphina answered tersely. "I'm more concerned about Noah's behaviour than anything else. He seldom wanders off without telling me."

"I don't think he meant to," Tabitha said quietly. "He just doesn't know how to tell us what's bothering him. He needs to know that we are aware of this new demand on his life, and that he has our full support."

"Agreed, but where is he?" Seraphina exclaimed.

"Down there," Shem answered. The group turned to see the Patriarch[23] trudging up the mountain, his back bowed by a burden heavier than his laden sack. Relieved, Seraphina ran to meet him.

"I'm sorry I was gone so long," Noah said, embracing her. "There's something I must tell you, something you must see."

"There's no need," she answered softly. Noah blinked at her.

"You know about the sacrifice I've been told to make?" he asked tentatively. Seraphina nodded.

"Thank God! I've wanted to tell you all week but didn't know how. It's a hard thing, Seraphina. I don't understand why Elohim[7] requires it of us."

"Even so, we must obey," she said. Sighing, Noah pulled her back into his arms.

"You might not be so willing to obey when you realize God has commanded me to go one step further than Abel."

"What do you mean?"

Noah hesitated, then haltingly shared all he had been told to do.

"So you see, dear heart. The Most High has commanded us not only to sacrifice the lamb, but to also eat it," he concluded.

Seraphina covered her eyes and began to cry. Noah reached for her, but she impatiently pulled away.

"You don't understand!" she wept. "It's God I'm crying for, not us. This isn't a sacrifice we're making to Him, Noah. It's a sacrifice *He's* making, to purify and cleanse us. That's why He calls Himself the Lamb that takes away the sins of the world. I don't like the idea of eating this sacrifice either. But it's right we share in God's suffering this way."

"You're not making sense!" Noah protested. "The only one who will suffer is the lamb."

"Not so, Noah. God hates bloodshed. The pain He will feel when the lamb is sacrificed will be greater than anything we can bear. Yet He will endure it for our sake, to cleanse us from sin."

"If this offering is so important to our salvation, why has the Most High not commanded us to make it before now?"

"I don't know," she admitted. "What I do know is that Elohim[7] would never have sent the Flood had there been another remedy. Perhaps this sacrificial lamb is a temporary solution to stay His hand from destroying the world again. It may also be a door to repentance and forgiveness, until He comes to abolish sin forever."

Noah suddenly understood what Seraphina was trying to say. He also knew what God meant when He spoke of the sacrifice of the innocent on behalf of the guilty. The penalty for sin was death. But the gift of God through the blood offering was forgiveness and life. Yet it would take more than the blood of a lamb to complete this work of atonement for all time. It would take the sacrifice of God Himself! How, Noah did not know. But it was the only way for Man to be restored to the place Adam had before he sinned. Overcome, he shut his eyes and raised his head to the sun.

Maranatha[15]! he silently cried. *Come Lord, come!*

"What're you thinking?" Seraphina asked, interrupting his thoughts. Noah opened his eyes and smiled sadly at her.

"I'm thinking what a fool I've been to keep all this to myself."

"Two heads are invariably better than one," she said.

"Come now, Seraphina!" Noah chuckled. "You only ever use your heart when it comes to God! But we waste time. We'll never get the altar finished before sunset at this rate."

"When will you make the sacrifice?" Seraphina asked with a catch in her voice.

"At dawn tomorrow," he answered. "Heaven help me, dear heart. I hope I have the courage to do it!"

"The Lord will help you," she said, reaching for his hand.

It was with a heavy heart that Noah stooped to retrieve his sack. Seraphina would be shocked when he told her the lamb was not the only creature to be sacrificed. Little did he realize that burnt offerings would become a way of life – as would the eating of flesh.

Noah laid the heavy stone in place, then stood back.

"We're about three short," he said, turning to look down at the rock-strewn ravine below. "I hope we've enough time to haul them up before sunset."

"Why go down there when all the stones you need are close by?" Japheth asked quietly. The thought of wasted time and energy sparked Noah's anger.

"Close by where?" he jibed. "I see nothing but pebbles."

"That's because the stones are hidden," Japheth explained. "I found them yesterday, when I was looking for a more sheltered spot for Tabby and Gomer. The place is only a short walk from here. Come, I'll show you."

He led the group down the slope, to where the scrub grew thickest, and began pushing his way through it.

190

"Watch your footing," he cautioned. "The foliage hides a gully we need to descend into." Clutching at the hardy mountain bush, he started edging his way down and was eagerly followed by everyone except Dinah. She disliked dark, shadowy places, but her concern at being left alone soon outweighed her fear. Gingerly, she pursued the others through the dense, tangled shrubs.

Ham anxiously waited at the base of the gully and cursed his thoughtlessness at not staying with Dinah. She was large with child and could easily fall. Fearing the worst, he began clawing his way upwards and was relieved to see her a few cubits[5] above him.

"Where've you been?" he chided, opening his arms. Dinah was close to tears and clung to him tightly.

"It's alright. You're safe," he murmured as they rejoined the others. Looking about her, Dinah saw the gully appeared to be a dead end, full of nothing but suffocating bush. Annoyed, she turned to Japheth for an explanation.

"Not everything is as it seems," he grinned, pulling aside the branch of a leafy sapling. "Behind is a cave like none you've ever seen. Come, see for yourselves." Ham eagerly stepped forward, but was restrained by Seraphina.

"No!" she exclaimed. "There's something hallowed about this place. I can feel it." The group stared at her.

"Are you saying we shouldn't enter?" Noah asked.

"Not at all, but it must be you who leads us in, not Ham."

Noah looked intently at his wife, then nodded.

"You'll need this," Japheth said, lighting a small lamp. Holding the light before him, Noah preceded his family into a high vaulted cavern and felt a tingle of excitement when he saw the rocks Japheth had spoken about, neatly stacked against the wall. God Himself must have protected this cave against the Flood!

"Perhaps people lived here," Japheth suggested, as Noah ran his hands over the dressed stones. "The tunnel over there may lead to another cavern, maybe even several."

Although it was too late in the day to investigate thoroughly, the urge to have a brief look was irresistible.

"We've no more than a few minutes to explore this tunnel if we're to finish the altar before nightfall," Noah warned. Leading the way down the narrow passage, he entered a chamber even more enormous than the first. It was immediately evident from the furnishings that the cave had once been a home. Noah's chest swelled as he ran his hand over the curved arm of a chair.

"This was made by Jasper," he said hoarsely. "I'd recognize his craftsmanship anywhere."

"Jasper?" Seraphina gasped. "But how is that possible?"

"He was headed for Ararat, in search of his sister," Noah reminded her. "This may have been the home they shared. Or perhaps he never found Jesse and ended up living here alone."

"I don't think so," Dinah said, so quietly that only Noah heard her. Joining his daughter-in-law at the entrance to a small alcove in the rock, Noah saw the skeletal remains on the bench within and knew they had found Jasper and Jesse. The woollen blanket covering the woman had been one of Seraphina's gifts to the carpenter.

"I've always wondered if Jasper found his sister," Noah mused.

"She was a demoniac, wasn't she?" Dinah asked. Noah nodded sombrely.

"Jasper wanted to tell her about the love of God in the hope she would repent before it was too late. He seems to have succeeded."

Dinah smiled. The peace pervading the cave strongly indicated that Jesse had indeed been healed both spiritually and mentally.

"I think Jasper and his sister must've been very happy here," she murmured. "I'm glad. It makes up for my lack of kindness to him in those early days."

"Enough!" Noah scolded gently. "Jasper wouldn't have you dwell on past mistakes. Now, it's getting late. We must pay our respects to the dead before hauling the stones to the surface." Nodding, Dinah left the alcove to assemble the others.

Seraphina tearfully watched Noah lay the final stone of the altar. Her experience in the cave had revealed an astonishing aspect of the Lord's goodness. An understanding of what the Ancients meant when they said Elohim's[7] gentleness made them great.

Her thoughts took her back to those early days when Jasper had been an integral part of their lives. She had felt such heartache when he had left. Fear, too, at not knowing how he would fare in a world fraught with danger and on the verge of God's judgement. The Flood had been an onslaught that nothing but the Ark and the creatures of the deep had been able to withstand. Yet Jasper and his sister had been miraculously protected against its ravages and had left behind an inheritance. The old man's furniture and tools would be cherished for many years to come.

Seraphina suspected Noah would entomb the bodies in the cave that had been their home. She hoped so. Jasper deserved a princely burial. In the meantime, there were other, more pressing matters to attend to. Sighing, she joined her troubled husband at the altar.

"God never asks more than we're able to give," she murmured. Noah did not respond and Seraphina reluctantly withdrew. She was bone-weary but doubted they would get much sleep that night.

Seraphina slept surprisingly well, but awoke just before dawn to an unwelcome sound. Startled, she pulled back the tent flap and stared at the sheet of water falling from the heavens.

"No!" she cried. "No! Not again! Noah! Where are you?"

"Hush! I'm here," he answered, walking rapidly across the wet rock face towards her. Relieved, she clung to him.

"Careful. You'll soon be as wet as I am," he said, stroking her tussled hair. But his warning was ignored and it was several minutes before Seraphina calmed down.

"Surely we're not in for another Flood?" she asked fearfully. Noah shook his head.

"This is nothing like before," he smiled. "Come. Feel how softly the water falls." Seraphina put out her hand, then looked at him in wonder.

"You're right," she said. "But how can this be?"

"So much is different since the Flood," Noah replied. "Perhaps this is God's new way of watering the earth." Intrigued, Seraphina again stuck out her hand.

"It tastes good," she said, licking her fingers.

"Better than a mountain stream?"

"Much. I think I will soon get fond of this Heaven-sent gift. Come, let's wake the family. This is exciting."

The others, however, were not as enthusiastic.

"I'm sure we'll find it different from what we endured on the Ark," Noah argued.

"I still don't like it," Ham muttered. "It's cold, and we can't even light a fire because the wood's too wet!"

The tacit remark made Noah groan. He had hoped to offer the lamb at dawn, but the wood would take time to dry once the sun rose.

"God will make a way in His own time," Seraphina consoled. "Just trust Him, Noah. Trust Him." Not having the heart to respond, Noah glumly watched the gentle fall of water.

"The sacrifice must be made," he finally said. "We will use oil to light the wood. Elohim[7] will do the rest."

Seraphina sadly slipped back into the tent and returned with a cruse of oil. Now that the moment had come, she wasn't sure she could stomach it. Taking the oil from her, Noah tenderly lifted the lamb from its pen and walked to the altar. The little creature looked up at him with such trust that it was several minutes before he had the courage to do what must be done. His eyes swam as the warm blood ran over his hands and stained the stones.

"I'm so sorry," he whispered as he poured the oil over the wood on the altar and lit it. The wet kindling reluctantly caught fire, but Noah was no longer able to watch. Turning his back on the sacrifice, he buried his face in his hands and cried out for mercy. And slowly, imperceptibly, an indescribable joy began filling his heart – the joy of redemption.

Laughing, Noah raised his hands and revelled in the warmth of the rising sun before turning to face his subdued family. The bow spanning the vault of Heaven above them made him gasp. Not even the bejewelled spray of a waterfall could compare to this!

Awestruck by the glorious arc in the sky, the small group of survivors fell prostrate before the Lord and trembled when the Voice like no other rang out across the *shamayim*[27].

This is the Covenant I make with you and all of creation. Never again will I destroy the Earth and those who dwell in it with the waters of a flood. To seal my promise, I place within the clouds my rainbow. When I look upon it, I will remember the everlasting Covenant between me and every creature upon earth. This rainbow is the sign of my Covenant with you. I, your Sovereign Lord, have spoken and thus will it be[44].

Elohim's[7] declaration made the rainbow pulse with an intensity that filled Noah with greater hope for the future than he had ever had. Rising to his feet, he reached for Seraphina's hand. Together they watched the rainbow fade against the backdrop of the early morning sky.

GLOSSARY

1	Abba	A Hebrew expression, meaning *Daddy*.
2	Assessor	In law, an assistant to a judge or magistrate.
3	Bet midrash	A Hebrew phrase, meaning *house of study*.
4	Chicle	The gum or sap from the *Manilkara chicle tree* has in modern times been used to make chewing gum.
5	Cubit	An ancient measurement equivalent to 18 inches.
6	Cypress	Genesis 6:14 states that Noah built the Ark out of gopher wood, a word not otherwise known in the Bible or in Hebrew. According to Wikipedia, possible translations include *squared timber*, *smoothed* (possibly planed) *wood* and *cypress*.
7	Elohim	Elohim is the first word in the Bible used for *God* (Genesis 1:1 refers) and occurs 2,570 times in the Tanakh (Jewish Bible).
8	Flux	An ancient term for *dysentery*.
9	Gossamer	Gossamer, also known as *spider silk*, is made out of a fibre spun by spiders. Spider silk is remarkably strong, its tensile strength being comparable to that of high-grade steel.
10	Ham	The third son of Noah. His name means *hot* as well as *black*. From him are descended all the African and Canaanite peoples (Genesis 10:6–20 and the Online International Standard Bible Encyclopaedia refer).
11	Japheth	The second son of Noah. His name means *wide-spreading*. As the names of his two brothers mean *dusky* and *black*, it is thought that Japheth might mean *fair*. From him are descended all the European and Nordic races, the Indians, Medes, Persians, Afghans, Kurds and Iranians, the Russian peoples, Anglo Saxons and Celts

(Genesis 10:2–5 and the Online International Standard Bible Encyclopaedia refer).

12	Jesse	A Hebrew name meaning *God exists*.
13	Lamech	The father of Noah. The meaning of his name is uncertain. Possible translations include *man of prayer, one who overthrows* and *despair*.
14	L'chaim	A Hebrew expression, meaning *to life*.
15	Maranatha	An Aramaic phrase meaning *come, O Lord*.
16	Methuselah	The father of Lamech and grandfather of Noah. The exact meaning of his name is uncertain. Possible translations include *when he is dead it shall be sent* ('*it*' referring to the Flood), and *man of the dart or javelin*.
17	Mil	One mil is equivalent to 2,000 ells or cubits. In modern terms, this equates to 1,000 yards.
18	Morning glory	The heavenly blue morning glory, otherwise known as *jalap*, has turnip-shaped roots that are the source of an ancient purgative still in use today.
19	Nephilim	The Nephilim were a pre-Flood race, referred to in the Bible as giants. They were the children born from the daughters of men and the sons of God (possibly fallen angels). Genesis 6:1–2 refers.
20	Ne'um	Is a Hebrew word meaning *oracle, word* or *utterance*.
21	Night soil	Night soil is a euphemism for *human faeces*.
22	Omer	One *omer* is equivalent to seven pints.
23	Patriarch	A man who exercised autocratic authority as the master of the house over an extended family.
24	Red lavender	A cordial composed of the oils of lavender and rosemary, cinnamon bark, nutmeg and red sandal wood, macerated in spirit of wine. It is still in use today and is used to remedy faintness and other similar conditions.
25	Sabbath	Instituted by God on the sixth day of Creation as a weekly day of rest.
26	Shalom	A Hebrew word meaning *peace*, and often used as a form of greeting or farewell.
27	Shamayim	A Hebrew word meaning *the vault of Heaven*, but commonly interpreted as *the sky*.
28	Shekel	One shekel is equivalent to 0.4 ounces and is the measure used for tender and valuable metals such as gold.

29	Shekinah	Shekinah is the English spelling of a Hebrew word denoting *the Dwelling* or *Settling Presence of God.*
30	Shem	The firstborn son of Noah. His name means *renown,* as well as *dusky* or *dark.* He is the forefather of the Semitic peoples (viz the Arabians, Assyrians, Armenians, Syrians, Mesopotamians), Arphaxad, the forefather of Abraham, and all the Aramaic peoples (Genesis 10:21–32 and the Online International Standard Bible Encyclopaedia refer).
31	Tree hibiscus fruit	Otherwise known as *'snot' apples*, are found on spreading evergreen trees (*Azanza garckeana*) growing 3–13 metres tall. The slimy fruit is commonly boiled and used as a relish or made into porridge, while its hard skin is fashioned into implements.
32	Talent	One talent weighs 34.3 kilograms or 75 pounds.

BIBLE CROSS-REFERENCES